THE THREE KINGDOMS

BOOK I: THE SONS OF FREEDOM

BOOK II: THE SHARDS OF THE CROWN

BOOK III: THE SINS OF THE FATHER

KEVIN R. ESSER

Cover art design by Saikono
https://saikono.deviantart.com

ISBN: 978-1-720-51945-4
Title ID: 8557236

Published by CreateSpace
CreateSpace is a DBA of On-Demand Publishing LLC, part of the Amazon group of companies.

Ordering Information:
Quantity sales. Special discounts are available on quantity purchases by corporations, associations, and others. For details, contact the publisher at the address above.
Orders by U.S. trade bookstores and wholesalers.

Printed in the United States of America.

www.createspace.com
www.facebook.com/thethreekingdomsthesonsoffreedom

"I wrote this novel for anyone in the need of self-motivation and determination to succeed in life, and not give up on their very dreams just because things look bleak. Even when odds are against you, there is always hope."

CONTENTS

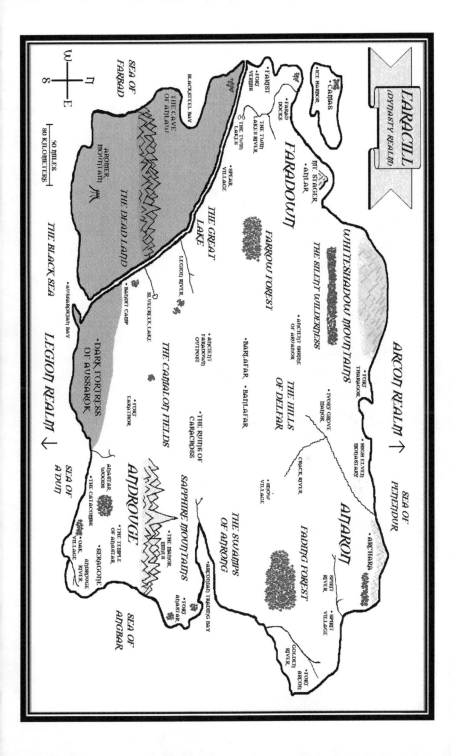

THE SONS OF FREEDOM

BOOK I

PROLOGUE

"How far would you go to save the world?" This was a question I once asked myself upon seeing the very world I lived in, torn apart by war, a war that has torn through these great lands for its entire existence. It was a war that I had for all my life, envisioned an end for just to see the freedom and valor which we so righteously deserved. Well the answer to that question lies in the tale, of which, the intricacies and details I am about to impart upon you.

My story will take us back during the start of the Third Century, the Century of War in Earacill. The eternal struggle against the malicious Saratrox, and his venomously evil host of Sarugs. You would have certainly known him; we all knew him. He became infamous by his limitless cruelty, and most evil of seduction. He was well known for the very own crown that had betrayed him, to which he had destroyed the crown and hid its shards deep within the early dark and perilous caverns, of which became appropriately named the Cave of Anlaw.

However, more so, he was known and hated for his corruption of the vast hosts of innocent men that, by force, of his demented will to take up arms against their very brothers of flesh and blood! It was with this wicked host, and his cruel ambition, he had almost destroyed the world we knew.

Moreover, who could forget the wicked beast, known as Arush'n'aug? Surely, you knew of the great dragon that roamed in our lands before the time of Saratrox? That horrible menace, which itself was considered our greatest threat to our freedom, our sovereignty, and our very lives?

My tale begins only days before the beast's third attack upon my hometown of Seragone in the kingdom of Androuge, back in the year 2935. Yes, I was an eager Hero-knight back then, in my youth driven by a distinct sense of cockiness, to which I may have been so foolhardy as to take on such a threat, with a naive disposition.

This is my story of the Three Kingdoms, and how they survived during the Century of War, to become what great civilizations they are now...

-Caradorian Saladar Caracross, 2965, the Third Century-

Death was the shadow, which followed ever diligent. Preventing it seemed impossible, yet deep in their hearts, the two allied armies of Earacill mustered together enough courage to fight and keep their fellow man alive. Even in the face of certain death, the morale of the two armies remained unscathed. They stood gallant, waiting for their enemy's next attack...

The dark red sky overshadowing the battlefield briefly flashes bright as lightning cracks through the clouds, followed by a thunderous booming sensation which shook the earth below abruptly. The standard issued steel armor worn by the soldiers illuminates an unnatural bright red from the flash. Some of the men have a feeling of uneasiness begin to overshadow their conscience, to little avail.

"Watch out!" a soldier from the eastern kingdom of Androuge shouted to a fellow knight. Although this "fellow knight" was not a mere enlisted patriot, or a drafted peasant sent to war by the High Council, no, this was a Hero-knight, the title given to the highest ranked soldier. On top of that, this Hero-knight was in command of the assault and oversaw his countrymen, this was the highest honor a knight could be offered. In a monarchy ruled without proper royal authority, there is no king to command his troops, therefore the High Council would issue this honorable authority to the soldier they see fit with the proper leadership and combat skills.

Alert and focused, the fully armored Hero-knight responded to the warning issued by the knight. He looked straight forward, fixing his gaze upon a host of about two dozen enemy soldiers appearing from the black steel gates of the dark fortress of Aussarok. These soldiers, in relation to their whole army, were entirely unarmored, dressed in a tattered and often torn black garb, this was their traditional raiment, and each wore there garb differently. Some men would wrap their face up entirely, others not at all. These soldiers had no proper uniform, their army had neither formality, nor any strategy or order. They are mindless brutes, with no conscience or soul, commanded only by the tyrannical dark lord Saratrox.

They are known only as Sarugs and each of them being over two hundred years old, cursed with immortality to forever be slaves to Saratrox. He had manipulated them to kill on sight, and being now long mindless slaves, they have no choice but to follow any order he commands. Their current assignment through their slavery: obliterate Earacill.

These Sarugs were each armed with a long sword, every blade appearing dull, and the steel had become worn from the slow decay over the past two millennia. Their faces are gray, years of rotting flesh, the natural skin tone they once had had all but faded. Their blackened eyes had no life left in them whatsoever, lifeless zombies if you will.

The host of these Sarugs had locked their gaze onto the him and they at once sprinted towards him. The noble Hero-knight charged out in front of his men and was prepared to counter their attack. They would not expect such a swift and cunning opponent to put them out of their misery on this hour, let alone singlehandedly. Their quick and deserved death would come if they dare challenge him.

They were once men, normal citizens from towns or cities, where they once lived back in their old land. They used to have a reason for living, they could have been great warriors or inventors, men of prosperity. Although now the Lord Saratrox had drained all the virtue, they once had out of them. Hate and sorrow was all they had left to feel, remembering the great suffering they experienced, they could never forget it. Now they are dead inside, they deserve death, and to be out of their desolation, and solitude.

They stared darkly into the knight's grim eyes. They once had clean and healthy skin, their vice had taken that out of them too. Gray and rotting it appeared now, their eyes, black and corrupt like the Lord himself.

The Hero-knight made the first move, he swung his sword at the first two he saw, beheading one, and cut across another's neck. A few more came upon him, five to be precise. He quickly ended their reign without even breaking a sweat. His tactics were high, he fought using combos, and he studied the Sarug's fighting style.

One more Sarug came, this one had a bow. He fired his bow upon him, although he quickly deflected the arrow from piercing him. The archer shot again, and parallel to before, the Hero-knight blocked the arrow using his own sword as the shield. Three more Sarugs approached, and he fought them swiftly, and they fell to the Earth.

The Sarug armed only with the bow fired at him once more, and this time, to his advantage, he missed his target. The Hero-knight grinned and threw his sword into the archer's chest, the adversary fell. The Sarug, and equivalent to many before him, was now free of their misery.

"Carador!" yelled Alos, a friend of the Hero-knight from Androuge. "We must fall back! Our casualties are too great, the enemy reinforcements won't cease. We are being overrun!"

"No!" cried Carador as he continued his duel with more Sarugs. "Not yet! Victory still lies within our reach, we need to push through!" The battle before them erupted with more sword fighting and cries of death.

Carador threw himself upon a group of advancing Sarugs, protecting his fellow soldiers. Alos and others joined him. They began killing a large amount, clearing a path.

A loud, high-pitched cry of morale breaking and fear inducing decibels emitted above the black clouds of Aussarok. The armies of Androuge and Faradown quickly stared up to the sky in fear, knowing where the sound had uttered, and out of the dark clouds appeared a large black figure. Everyone knew what it was, was Saratrox's greatest warrior, the Great Black Dragon known as, Arush'n'aug.

The army assumed this was the end of the battle. The great dragon soared down from above and breathed a great flame at the army, many fell in a heartbeat to Arush'n'aug. The host of Androuge panicked and began to retreat, although Carador himself stood his ground, hoping to do some major damage to one of the two enemies.

Sarug archers moved forward, firing a cloud of black arrows at the fleeing soldiers, striking many. Carador heard a sudden cry. He looked downward and saw that Alos stricken with a black-feathered arrow, directly in the chest. Alos still grasped for life, coughing for air. Carador knelt beside him. He plucked out the arrow that had pierced Alos. Carador was going to speak but. Alos died there instantly.

"Be at peace, Alos. Away from here and our suffering," said Carador standing back up. He shed a tear.

"Retreat!" yelled Carador raising his sword above him, and looking around at all the warriors, he was in command of the remaining soldiers of Androuge. "Retreat!" he yelled again, viciously attacking more Sarugs, easing their retreat, and at the same time avoiding Arush'n'aug and its great fire.

The host was retreating. They had too. There was no other way. In return, the golden light of day would never shine on them again, and they would all but perish from this world...

PART I

* * * * * *

THE RISE OF A HERO

*"The days in Earacill grow dark.
Two great threats endanger the world and all in
surrounding. Earacill needs a savior whom can stop these
threats. And bring peace back to the land..."*

CHAPTER I

* * * * * * * * *

THE WEEKEND IN FARADOWN

One year later.

"Checkmate!" announced a Squire of Androuge proudly as he pushed his Bishop chess piece a step forward, trapping his opponent's Queen in its final position, leaving the opponent in utter disbelief. "Well, Carador I believe we are evenly matched now, for you had bested me yesterday, and today I claim your victory. I propose during our third match, we shall discover the true chess champion," boasted the young redhead.

The opponent cracked a smile, "well, the competition was certainly there, a fine match indeed.

I thank you for a fine challenge, Sarford," said the Hero-knight to the Squire.

Sarford gave a short nod in acknowledgement. "The very same, Carador," he said as he reached his right hand over the small oak table towards him, and Carador met with his left.

Carador released his grip and looked out into the distance above the snowcapped white mountains of Androuge, where he observed a glorious orange sunset over them. "Well, the hour grows late, the sun is setting, and nightfall is imminent."

"Aye," Sarford nodded. "It happens too early if you ask me. All I desire is a couple more hours of daylight and I would be content." He let out a sigh as he picked up one end of the chess table, opposite to Carador's, and returned the table through the fifty-foot Great Gate of Androuge's citadel: Seragone, in which they held their competition. They placed the table down inside the courtyard slowly.

"What say you to a rematch, the same time tomorrow?" asked Sarford.

"I'll be present," said Carador confidently.

"Not to worry, I'll go easier to match your skill, no need to feel deterred. Remember, you had defeated me yesterday, you have plenty of skill in you."

He laughed. "Deterrence is for the weak, Sarford. I will see you at dusk!" he pointed one finger at him while taking a step back.

"I will be looking forward to it," he replied with a nod of acknowledgment and began to turn his back but still had some boast in him he needed to release. "As you well know, Carador," Sarford added before Carador could even depart. "I will be proclaimed master of chess in all of Androuge. Everyone will know me as an ordinary Squire who had bested a Hero-knight of Androuge... Twice!" Sarford stated boldly, placing a fist upon his chest. "Well, in chess at least, I'm not quite prepared to challenge you in combat." He lost his boast.

Carador cracked a smile, "well, only time reveals all, don't let your overconfidence get the best of you, it may come crashing down," said Carador with a wolfish grin, and Sarford smiled nervously.

Without another word, Carador turned his back to Sarford to take a moment to admire a radiant orange sky of beginning nightfall, only to have the tranquil scene be abrupted by an unknown soldier's blunt voice.

"Lord Caradorian! Caradorian!" yelled a knight of Androuge, before him.

Carador took one step towards him, "yes?"

"This was sent to you from King Faraduel of Faradown," announced the unarmored knight breathless, handing him the sealed letter. It was in a teal colored envelope, crumpled and slightly torn. The knight was dripping with sweat and panting for air. He sported brown leather armor, a chainmail cuirass underneath, and a sheathed steel long sword at his right side. This was standard attire for off duty Seragone knights.

"Breathe, Soldier. Unless this is an emergency, there is no need to exhaust yourself."

"Yes, Sire," he promptly replied and took a few deep breaths.

Carador opened the letter and glanced over it. Sarford curiously stepped over to him, and Carador read it aloud:

Carador,

As you very well know, my Birthday is in two days. I would be honored if you can make the time to travel to Faradown for the weekend. I feel it would be an excellent time for us to catch up on current affairs, for we have not had the pleasure to communicate in person for a few seasons.

If you have previous engagements or are unavailable, I understand to the fullest. If you do intend to arrive, however, please leave as soon as you receive this invitation, for the road ahead is long, and Vialo and I would expect you before tomorrow evening. This message should arrive to you by six. I certainly hope you will be able to make it.

-Lord Faraduel-

Carador put the letter down and focused his gaze towards the horizon. He located the sun, which was accurately six inches above the summit of Mt. Stager. As Lord Faraduel predicted, the letter had arrived on time.

The King of Faradown, Faraduel Sildorian, Carador's old childhood friend. Both Caradorian and

Faraduel had come from royalty, and their friendship was destined. The Caracross and Sildorian bloodline have had a long history of fighting side-by-side against Arush'n'aug and Saratrox. The two kingdoms have kept peace with one another since their inceptions in the First Era.

Faraduel received the nickname, "The Dragon King," from his own kin and friends. He received this profound and almost controversial name for his fixation of dragons. He most admired Arush'n'aug, not for its deeds, but for what a magnificent creature it proves to be.

Carador turned to Sarford. "Well, my friend, it seems that I must depart before the hour draws too late. Farewell, Sarford," he said walking off, but not before laying a hand briefly on Sarford's shoulder.

"Farewell, Carador! I feel that next week will be a sounder time for chess," finished Sarford, as he turned around and walked south towards his village.

Carador dashed into the main hall of Seragone, his quarters branched off to the right. The halls of Seragone were chiseled from stone, each arch and pillar defined to the highest detail, chiseled down and smoothed to emulate steel. The glossy stone helped reflect torch light and would keep the room illuminated always. The floor of the hall was stone as well, but not as defined such as the walls and ceiling are. The floors were covered in deep red rugs that bore the silver sword of Androuge.

The main hall was occupied with residents conversing blissfully. In Androuge, only the wealthy and royalty are gained access to the great hall limitlessly, with exceptions for special occasions, meetings or weddings. Hero-knights and Paladins are gained access to the great hall as well as own private quarters in the citadel. At all times, eight Paladins guard the great hall, three on both the left and right side, and two at the door.

Carador made his way past most of hall's residents but stopped in his tracks as one middle-aged woman approached him with a basket in one hand and a bottle of red wine in the other.

"Hail, Carador! Where are you off to in such haste?" she asked almost excitedly. She had quite the optimistic tone to her voice.

Carador smiled "It's very lovely to see you, Merriam. Never a day goes by that you show age."

Merriam's cheeks blushed red, "and you have only aged into a respectful young man."

"Alas, duty calls, Lord Faraduel requests my presence in the west. I must depart at once as to not disappoint my old friend. Take care, Merriam!" He bowed politely and went forth.

"Godspeed, Carador!" He heard behind him.

He took his first right down the hall and entered the fifth room down, his own. Without a moment's hesitation he gathered his supplies, knowing full well what he would need for a weekend away. His stonewall room was kept orderly and mostly cleaned, castle servants and maids kept every room within the walls as clean as possible.

After packing a change of clothes, he retrieved his old, yet faithful, steel long sword, as well as a red journal with the title faded from age, and some rations for the road. He threw his pack over his shoulder and bolted out of Seragone.

Caradorian Caracross is in his mid-thirties, thirty-five to be precise, and is the only descendent of Caragorian Caracross, the former fifth and last King of Androuge, and Morwen Caracross. Other than Faraduel, who respects Carador's wishes and keeps his true destiny silent, none are aware that Carador is the son of former King Caragorian. If they knew the truth, he would have been already crowned king. Except for Faraduel, all who knew the truth about him are all but deceased. After his parent's death, Carador went into exile to forget his past, and when he returned, he kept the truth about himself, silent, none ever expected any royalty from him. He feels that he does not have the responsibility or leadership to control a kingdom, especially in these dark times. He wishes to remain a Hero-knight of Androuge, nothing more.

His armor was of a dark, slate gray color, the color of Triton, which is known as the strongest armor forged in the world. Triton armor was protective, although it is vulnerable to damage, hardly anything has successfully penetrated it. Only high-class soldiers have the honor to wield Triton, since it is such a rare ore to mine, and Triton is mined in the Black Mountains in the Aussarokian territory. The dwarven populated Manor Mines contain Triton as well, however, negotiating with the dwarfs to purchase some, does not come easily. He wore a maroon cape, tattered on the bottom, from miles of trekking, this cape symbolized a Hero-knight from lower class knights. His helmet concealed half of his face. Carador's hair was long and wavy, dyed a dark blond shade, and whiskers of a darker color protruded from his face. He has a fusion of green eyes, with a hint of blue, appearing silver. His build was of fair strength, he had prepared his body daily, all in preparation for when the task of maintaining order was to fall upon him, in this deed, he was destined to succeed.

Carador departed from the citadel entrance, and now headed to the stable to prepare his steed. His horse, Azaful, who upon noticing Carador's presence, neighed loudly in excitement. Carador smiled at the sight of his old companion, having raised Azaful from his days as a mere pony. Carador opened the stable, and gave Azaful a light pat. He mounted his steed, and with a gentle touch to the horse's side, they set off, to the west.

* * * * *

It was the Third Century. The Age of War, as some had come to call it, due to the chaos and misery that now commanded the land. The tyrant Saratrox, along with his so-called *pet*, Arush'n'aug have been nothing but a terror for everyone for as long as the citizens have remembered. The year is 2935, dated as the 2935th year since Earacill's discovery, and in those years, no successfully accomplishment to rid the land of them has ever been successful.

Twenty-four grueling hours of non-stop travel later, Carador had arrived at Faradown. Riding through the night and all that day, weariness became to fatigue. He refused to rest until later that night.

With the sun diminishing behind the Whiteshadow Mountains, Carador rode into the realm of the western kingdom of Faradown, and just as the letter had stated, *"Vialo and I would expect you before tomorrow evening."*

Faradown's appearance had not differed much then that of Androuge's. Both kingdoms contained a forested areas and mountains surrounding them. The main castle of Anlar had a predominant color of sky blue. Carador rode to Faradown's capital: Anlar, which was promptly constructed upon the highest peak, residing under Mt. Stager itself. The base of the city lies upon the base of the mountain. The upper city starts on the mountainside and ends at the summit of the mountains. Anlar rests upon the summit. Behind Anlar is Mt. Stager striking a magnificent five hundred feet into the sky, it was a site all had to see. Faradown lengthened one-mile-long from the top of the mountains to the plains below. The radius of Anlar had also lengthened overtime, one mile.

Carador's horse came to a halt after a sharp tug at the reigns, with a slight jump, he dismounted and tied up his exhausted steed. He made his way to the castle doors, and with relative ease, he opened them, and walked inside. Ahead of him, he saw his old friend, the King of Faradown, Faraduel, whom he overheard instructing a knight to look out for Carador.

"That will not be necessary!" he announced with a grin on his face, while curling his arm to hold his scratched helmet against his hip. Faraduel turned his head in surprise and spotted him.

"Ha!" blurted Faraduel joyfully, walking towards Carador. "I knew you would make it!" cried

Faraduel joyfully.

"Well, I would certainly not want to miss your fortieth birthday," he explained shaking hands with his old friend.

"Come on in!" Faraduel replied, happily waving his hand to beckon him. "The celebration will begin soon, even though it's not quite my birthday yet!" he sniggered, walking towards the great hall of Faradown. "Though the preparations are in work," he added.

Faraduel wore a dark blue robe, with a sky-blue sword embedded on the chest. He wore a silver crown upon his brow, with also with a sky-blue sword embedded in the center. The sword was Faradown's symbol. Faraduel had dark brown hair, almost appearing black, with a tint of gray to it. He also had a short-trimmed beard that went across his whole face. Faraduel is the son of the former Steward: Arog. Faraduel was born in the year: 2695, Faraduel was Carador's closest of friends, since early childhood. After the former King Silithor and his son are slain in battle, the Steward Arog is made king after his passing, Faraduel then takes the throne of

Faradown.

Carador walked with Faraduel to the main hall's table, there rested a variety of foods. From turkey, to corn, and mashed potatoes, resting in the center of the table, stood a large vanilla cake. With chocolate icing surrounding the edges and decorated in the center of the cake appeared a large "40."

"Please, take a seat!" pointed out Faraduel eagerly, to ease Carador after his long ride.

Carador gradually took a seat on the end of the lengthy table, in front of him, a variety of kitchen utensils were laid out before him.

"Attention, attention please!" a woman's voice was heard emitting from the castle's kitchen in the eastern corridor. The voice was that of Faraduel's wife, Vialo. She emerged from the kitchen drying her hands with a brown tattered rag. Behind her, a six-foot-long wooden trolley filled with various dishes was rolled out by four chefs.

"The main course is prepared for the king!" she announced tucking away the worn rag. "Hello, Carador," said Vialo as she saw him patiently standing next to his chair.

Vialo laid out plate on the table, it was a

platter of beautifully decorated King Salmon. The four chefs took care of the rest.

"We have not seen you in such a long time. How are matters back in Androuge?" she asked with a concerned tone in her voice. Queen Vialo was a beautiful woman with long blonde hair that shines like gold.

"My lady, the years have been kind to you, age has not affected your beauty one bit. It has been too long since my last visit," he said gesturing politely. "Androuge is going through its usual episode, as it has been through the years," he replied standing back up to straighten his posture.

"Yes, I would agree! It's always wonderful to see you, and I am pleased to hear the kingdom is well," she replied merrily.

"The pleasure is all mine!"

She smiled, "please excuse me," she then turned around and walked to her seat, as it stood at the opposite end of the king's.

From each section of the main hall, twenty of Faradown's finest knights and Paladins emerged, who all promptly proceeded to take a seat. Last came the king himself, walking in a slow and quiet manner with the best of posture, with hopes all would remember the extravagance of this day. He sat down without uttering a word, however, a big smile began to grow from ear to ear.

"Let us eat!" the king suddenly roared cheerfully from across the table to everyone, smiling as he has been all day. "To celebrate my four hundredth Birthday!" he added.

The group sat in silence and confusion.

Faraduel gave a grin. "Nah, it's only my fortieth! I'm just getting old, so there isn't much of a difference!" he laughed comically.

Everyone at the table joined in laughter, including Carador, although he laughed sarcastically, wondering if the others were genuine in their laughter. Faraduel enjoys telling jokes, though majority of the time, they had no humor behind them.

The variety of foods, which lay before him, was so mouthwatering, that Carador did not know where to begin eating first. In this situation, he knew that he must begin somewhere. He grabbed hold of a bowl of mashed potatoes and dropped them on his plate, with great vigor, he placed the bowl back down. After that, he took a great hunk of the turkey, although he was considerate as to leave some for the others, turkey has long been Carador's favorite of foods. After that, he applied himself with some corn, and lastly, a hefty piece of apple pie for dessert. The long table quickly erupted with chatter and laughter.

"Ladies and Gentlemen!" announced Faraduel loudly retrieving his silver goblet of red wine, a handcrafted wooden spoon, and brought them together repeatedly, producing a chime sound as to have the company hearken to him. "I would like to propose a toast, to Carador, whom I have known for many long years and would never miss out on the opportunity to adventure with!"

The men of Faradown shouted with pride and gave Carador a congratulatory hand, in response to the king's statement.

"Nor would I miss out on such a chance for the world!" he retaliated from across the table and he raised his golden goblet of red wine to him.

They all laughed roughly and returned to their meals to eat for the remainder of the hour.

* * * * *

That night, it had taken Carador much longer to fall asleep, because the food resting in his digestive system did not settle easily with him. While trying to fall asleep, he remembered he could not stay all weekend, for he would have to leave in the morning to run some errands and attend to business in Androuge.

Carador soon resorted to lie in his bed, reading the matured, red book he had brought along with him entitled: *My Extraordinary Journey*, a journal written by Tharagor: the discoverer of Earacill, or "Dynasty Realm". He opened the book and read the first page.

Day 1

Days in Arcon Realm grow more tiresome each day. I see the same faces each day. I see the same lands every day. I desire it. I desire more. I should become a traveler and visit distant lands. Perhaps discover new ones. That is what I'll do! I will cross the sea, past the horizon under the setting sun, never to return to my home here. I will find a new and peaceful place to settle. Somewhere I could pick up a book and read it under a tree in a peaceful bliss.

Alternatively, I could paint a picture of my image. Yes, a quiet and peaceful place, undiscovered, for only me...

-Tharagor

* * * * *

The night had come and gone, and a streak of the early morning sunlight came through the window, onto Carador's face, awaking him. He was prepared to explore the city of Anlar. He had breakfast with Faraduel and later left the castle to explore the city. Faraduel hoped Carador would not depart back to Androuge too early, because they have not seen each other in a lengthy time.

The first place Carador found himself heading was into a bar in search of a fine and refreshing ale. He located a bar east of him, south of Anlar. The buildings outer appearance stood out from the other ones in the city, it appeared poorly constructed, almost decaying away, he wondered if it was even built properly or if the awkward appearance was some constructional error. Anlar could be described as a city with a constant clear sky during the day and night. It had sparkling green homes, shops, and great halls. Anlar was a beautiful city. It had stone paved roads, and every road seemed to be designed to perfection.

He walked towards the front of the obviously aged bar, Carador walked up several wooden stairs that creaked so badly, he sensed he might break through them, Carador entered, *"The Wheezy Wizard."* He walked through the old walnut doors and appeared inside the bar.

The bar appeared small, for it had only ten wooden tables, akin the bar, the tables were as faulty in design. Each table was filled with people, only men. Carador noticed the thick scent of ale. It had the smell of ale in the air. The bar's structure was rotting wood.

The bar was surrounded with people everywhere. Most of the men inside were from Farist, a small town by the sea owned by the dwarfs, and the rest of the drunks were Faradownians.

Carador was used to the way men were prone

to behave in bars like this, always laughing passing out and spilling ale on the ground. It was the same in this bar. He walked forward towards the counter, the floors creaked as badly as the steps outside.

Carador walked over a pool of ale that someone had spilled on the ground. The spilt ale was not helping the wooden floor much, it created a soft spot, and even more unstable. He quickly made his way to the bartender.

"Good afternoon, Sir," the bartender said politely upon noticing the presence of Carador. "How may I serve you today?" the bartender questioned while drying a stone beer mug with a stained cotton cloth.

The bartender had brown and worn clothes that had two tears in it, one on the shoulder and the other on his collar. He had a brown curly mustache and dark dreary eyes. His face was well weathered and full of wrinkles. He appeared to be in his late forties.

"I'll have an Androugen ale," Carador replied.

During the process of ordering the drink, a man around twice the size of Carador, pushed him with great force, clearing the way to the bar hard out of the way, as if Carador were a simple fly, an annoyance to the man.

Carador stumbled almost falling over. A nerve in his temple twitched angrily. The bartender watched Carador in surprise. Carador fumed from the surprise attack. He is not one who is easily pushed around. Carador does not take kindly to bullies, as he did not care at the man's evident physical advantage.

Carador stood back up, walked over to the counter, and he pushed the immense man out of the way softly, so he may appropriately retrieve his drink.

The prodigious man swung around, and punched Carador in the face, nearly knocking him down. A few drunks gathered around them, to watch the inevitable brawl.

Since Carador had applied his helmet and armor, his helmet only received a dent on the left cheek from the man's mighty blow. Carador swung a punch into the man's stomach, obviously to little effect.

All the drunks had gathered around the two

THE WEEKEND IN FARADOWN

now. Carador grabbed an empty ale mug and smashed it in the man's face so hard the mug shattered in all directions, placing three small cuts on his fat face. The man was enraged, many of his veins and nerves were apparent throughout his face. He began to sweat, and his forehead turned red. The man obtained a wooden chair and started swinging it around swiftly and violently in Carador's direction. Carador ducked quickly, thus avoiding the blow.

The chair narrowly missed and closely striking another drunkard, who appeared amazed. Still enraged with anger, Carador's adversary swung again, this time the chair hit the intended target, Carador's head. The impact was so fierce, that the chair broke in several pieces and allowing Carador to stumble several feet backwards before falling to the ground.

Carador scrambled to get back on guard as he shook his head in disbelief. *This fellow needs to be taught a lesson in proper etiquette!"* Carador thought. He charged forward towards him. Carador rapidly punched the giant in the stomach, taking him by surprise, while at the same time, taking his breath. After about fifteen blows Carador directly uppercut him in the face, making him rise a foot into the air, he landed on a table that broke instantly due to his size. The man was now unconscious.

Carador rose, cracked his neck, and uttered, "What are you all looking at? Go back to your drinks," he ordered. His head was starting to ache, from the first blow he received.

The unruly mob did as they were told, instantly. They never spoke to Carador or dared utter a word of the previous debacle to each other.

Carador headed back to the bartender.

"Now that the show's over, I'll have my drink please," Carador sighed wearily resting his head on one hand.

"That was some amusing fighting there, Sir," the bartender announced slight nervously while passing Carador his drink.

"Don't mention it," Carador stated with a sigh, looking into his mug of Androgen ale, one hand rested on his helmet. "Please," he added. He stared blankly into his ale, watching the foam swirl around and around, almost hypnotizing him, however; he did not desire to intake just yet.

"I'm quite sure I will have much challenging

adversaries to overcome in my days, much more dangerous, merciless, opponents then him," he said straightening his posture. "Namely, fighting Sarugs, or slaying hordes of Aussarok. Not the mere task of ending a brawl."

"Have you heard about the tournament at the Faradown Arena?" the bartender asked gingerly.

"No... What about it?" Carador yawned.

"Well, it's supposed to be the highlight of everyone's day, rather choosing to watch, or compete in. I think you have the skills to survive the obstacles, I see the possibility of you winning!"

"No, thanks, competitions are not my style," replied Carador. "Thanks for the invite though."

"Did I mention that the grand prize is eighty thousand Bansers?" the bartender added with a smirk.

"Well, that does sound convincing, however; I am not in the need of wealth at this time."

"Oh, well, if you decide to participate, count me in as one of your viewers."

Carador quickly approached boredom of staring into his ale, he decided to finally open his helmet visor, and grasp his ale mug on the counter,

THE SOITS OF FREEDOM

and he drank it in one breath. He gave a polite burp and lightly slammed the mug on the counter.

"This is the best ale there is!" Carador rejoiced cheerfully, the alcohol's effect quickly setting in. "Everyone back home drinks it, it is a most popular ale," he continued proudly.

"Not too many people here buy it, they mainly buy Barion ale, which is ale from Barlafar in case you did not know," announced the bartender, while refilling another patrons mug. "Men from Barlafar come here often, they bring their ale here commonly as a welcoming." The bartender continued. "Not to get confused with Banlafar, Barlafar is the town of humans, next to it," he added.

"I know," said Carador slightly annoyed.

"Quite popular in these parts! My barrels are tapped within the first few hours of a receiving a new shipment," the bartender stated crossing his arms.

The drunken crowd in the background exploded with laughter, startling Carador. He wanted to rest easily and avoiding surprises or chaos for a while yet. Most of the drunks did not have the cheeriest disposition of Carador due to the previous ordeal. They started throwing small items at him, such as of chips from broken ale mugs, as they spoke ill of him, uttering that he's a show off, and a nut. Carador was not going to stand for the insults that flooded upon him, his nerves were twitching like an overrun heartbeat.

He reached over the bartender's counter where he discovered a throwing knife, which was most likely there, in the event of anyone trying to rob the bar, or an attempt to harm anyone, although the chances of such an event occurring is low.

Carador grasped the throwing knife, wheeled around, and with much strength and grace, in one motion, he threw it. The knife soared through the air and stopped when it lodged into the wall, coming inches away from three drunks who froze in their stops and turned white. Carador smirked as he saw the knife hit his desired mark.

The drunks appeared pale, looking at Carador with a frozen look, and now were silent.

"Now, if anyone talks ill of me again, I will not be so merciful in my aim!" thundered Carador angrily.

Carador rose from his stool and walked to

where the knife was planted in the old wood. The drunks remained pale as Carador walked over, glaring at the drunks wrathfully.

With a sharp tug, he removed the knife, which wedged a good three inches in the wall. Carador proceeded back to the counter. He handed back the single bladed throwing knife back to the bartender.

Carador breathed, "Sorry about that," he said dropping the knife on the counter and attempted to slowly relax, as he sat back down.

The Bartender chuckled, "no apology needed, honestly I would probably have done too, if I knew how to throw a knife anyway near as precise as that," he said cockily, trying to impress Carador, while failing in the process.

"Uh, so what's your name?" the bartender asked trying to make small talk.

"Carador, Hero-knight of Androuge."

"Carador..." The bartender recited. "A name I shall not forget!"

The drunks were quietly talking again amongst each other, now knowing better not to talk of Carador anymore.

Through the doors of the tavern, four of

THE WEEKEND IN FARADOWN

Anlar's city guards entered, each formally dressed in blue patchwork with ring mail armor underneath. Carador turned around to witness one of the city guards taking report of the incident, while interrogating a group of the drunks, who were too fearful to claim that Carador was a part of the conflict, and instead claimed that the man attempted to assault the bartender for not serving him, and Carador was there to retaliate, and knocked him out in the process.

Carador smirked, at the story he heard them tell, almost chuckling as he watched his lifeless adversary being taken out by the other three guards, and that he was now clear of a bounty, all because the drunks were too intimidated by him.

His former opponent would live, nevertheless, due to his overconfidence, he had sustained a broken nose and a batch of bruises. The city guard in the past had reported various public disturbances from the same man and they were now planning to stop them. The guard, who had taken report, was now heading towards Carador to hear his side of the story.

Carador quickly noticed this, and didn't want

to be a part of it, despising any type of interview. "Well, I better be on my way," he said while standing up from his stool, and to avoid interrogation, he attempted to walk out, only to be stopped by the guard's low voice.

"Excuse me," he announced loudly from behind, assuring Carador heard him.

Carador stopped in his track, gave a quick smirk and took a deep breath. He wheeled around and faced the guard. "Afternoon, soldier," he gave a polite nod.

"I have here reports indicating an attempted assault towards this here bartender," the guard spoke pointing his ink-tipped feather towards the bartender. "And that you," he now said pointing the feather at Carador, "retaliated and took control of the situation, and successfully took him down, can you confirm this?"

Carador nodded. "True to every word!" he said. "I was residing here-" he said, pointing to his former seat, "when he entered the bar, and drew this knife-" he took a hold of the bartender's knife he had thrown towards the drunks before, "at the bartender for not serving him."

The bartender had a confused look on his face, knowing none of that had happened.

"As I attempted to stop him, he gave me a hard blow to the face, denting my helmet," he said as he should the guard the deep dent on the side. "So, I picked up my mug and smashed it on his face, causing him to stagger around a bit before falling backwards and breaking through that chair," he ended showing the guard the broken furniture.

"Understood, and what is your name?" the guard asked. Carador smirked. "The name's Carador," he replied short and simple.

"Carador? You mean the close friend of our King Faraduel?"

"That is correct, he would be happy to know this city is now clean of yet another criminal."

"I agree, and all thanks to you," he smiled and nodded. "Have a good day now, Carador," the guard ended and now walked over to the bartender to check on him.

Carador gave a quick nod to the bartender, giving him the signal to agree with the story he told, and the bartender got the idea, and agreed to it.

Carador gave a last quick grin and wheeled

around, heading out of the bar. He needed to find the nearest blacksmith, and get his helmet repaired from the brawl. He would appear strange walking around with a damaged helmet. He took his helmet off and walked around for a couple of minutes until he found a blacksmith.

He approached the blacksmith. "How long would it take you to repair this?" He asked throwing his helmet to the blacksmith, who unaware of his presence caught it at the last second.

He looked about the helmet for a few seconds. "Two hours," he assumed looking at the helmet. He had a grumpy tone, although, he was not grumpy. "It'll cost ya' fifty Bansers," the blacksmith continued. His mustache seemed to be twitching back and forth each second.

Bansers are the currency in Faradown. Carador had a sack of Bansers along with him. He opened it, and took out two twenty-five coined Bansers, and tossed them to the blacksmith.

"Come back within two hours, it will be fixed, ya," ordered the blacksmith snorting as he placed the helmet on a shelf above him.

"Thank you," replied Carador, and he left the blacksmiths tent with a grin on his face.

He walked onward to new sights he had not viewed before in the city. Faradown was larger than Carador had thought of, at his first glance, long ago. Carador had come across a long street crowded with people, a sale was occurring on every store located on the main street, from groceries, to household appliances and armor.

Carador shrugged and entered the sword shop on the street, to examine what exquisite weaponry Anlar contains, his current swords recent signs of dullness and wear convinced Carador to purchase a new one. He walked for a few more steps south of Anlar until he came across a metal sign that stated, *"The Sword and the Shield."* On the sign was a large circular shield, underneath, a silver Bastard sword. Carador knew right away that that store was an armory. He carefully made it to the entrance with a couple of "excuse me" phrases in the way.

Carador walked inside the armory. He entered the shop faintly confused, because the areas were absent of any piece of armor or weaponry. There was no one else in the armory, besides him and the shopkeeper.

He walked to the counter and approached the merchant who was examining a new shipment of swords he had just received. Surprisingly, the merchant was an elf, old yet wise. He had black hair, blue eyes and a green cloth shirt with gold linings surrounding it, and upon the shirts chest, was a sword, the symbol of Faradown.

"Hello, there," Carador notified the merchant politely.

The merchant eyed Carador inquisitively, as he placed the sword lightly on the counter. "Ah, welcome! It's good to see you, Carador," the merchant said with anticipation.

"Do you- wait! How do you know my name? We have not met before," broke off Carador with suspicion.

"Everyone knows of you here, Carador," the shopkeeper replied wisely. "You are King Faraduel's oldest living friend, the heir to the dynasty of Androuge, and earlier, you fought a criminal twice your size, and defeated him."

"Yes, however, that only happened not even fifteen minutes ago! How could you have known this so fast?" Carador asked puzzled.

"Facts spread like wildfire in Faradown, Carador," he stated. "You'd be surprised."

"Yes, I am!" he replied, nodding his head. "And what are you implying by: heir to the throne?" he questioned suspicious of the merchant.

"Surely you know, Carador?" asked the shopkeeper disappointingly. "If you were to slay Arush'n'aug, you will become king over Androuge, restoring your bloodline that has been broken for the past thirty years," he continued.

"You know nothing of my bloodline, do not speak of it again," he said sternly.

The merchant nodded. "In time you will see what I see. Know that the slaying of Arush'n'aug will bring great leadership over you, in more than just one way. It is your destiny to free your people and bring peace upon them. It runs deep in your blood, Carador, you cannot fight it, I'm afraid."

"Well, yes, I too have heard the rumors that if one was ever to successfully slay the demon, Arush'n'aug, they would be a worthy being to be crowned king. Although, where you are wrong, my friend, I have no intention of obtaining such a high rank upon my people, I am a Hero-knight, I do all in my power to protect, and lead our people. I would not seek lordship over my kingdom, unless, of course... drastic times would call for it, in which case I would," he finished catching a deep breath. "Anyway, I am here to shop, what weaponry do you carry?" he said giving a quick glance around the shop. "Or are you out of supplies right now?" he said, seeing no merchandise displayed in the shop, only the few new swords in the crate upon the counter, which held Carador's gaze.

"Weapons, eh?" questioned the merchant raising his brows, as he turned around and walked into a backroom, leaving Carador.

Carador opened his mouth to utter a complaint, but then closed it again as he saw the shopkeeper coming back with a big green leather-bound book, the book appeared worn from age of its previous viewers.

"Here you are, Carador," he breathed placing the book in front of Carador. Carador gazed upon the book, not knowing what the book was for, yet as he opened it, he was able to identify it right away.

"Ah yes, amulets," Carador whispered quietly to himself.

He flipped through the book for a minute until he came across the amulet page. On that page were around thirty sorts of amulets. Ranging from those intended for healing, strength, defense or anything else:

AMULETS	BANSERS
Anaron Amulet of Elves	100
Anastar Amulet of Life	500
Androuge Amulet of Mankind	100
Anlaw Amulet of Death	500
Crimson Amulet of Dexterity	500
Crystal Amulet of Power	2000
Diamond Amulet of Sovereignty	1000
Dragon Amulet of Omnipotence	2000
Dynasty Amulet of Leadershup	2000
Emerald Amulet of Defense	500
Fire Amulet of Strength	500
Firestone Amulet of Kings	5000
Gold Amulet of Wealth	3000
Green Amulet of Luck	500
Ice Amulet of Wisdom	500
Jade Amulet of Nobility	500
Light Amulet of Stamina	500
Manor Amulet of Dwarfs	100
Onyx Amulet of the Mines	500
Red Amulet of Intellect	500
Ruby Amulet of Courage	500
Sacred Amulet of Old	1000
Silver Amulet of Charisma	500
Steel Amulet of Resistance	1000
Triton Amulet of Toughness	3000

"Where did you get these?" Carador asked surprised at the value of the various amulets.

"The majority of them I handcrafted myself," said the merchant polishing the single blade. "And the others," he chuckled slightly. "Well, the others I found in the ruins of caves, mines, and even some were buried underground."

"I see..." acknowledged Carador. "If you truly found those, then why do you not sell them at a much higher cost? I mean, five-hundred to one or two thousand Bansers is a low price. I can afford to purchase any of them right now. Don't get me wrong, I favor a good bargain as much as the next man, although if you were to raise the prices, well then you get easily become the richest elf in Faradown, or maybe even in the land!"

"I do not need wealth to enjoy my life," responded the shopkeeper. "Especially not with this thousand-year-long war going on, Saratrox and Arush'n'aug could strike anywhere at any time. Imagine waking up one morning and at your front door, are hundreds, or even thousands of armed Sarugs prepared to strike you down, and you watch as your city burns before you, and the dead of those all innocent now surround you. Have you ever felt it? That horrible feeling of not knowing which day in your life will be your last! I have that dreadful feeling every morning, and believe me, it is not comforting," the merchant explained. "I am sorry," the merchant continued regaining his previous posture. "Days in Earacill grow dark, we are in a desperate need for heroes."

"All you have uttered is the truth, my friend," said Carador in agreement. "Bansers hold no value if you have no use for it."

Carador returned to the book and observed the remaining words. He closed the book, looked back at the merchant.

"Well, since I am here, I'll buy the Firestone amulet, please," he said with enthusiasm.

"Ah, just like your father, it truly does suit you" the merchant announced wisely.

Carador stared up at him alarmed and surprised. "My father?" chocked Carador surprised. "No, no my father is no king, and he never will be, he is a blacksmith, back in Androuge," he lied trying to steer the conversation away from his former life.

The merchant looked blankly at Carador.

Carador thought his lie would destroy the merchant's faith in his previous implication, though he was too wise for Carador's ploy.

"A new King of Androuge would reunite *the Three Kingdoms*, Carador. And Aussarok will fall if they reunite and strike as one, with the proper tactics," he said knowing Carador's true destiny.

Carador appeared lost and confused, he took another glance around the shop. "You never answered my question. Where are all your supplies?" questioned Carador eagerly trying to change the subject.

"Look for yourself," replied the merchant quick and demanding.

"I already have, there is nothing," mumbled Carador.

"Look again," pointed out the merchant.

Carador turned back around, rolling his eyes annoyed.

The merchant waved his hand slowly in the air, unbeknownst to Carador. Light blue smoke slowly creped out of the shop's walls, and counters, quickly, the supplies appeared from the foggy blue smoke, everything in the book emerged.

Carador turned back around, surprised.

"Surely, you have heard of the elven magic, haven't you?" questioned the merchant with mild curiosity.

"Well, yes," admitted Carador. "However, I failed to realize that the elves knew this kind of magic, this is high wizardry magic," explained Carador.

"Yes, although some of us have learned certain amounts of their magic too," the merchant professed.

"Ah, I see," acknowledged Carador, with a touch of laziness.

"I used a vanishing spell, to prevent thieves from stealing, the objects were cloaked."

"Hmm, rather wise thinking," complimented Carador. "Well, you know my name. What is yours?" he questioned curiously.

"My name is, Morler, founder of the Sword and the Shield," he answered with a hint of cockiness in his voice.

"So, why is an elf living in Faradown, let

alone, the capital?"

"Live anywhere too long, and life there begins to grow dull. Seeing the same faces day after day, nothing but fellow elves," he replied shaking his head. "No diversity."

"I see, that's reasonable enough. I can't say I can relate, but I can understand," he said crossing his arms.

"When you live to be over six thousand years old, you come tell me if you still feel the same," smirked Morler.

Carador let out a nervous chuckle. "Excuse me for a minute, Morler," he implored politely as he walked away from the desk and walked towards another counter.

He walked towards the front of the counter, presented in front of him, several amulets as seen in the book. He quickly identified which of the amulets was the Firestone, remembering the red flaming shape of it, and its Triton polished stone. Carador took the amulet by the necklace and proceeded to walk back with it to Morler. Carador placed the amulet slowly on the counter next to the sword.

"Okay, your total cost will be five-thousand

Bansers, Carador," he announced.

Carador nodded, and he opened his sack of Bansers and poured out the coins on the counter. He paid Morler with some of his gold, with a great sum remaining.

"I'm in the market for a new sword; may I see that book again?" asked Carador eyeing the book.

"Certainly," answered Morler as he handed the green leather-bound book back to Carador.

He began to search through the book again, searching in the index section for swords. The swords were located on page fifteen. Carador turned the book to page fifteen and noticed that the swords ran all the way to page thirty, one sword per page. Carador studied each sword for a moment until he came across a sword, which was one that he never imagined, could be real, nevertheless, his eyes played no tricks and he began to thoroughly read the details of the sword:

THE EMERALD-STAR: THE SWORD OF LEADERSHIP

The Emerald-Star may be considered the most historical and the most famous of all legendary swords. It was forged by the greatest Elven blacksmith of all time, in the mysterious Cave of Anlaw. It was forged for King Tharagor in the year 19 of the First Century. It then became an heirloom to Tharagor's dynasty. This sword has seen its share of battles in the past. Its high polished Triton double-bladed edge glows Emerald green when its user is enraged with anger, for the benefit of superhuman strength. Its Emerald handle regains your strength when weary of war or traveling.

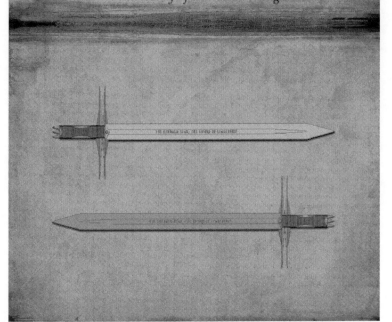

Carador had been in the market for a new sword quite some time now, to find such a marvel now only seemed fitting. He tried not to comprehend its expensive price tag yet but just as he feared, the price was in fact way above his limit. Down on the bottom of the page stated its price: One hundred thousand Bansers. Carador needed to find a way to make seventy-five thousand Bansers.

"Well, I found what I am looking for!" announced Carador. "Although, its price is much too high for me," he said disappointingly. "Err- I might be back," informed Carador a little discouraged. He placed the book back on the counter and headed out the store.

"You will be back," Morler said quietly to himself as he placed the book away.

CHAPTER II

* * * * * * * * *

THE TOURNAMENT

With his unexpected experience at the "Sword and the Shield" Carador walked for close to an hour around Anlar, enough so that he was sure he had crossed with everyone at least twice. His focus was straightforward on the Emerald-Star, nothing else mattered to him after seeing it in all its glory. He was willing to do anything to obtain it, like a child begging their mother to buy them a new toy. Carador was so anxious and hellbent to earn some extra gold now. He made his way into local businesses and shops, asking merchants if they needed any extra labor for an hour so, unfortunately, he was turned down. He resorted to reading signs and the local prints for any sort of luck, still, to no avail.

Carador continued to walk the streets of the glorious golden city, from a distance he could see a sign, hastily nailed onto the right side of an archery store. Not expecting much, he headed for the sign at the off chance it was requesting work for a shop or service. He approached the sign with a sigh of relief as it was beneficial to his current state, the sign stated:

*Come and test your skill at the new tournament
This week only! At the Faradown Arena.
One impossible course. One brave winner.
One man to walk away
eighty thousand Bansers richer!*

Carador grew a grin on his face. "This is what that bartender must have been talking about!" Carador whispered to himself, remembering the bartender mentioning a city tournament. He knew he must compete in the tournament, to buy his dream sword.

Carador headed immediately in the direction of the grand Faradown Arena, it was north from the sign he had read. He recollected from his memory of passing the arena, although he failed to notice the tournament being held there. Carador made a brisk stride north. He came to a quick halt, remembering his helmet, which he had given the blacksmith to repair. He was so anxious about the tournament that he had almost forgotten about it. He was told that he could retrieve it in two hours, and judging by the numbness in his legs, for lack of resting, those two hours had indeed come and gone.

He wheeled around, and headed south, where the blacksmith's shop was located. He came back across the shop. Walking into the blacksmith's tent, he stared at the blacksmith, whom to his surprise, was fast asleep. Sleeping deeply in his chair, his head was upwards, the bright sun beaming down on his face.

Carador crept a bit closer, quietly stepping into the tent, making sure he would not wake the blacksmith. He located his helmet, standing on display, along with three other objects: two were swords, and one was a steel breastplate. He slowly reached for his helmet and grasped it from the counter. The helmet appeared in better condition than he had ever seen it. It was neatly and precisely polished along the edges and markings. The dent it received on the cheek was all but gone. Carador happily equipped his new helmet. Even the inside of it smelled of new leather.

"Thanks, mate," whispered Carador joyfully to the sleeping blacksmith while adjusting his helm. Carador stepped silently out of the smoked filled black tent.

Carador's thoughts soon returned to the ongoing tournament. Almost forgetting, Carador promptly sprinted off north again, at great speed. His only companion: the desire for his new sword.

Sometime afterwards, Carador arrived at the Faradown Arena. He stood at the entrance of the black gateway, calmly walking into the arena, mental fixation of the Emerald-Star still present. He noticed a sign, explaining the tournament. His heart sank as he saw the tournaments challenge, he was to overcome obstacles constructed with larger than average blades, axes, and other forms of maliciously innovative weaponry.

"If you do not succeed to the end, you will die

by steel," Carador mused to himself. *"I will not end my life by man-made material, and that's a promise!"* He thought clenching his teeth and walking closer to the obstacle course.

Courage is the key to win over the others. Skill will strongly be required to stay alive, to win the prize and buy the Emerald-Star. Carador went through the gates, walking tall and courageous. He was required to enter weapon storage before entering.

Carador stepped into the weapon storage. There were a variety of weapons, many swords, axes, knives, and halberds. Carador bluntly equipped a sword and a knife, since his was residing currently in Anlar. He could not figure out why he would need to use weapons in an obstacle course, but he would find out soon enough he thought. Carador headed back out of the weapon storage, he carefully checked over himself, making sure his armor was secure, proving to himself that he was worthy. With a last breath, he walked in front of a spiked black gate, the entrance, and entered.

At a full three-hundred-and-sixty-degree angle, he was surrounded by a crowd of several hundred. Citizens of Faradown made up most of the attendance. They cheered on a contender whom had the moment was taking the course. Carador could not decide if he should hope the participant ill fate in his trial, or if he wanted him to survive, win the tournament, and claim his prize.

Carador stood behind two nervous looking men. One was armed with only a sword, and the other, strangely enough was weaponless. They both stood prepared to take the tournament, their fear for life and limb, shamelessly evident.

"OOOOHHHHH!" Yelled the excited crowd as the participant received a harsh blow from a large axe. His lifeless corpse satisfied the ground with a loud thud.

The gate opened wide for the next competitor, the unarmed Man, he slowly took a step inside a lengthy and darkened cave, and his hands were trembling nervously. A long silence from the crowd had overcome them, as they waited ever diligently to witness the outcome. Seconds later, they broke out into applause as they saw the human appear out of the darkness of the cave, sweating frantically. Carador speculated what devilry lay about in the cave, nevertheless, knowing full well, he could experience it first hands soon enough.

The participant leapt past two threatening, swinging axes, which stood near the exit of the cave. After the quick run, the fellow lost his balance, and he fell onto the platform, right at the edge of the course. Underneath him, a commanding lake of fire rested, on which the tournament stood.

The competitor slowly picked himself back up, the hopeless fear still in his eyes, although he was relieved, he did not fall off. He gingerly walked a little further, looking upwards at the swinging axes. He, however, was not watching where he was stepping, in return, a concealed blade hidden in the floor, pierced upwards, and stabbed the fellow in the foot. He yelled painfully grabbing his wounded foot, again he lost his balance, and he backed up, falling into the lake of fire, scorching in the flames.

There was a loud, "AAAWWWEEEE!" from the crowd. The gate opened again, to beckon the next participant. The man, armed with the sword, who stood in front of Carador, slowly walked forward towards the gate. He trembled more so than the previous competitor. This was quickly followed by a loud yelp, dropped his sword, ran off, out of the arena, and vanished. A lot of "boos" from the crowd quickly erupted, as they witness the coward run off.

The gate remained opened for Carador. He gave a last deep breath, bravely, Carador headed towards the opened gate. He slowly stepped inside the cave, shielding himself with his sword as he cautiously walked about. The gate slammed behind him, there was no turning back now.

He looked ahead, where he examined ten torches, five were on either side of the cave. Carador contemplated taking one, debating if they would in any way become of an accessory to victory. No previous competitor took a torch, thus Carador applied himself one, being diverse. Now given that, Carador could see the sides of the cave, and the ground, ahead of him. Thankfully, he did not locate any concealed blades, let alone, see exposed ones anywhere. He prepared his weapons, if a ploy was in order, to catch him off guard.

Carador slowly walked down the center of the cave, observing hesitantly for any sign of concealed weapons. He continued to walk down the dark path, so far, it remained well for him. A few more feet down however, six large swords sprung out of either side of the walls, coming inches to Carador's head, body, and legs. He froze in his position. Unfortunately, one of the large swords however, had struck the blade of his knife; separating the blade from the hilt. Carador now, was only grasping the hilt of the knife.

"Great!" he groaned angrily, as he dropped the bladeless knife. Carador brought his sword closer to him, now being one weapon short. The torch remained grasped in his other hand.

Carador walked further on and came a few feet from the exit of the cave. The gate went ajar, and he blissfully stepped out.

He was relieved he was outside again. The torch was now useless, so he dropped it. Carador was still not going to take any chances. He quickly made a run for it, the fastest he could, running out of the cave. At the exit of the cave, two large steel battle-axes came down and collided with each other, erupting with a loud: Clang.

"Wow, what luck!" Carador thought to himself surprised, as he halted his sprint.

The crowd erupted in applause after witnessing his presence once again from the inside of the cave. Carador took a minute to catch his breath, as pacing was critical in an even such as this. Underneath the wooden platform in which he stood, Carador observed the lake of fire, which lay deep below. The support beams of the tournament were constructed of steel, angling forty-five degrees away from the lake; therefore, avoiding the flames. The fire also resided low enough that only minimal heat could be felt by those on top.

Carador again, looked everywhere for concealed blades. On the floor, the walls, and even if something was going to harm him from the sky, he could not be too careful. Carador located the hidden blade that struck the last competitor, it stood in the center of the walkway. There were other ones similar, all around. Carador carefully avoided those blades, by taking a large leap over them.

Carador walked further onwards, one thing leading to another. Two fierce swords came swinging, head on towards him. Carador quickly dropped to the floor, and stayed low, avoiding the blow. The swords were swinging freely above him, akin to a giant pendulum. He calculated the time it took the swords to swing from one end, to the other. With that, he leaped back up.

When the two swords passed over him, he remained standing, preparing to jump. The large swords came swinging backwards, Carador quickly jumped onto the blade of the sword, and grabbed a hold of the metal pole they were smelt together to keep his balance. The swords were not sharp, though by no means did this nullify them as a threat.

He carefully kept his balance, as the swords swung back and forth. Carador jumped off the sword from the back. Without giving him any time to catch his breath, two large axes came heading his way, he dropped to the floor at the last second. The axes were now swinging above him. Carador groaned and started to crawl away.

Once the swinging axes had passed, a large stone and rectangular boulder came smashing to the ground with such force that if it were able to match Carador's speed, it would have no trouble flattening him. There was no way around it. As soon as it went up, it came back down.

Carador mentally timed how long it stood in the air until it came back to the ground. The boulder went back upwards, as soon as it was above Carador's head, he made a run for it, reaching the other side safely. There was a greater applause from the crowd.

After a few more jumps, ducks, and dodges, Carador confronted two men, who judging by their looks, had been captured, and forced to resort to violence on whomever they see upon the platform. They both wielded battleaxes. Carador gave them the title of "Crazed Axe-men." The crazy axe-men sprung forward at Carador, with savage force. One of the axe-men swung furiously at Carador. He shielded himself with his sword and successfully deflected the blow. The force of the axe-men's swing was so massive, that it shattered Carador's sword into countless shards. The pieces of the sword came falling to the ground resembling hail. The axe-man swung again towards Carador's head.

Carador reacted fast, he back flipped away from his current state, therefore; the axe-man missed his intended target. Carador landed inches away from a large sword that swung reverse and forward like the other blades Carador encountered.

The axe-man walked towards Carador again, wielding his weapon, threateningly. The axe-man that was trying to kill Carador charged towards at him. The other axe-man was indifferent to Carador, looking for an escape for himself. Carador quickly looked behind him and witnessed the giant sword, the same one that was swinging freely, came close to striking Carador, by the time the axe-man was in front of Carador, the massive sword swung towards them.

The axe-man approached Carador, he pulled his axe behind him, and prepared to swing. Carador could hear the sword slice through the air in its approach. Carador grinned and quickly jumped out of the way, and instead of him getting hit, the sword found sanctuary deep within the poor fool's stomach. Carador turned around in curiosity as to the fate of his plan. The corpse confirmed this.

"Excellent!" he thought to himself. Carador turned back around to get the next axe-man, when he wheeled around, the opponent's axe, had slashed

Carador in the head with his mighty swing, Carador fell on his back in shock. He was quick to return to combat stance as he felt his helmet, feeling a long deep slash in his helmet, not deep as to have pierced his flesh, though the exception of a small cut that went from his right eyebrow to the top of his head. The hole was most obvious. Unfortunately, because it was Triton armor, the slash did not go too deep into his helmet.

"I just had that fixed!" Thundered Carador with furious anger, his face had enlightened bright red, he was breathing heavily.

He charged at the axe-man with such force, he speared him in the stomach, forcing the two to the ground and both began to roll towards the edge of the stadium as a result. They both landed a few inches from the edge. The axe-man's battle-axe fell off the stage, melting in the lake of fire below.

Carador grabbed the axe-man by his shirt, and with a mighty push, he tossed him off. The axe-man quickly grabbed Carador's leg to bring him down as well, causing both to fall. Carador was able to grab the wood of the platform with one hand. The axe-man was not so fortunate, as he burned to death.

Luckily for Carador: he remained hanging, nevertheless, his grip was slipping. With all his might, Carador punched a hole in the platform, he was now hanging by two supports.

The intense heat of the fire below was so hot, that Carador's leg plate began to heat rapidly, burning his legs. Carador grabbed with both hands on the edge of the platform, he quickly pulled himself to escape the raging heat. He got himself back onto the platform, only to be knocked back down by the roaring cheer of the audience.

Carador noticed that in front of him stood the finish point, marked by a series of vibrant flags and banners. Yet, Carador noticed that there were blades sticking all around the finish point. There would be no easy way to get around. Carador turned around and headed to the dead axe-man's body. He took his mighty axe and walked back to the finish point. He threw the axe on the blades, forcing them to all emerge upwards. The axe split apart and was sent flying two different directions. One right above him, the other went soaring the opposite way. Carador carefully grabbed hold of one of the emerged blades and jumped beside it. He safely landed on the finish point.

The audience had broken out loudly in applause, they stood up, and clapped constantly for the winner. Carador stepped down the wooden steps, and on to a stand.

Carador noticed half a dozen city guardsmen protecting the prize money, which was carried by a wobbly dressed man. He presented the bag to Carador.

Carador happily took the bag of Bansers. He then began walking towards another gate, the exit. Carador took the exit and left the tournament.

"Well, that was easier than expected," breathed Carador, his eyes fixed on the bag of Bansers. "I wish I could do another of these tournaments," Carador spoke quietly to himself. "A more challenging one perhaps."

With the adrenaline flowing through his veins, Carador did not care enough to get his helmet repaired, he now sees the damage as charisma, and considers that the slash gives him more character.

Carador's heart had felt lighter than it has in years, euphoria filled his mind and he felt invincible.

He had enough money to buy the Emerald-Star!

CHAPTER III

* * * * * * * * *

THE RACE TO BANLAFAR

Today was one of Carador's greatest days. He headed out of the tournament, it was now closed for there has been a victor. Carador's heart was filled with joy knowing that he could now purchase the sword.

He ran as fast as he could, away from the Faradown arena, in a mad dash to the armory. He was sweating from the tournament, and now from running.

Carador later spotted the sign of the armory, and quickly approached the doors. He barged in with great anticipation.

"I'll buy the Emerald-Star!" shouted Carador breathless as he threw the hefty bag of Bansers to Morler. Carador had put his fifteen thousand Bansers in the bag already, he had five thousand Bansers remaining. Morler caught the bag with a loud "humph," because of its mass.

"In your hands you hold a bag of one hundred thousand Bansers!" cried Carador, being so worked up that he hardly gave himself time to catch his breath.

Carador turned around and he saw the wall full of swords. He visualized the Emerald-Star, he was able to identify immediately it was the Emerald-Star from the drawing. The sword looked far better up closely.

Carador took the sword off the plaque, which was mounted on the wall, and gripped it tightly, the sword regained Carador's strength, from the tournament and from running. Right then he knew the book did not deceive him.

He read the inscription that had been carved into the sword, the double-blade sparkled silver and blue from the Triton, therefore, no rage was within Carador.

Carador looked back at the display, from which the Emerald-Star was situated, next to it, laid the sword's scabbard, it was brown, assembled out of strong leather, and emeralds encrusted around it.

"I see you have won the tournament, congratulations," avowed Morler, grinning at him.

"Heard the applause, I'm assuming?" asked Carador. "Seeing as it happened minutes ago, there's no way you could have known otherwise!" he queried shocked.

"Well, aren't you holding the sack of coins that was being rewarded?"

"Oh," Carador blubbered with an embarrassed look as he stared at the sack of Bansers.

"And remember: facts spread rapidly in Banlafar," Morler assured calmly.

"Seems a little too fast," joked Carador taking the sword and the scabbard to the front counter, laying them with a great ease in front of Morler, prohibiting the quietest sound. "How did you get this sword," asked Carador, still heavily eying it.

"I believe that once it was in the possession of the elven King, Tharagor, whom unfortunately was slain in battle by Saratrox. The sword was passed on to his son: Morather. Although when Morather, was slain by Arush'n'aug, in the year 2305, of the Second Century, his sword was lost and almost buried in the

Camalon Fields. Once when I was exploring the Camalon Fields, I found it in the middle of the fields worn and dull. Though oddly enough, I saw nothing regarding the corpses those who had fallen, not even the late King Morather himself."

"I found the sword, I failed to realize that the sword was rare until I found a description about it in a book I had read. I then decided to sell the sword, in this shop, since I have no use for it. And for five hundred years, no one has possessed the Bansers to purchase it, or they never even seen it for sale, except you, Carador," Morler finished.

"So that is why it was so expensive and extraordinary," consoled Carador equipping the legendary blade, he held it tight. "Well, my friend, I best be on my way, nice meeting you," Carador informed Morler, as he concealed the sword in its scabbard, and he tied the scabbard around his waist. "Farewell, Morler," said Carador. And he left.

* * * * *

The hour was later than he had expected since he left the armory. Carador had finally equipped his new amulet, he had forgotten all about it during the tournament. The presence of the amulet had given him so much power, he felt that he could overcome any opponent with one hand tied behind his back. He was relieved at his new purchase, giving him self-esteem that would aid him in the future.

It was nightfall now, the town was silent, and the stars above glittered in the moonlight, and the moonlight upon Banlafar. The only sounds now came from whistling of the trees, bells ringing quietly from surrounding buildings, and Carador's footsteps. He almost fell asleep walking, "It's so peaceful and silent now," Carador thought weary to himself.

Carador headed back to the city, Anlar, one more night would satisfy both him and Faraduel. He approached the gate of to the city and entered. He entered it relieved that he could finally get some rest. Silently he walked through the halls, not allowing himself to make racket that would wake those already resting, Faraduel was not around; Carador assumed he was already sleeping.

He headed to his own guest room, and there,

he deposited all his belongings. From within his bag, he retrieved his pipe, a book, and some tobacco. He headed back out of Anlar and sat down on a bench outside, Carador lit his pipe and inhaled the tobacco, and he proceeded to sing a song about a former King of Androuge:

"Sa
Earicadal Mai ish Lan to Sah
Mali to sai noi to Dah
Gele shew noi shlaw sah sadarrow?
Hesie kish horlan kai sah madarrow
Hei shew noter hes da ganferies?
Kai mai hies ish tio sanferies.
Corien shew moeh sah faw?
Kai sah hese kai Man
Noe shew sti flish cazt larrow?
Kai fenies seret fah sah carrow
Sa
Earicadal Mai Ish Lan to Sah"

It was a song about the first King of Androuge: Earicadal. Carador had sang it in Androgen, the secondary language in Androuge. In common speech it would state:

"*Oh*

Earicadal Great King of Old
Founder of gems and of Gold
Shall you be heard across the land?
From the mountains to the sand
May you be blessed with many powers?
To build cities and sturdy towers
May you be heard across the land?
To the fountains and to Man
May you be blessed with many powers?
To crest land for the flowers
Oh
Earicadal Great King of Old"

The moonlight shone on Carador's face, and blackness filled the night.

"The stars are obscured, something lurks in the East, a sleepless terror, filled with fury, sorrow, and pain." Carador told himself aloud, these thoughts now commonly ran through his mind, he could only imagine what it could be, the dragon, Arush'n'aug.

A short while later Carador finished smoking his pipe and returned to his room. He went into his room, closed the door inaudibly and crawled into his bed. He reached below, under his bed and felt around for the book he was reading. He grabbed it and adjusted himself as to read another day of Tharagor's journey.

Day 2

I have made my preparations to leave my homeland of Arcon Realm. I have bought a boat with all my money.

I will use it to cross the sea. Alone I could not make this trip, so I will bring my family and closest friends who grow tired of Arcon Realm.

"Tharagor, where will we go? There have been no sightings of land around here within hundreds of miles!" said Arien, one of my closest friends, mind you.

"South. South has been explored only slightly. The South must have some land we have not yet discovered. Why not explore there? East is filled with land of humans. Let us find another land we can claim for ourselves."

"It is a foolish task, Tharagor, however; I too would like to explore for a new world."

"My words cannot describe the fortune I feel of your family's decision to follow mine. I promise you we will find new land."

"A new world? That must be one of the most ignorant of your crazy ideas ever, Tharagor!" yelled some of the town's citizens at me after I had enlightened them, as too my migrant aspirations.

"The land down south has never fully been discovered! Why not search it completely?" I yelled back to them. I didn't want to make them think of me foolishly.

"The sea northwards are empty! You are all going to die!"

"Don't listen to them, Tharagor, there will surely be undiscovered land waiting to be found," I told myself. I was not going to let my friends and family down. I swear it!

-Tharagor

Later Carador fell asleep listening to the breeze of wind crashing against his window.

* * * * *

Morning came with a stream of sunshine shining through the window of Carador's bedroom. Carador was awoken by the bright sunlight in Faradown shining in his face.

He yawned wearily, wanting to rest more. The swan-feathered covers would tempt anyone to rest longer, nevertheless, Carador fought the temptation. He rose up, stretching. He climbed out of bed, fixed it, and washed his face at a nearby fountain from within the room.

He hastily gathered his equipment from under the oak bed and walked out of his room for some morning grub. Carador gradually walked through the halls, greeting visitors or friends of Faraduel.

He walked along and sat down at the lengthy table where his breakfast was laid out before him, he equipped a knife and a fork and began to eat. On his plate sat three perfectly cooked sausages, two scrambled eggs, and a slice of crispy bacon. For a drink Carador chose Green tea, it was one of his favorites.

Carador quickly devoured his breakfast, and he said his goodbyes to Faraduel and Vialo. He was returning home to Seragone today.

Shortly later Carador left Anlar, he gathered his equipment, and mounted his horse and left the kingdom of Faradown.

* * * * *

Carador returned to his kingdom, the kingdom of Androuge in the West. He rode past the vivid landscape, the tall striking mountains securing Androuge from the north, acting as a shield to their defense. A beautiful indigo blue they shone in the starlight, and shone silver in the sunlight, it was quite a skeptical to view. The light green fields of Birchwood were located outside the capital city of Androuge.

With a steady pace, He rode further on until he would arrive to the kingdom's capital. Carador's horse was equipped with its master's items, while he himself grasped the Emerald-Star, still filled with virtue of the sword.

Carador rode onto a hill, his favorite hill, one of the highest peaks, where he can view each region of Seragone. Normally, it shone in the fiery daylight, and gleamed at the tranquil night. Although what his eyes had fixed upon was not what he had expected.

Carador noticed the city of Seragone, the City of Silver Knights. The capital city in Androuge, destroyed. It remained there as a scene of an assault committed by Aussarok. Nevertheless, they could not have besieged the city, for everywhere flames from the underworld had scorched the city. The city was crumbling, however; there were no signs of rubble from catapults or trebuchets. Something else had attacked the city.

Seragone, the capital of Androuge, Carador's hometown, had been attacked by, Arush'n'aug, one of the two of Earacill's most loathed and feared beasts. Arush'n'aug was also properly known as the Great Black Dragon.

This was the third devastating attack Arush'n'aug has accomplished in Androuge, and it would not be the last if, unless the beast is confronted and defeated in its entire devilry.

Carador felt a great deal of shock, anger, and depression, at the sight of this travesty. He nervously bit his lip hard enough that it began to bleed. He felt no pain from this, for the pain from the attack on

Androuge already sat in his heart.

The city's towers were burning, along with many homes, stores, and farms, most homes were razed to ash. The temple of Anastar was burning, it is Androuge's most sacred of buildings. Its foundations were found directly across from Seragone.

The city itself bore scars of battle, it still stood sturdy enough to enter, and repair could be done. There was a good quantity of survivors from the attack, soldiers making up the majority, having been armored and were well trained, although peasants managed to survive as well.

Carador rode down the hills as fast as his could go and kept going to the entrance of Seragone, and rode inside, avoiding fire and rubble as Azaful galloped on.

Carador rode to the uppermost sector of Seragone. Towards the top of the city, Carador had a palace room where he stayed. Hero-knights and Paladins have quarters in Seragone. He entered the public housing, and he headed to his quarters as to salvage some equipment from his room.

He headed through the main hall that used to

be bright red but blackened now from the fire and smoke.

"Carador!" yelled an elderly man running towards him, with one hand in the air, and the other gripping his abdomen.

"What happened here? Was it Arush'n'aug? Aussarok!" asked Carador eagerly, facing the man.

"Yes, it was Arush'n'aug! The shadow has fallen upon Androuge! It has destroyed us!" cried the peasant, sweating, blood gushing from his abdomen.

"Where is everybody?" cried Carador in disbelief, with a hint of woe, looking around angrily to all the corners of the housing.

"They have left, they have retreated to safer places, although I do not know as to where such fortifications are," he sobbed, his mind racing through the previous suffering he had witnessed.

"You're wounded," pointed out Carador. "Let me heal you," he said looking at the gash.

Carador stretched out his hand. White static shocks emerged from his fingertips and it built up into his palm into a large white orb, as bright as the sun, but as cold as ice. He positioned his hand on the peasant's wound, the orb entered the cut and vanished. The cut slowly closed, and he was healed.

"Aruanor's Grace has healed you," said Carador quietly gazing upon the newly healed wound.

"You know the arts of Aruanor?" asked the peasant cheerfully, looking down at his side.

"Yes, in my earlier years, I was a healer for the wounded and sick, such as yourself. Rarely I can conjure it, the power is far vaguer to me, than in previous seasons," responded Carador looking at his hand.

Behind Carador and the peasant, a large chunk of rubble fell to the ground, crashing to the right of the entrance. Both looked quickly.

"Get yourself out of Androuge! Make for safer havens, and do not come back to Androuge for some days!" cried Carador to the man.

"I shall! What about you?" asked the peasant half-panicked and half-curious.

"I have my own conflict to deal with," announced Carador scornfully not looking at him, the task before him controlled his mind.

"Go now!" cried Carador sending him off, with the motion of his arm.

The peasant swiftly took flight, out of the housing the castle, and away from Seragone.

The castle was now deserted, no knights or peasants anywhere to be seen. Carador turned left went through another hall, then turning right and entered his room. His room was slightly damaged. Shattered glass covered the floor and some of his belongings were burnt from the fire that managed to enter through the window. He picked up the items he desired to bring with him. Most of them were on his nightstand, next to his bed.

Carador headed out of his room, mounted his horse and left Seragone. He placed his items, which he retrieved, into the horse's saddle pocket. Carador, in his full armor, was now in possession of the Emerald-Star, a hatchet, hunting knife, sleeping bag, some food, book, his pipe, and some of his favorite tobacco weed.

Carador's thoughts told him to return to Faradown, to see Faraduel, to give him word on what evil deeds Arush'n'aug has accomplished in Androuge.

Carador raced out of the territory of Seragone. His horse suddenly threw him down.

Carador heard a thunderous crumbling noise. He crooked around to see: a watchtower of Seragone crumble and smash against the side of the castle, sending large rubble down to the ground. Carador, gritted his teeth, and whipped back around, mounting his horse with a great leap, and headed off towards his destination.

He rushed through the burnt fields of blackened crops while his eyes watered from the remaining, smoke, which fouled the air, for many miles. Shortly after, he changed directions, away from the field gaining more speed. Carador went over an undamaged golden bridge and reached a small forest. The trees still displayed their late summer greens, standing vibrant and proud in the afternoon sun.

Carador made it out of the woods and reached Faradown the next day, annoyed that he was forced to waste another day riding.

* * * * *

The next day, Carador had arrived in Faradown again, he headed straight to Anlar to inform Faraduel about Arush'n'aug's dark attack upon Androuge. Carador burst through the castles doors. Two sentries marked his arrival, each sounding a horn. His old friend appeared in front of him.

"Your lordship!" cried Carador.

Faraduel looked at Carador with keen, inquisitive eyes.

"Ah! Carador, you're back," he noted, his head nodding slightly. "What is the reason?"

"I must tell you of a great evil which has occurred," said Carador, his voice low and serious.

Faraduel looked taken aback.

Carador stepped in front of a large crowd of people: peasants, knights, farmers, and Paladins, talking amongst each other, some laughing with euphoria, they were still there for the celebration of their king's birthday.

"Attention citizens and soldiers of Faradown!" he began. Silence commanded the air.

Everyone in attendance looked at Carador, abandoning his or her previous conversations.

"Arush'n'aug has attacked Androuge earlier this week!" The audience gasped with fear, and the feeling of panic grasped the crowd.

"It has struck the capital, Seragone. This is the third assault upon Androuge in its history! The city lies in ruin. It's people dead in the streets! Most of the cities, homes and shops are destroyed, the Temple of Anastar rests aflame, and the peasants and farmers lie dead in the very streets!" he preached.

"We need to stop this vile creature, or it will continue on with destroying our cities, and killing our people! I am planning to slay Arush'n'aug, although I believe it will be impossible for me to stop this creature by myself! I need an army, Faraduel, a large army, and only then, can we put an end to Arush'n'aug's treachery! I need Earacill's finest soldiers and warriors to bring an end to the evil of our time!" He continued short of breath. "If there is anyone here that would join me, and slay Arush'n'aug once and for all, join me now!"

Whispers and murmurs became evident. Everyone voiced his or her opinion about Carador's freighting report. Carador slowly walked back to Faraduel, satisfied with his speech. Faraduel said he was impressed and that he would join Carador in slaying Arush'n'aug, although he could not go with him now.

"Carador," Faraduel stated seriously, which was strange for him to hear. "Ride to Banlafar, tell Count Arien about the attack, he will know what to do. There we will settle this matter and see who will depart with you. I will alert Anaron as well."

"I shall, my friend. This vile beast will be expelled!" Carador cried clenching one fist. "Farewell!" said Carador as he bowed, wheeled around, and left the castle.

Carador mounted Azaful and rode out of Anlar and away from Faradown to Banlafar, the first elven town.

It was too late to reach Banlafar before nightfall. He would have to make camp somewhere. Carador traveled south for two hours and approached the entry of a forest.

He entered a forest known as Farrow Forest. There unfortunately, Carador would have to make his camp. Farrow Forest was a lonely and silent forest in Earacill. Carador traveled through the forest, searching for a reasonable campsite. Soon enough, he came across a flat area within the woods where he could setup his quarters and rest. The terrain was suitable.

He tied up his horse on a nearby tree. He began to conceal his sword, his helmet and all his other possessions as he laid them down under a blanket as to protect them from the elements of nature. He then took two other blankets, to make a tent shaped shelter to keep him dry. His sleeping bag would keep him desiccated, staving off night chills.

Carador's horse was exhausted from the hard riding it had provided today. Azaful started to rest instantly and laid down on a soft patch of the pasture. As for Carador, he was sitting in front of a fire he made from nearby branches of the trees and recited an ancient Androugen poem:

"Hail Androuge the kingdom of Silver Knights! Where lies Seragone, the mightiest city in the land.
Great leaders resided there, our men look upon the kingdom's lords.
With great fortresses, blue oceans, mystic fighters and knights so bold.
Have them now last here before this mighty city of old.
Hail Androuge! Will you now crown us a new lord?
So that we may again look upon you as the mightiest

kingdom in the land."

Along with that, Carador took out Tharagor's journal from his bag and started to read another page of it.

Day 3

My final preparations are complete. I will set sail on the fifth day. Tomorrow I will have my going away party. I am not planning to return to Arcon Realm.

"We depart on the fifth day, Mother, Father. To the land southwards, where our new lives will begin," I told them.

"I am fortunate you have decided to do something well with your life, Tharagor," my father said to me earlier.

"Yes father, our trip will be worth it."

Therefore, I decided to enjoy my last days here in Arcon Realm. Maybe visit old towns I once knew avid well, which I will never see again. I was going to miss the arena, I practiced my archery and fencing there. If I ever were to fight, the training I received there would last a lifetime. I feel I would easily come over the loss of all things I loved, with time. My thoughts would be on my new lands, the new discoveries.

For the remainder of the day, I said goodbye to my friends and their families, for I was never going to see them again.

-Tharagor

After a short but much needed night's read, sleep had welcomed him, and with it, dreams.

CHAPTER IV

* * * * * * * * *

BANLAFAR

When sunlight first crept through the trees, Carador awoke, and crawled out of his makeshift quarters. Azaful was grazing in the pale light of the morning sun, which was attempting to break through the dreary overcast sky. The Hero-knight of Androuge started to make breakfast with a cooking pot he had taken from his home. He heated some water with a fire that was still burning from the night. He poured the water into the container, and added an onion like ingredient, called Orlies. These are found growing underneath trees, mostly in forests.

"You know, Azaful," said Carador, yawning, and turning to face his companion. "These Orlies only come around twice a year. So, you must keep track of that, and get as many as you can before they spoil, and that's why you can't purchase them in any stores," he continued pulling out a number of Orlies he found growing underneath a nearby tree. He threw the Orlies in his steaming pot. Azaful's head jerked as of to acknowledge Carador.

Carador also added some berries into the water, known as Gornberries. They had the combined flavor of strawberries and peaches. Next, he complimented the meal with a few common herbs known as Sorfoil, which is also used in various potions. Sorfoil contained caffeine, making the herb addictive.

Carador stirred his breakfast a bit, and then he added his final ingredient: Jaron. This was a sausage from Androuge. He took out his knife and cut the sausage into pieces and dropped them into his pot. He continued stirring and waited a few minutes until his meal was ready.

He hastily took in his breakfast, having a sense of urgency on his mind. Azaful, however, much to the contrary, peacefully grazed on the green pasture. Carador shared a ration of his water with the relaxed steed.

Carador gradually ate some more of his breakfast, enjoying his homemade meal. Nevertheless, his eating was interrupted when he heard some rustling of branches and leaves nearby his campsite. He got suspicious and armed himself with the Emerald-Star and slowly drawing it, his grip tightening, prepared for the worst.

Carador looked ahead, through some trees, although he spotted nothing, figuring it was the wind or a wild animal. He returned to his meal, still ever cautious. The rustling in the trees seized, and with a quick leap, a large, black-robed-man jumped from the trees, pointing his blade at Carador. Luckily, Carador sensed the man coming upon him from behind. Carador jumped up, turned around, and deflected the assassin's strike, with the most impressive of grace.

The attacker was a Sarug, although it wasn't a mere Sarug, it was one of Saratrox's finest. Saratrox's head Sarugs could be identified by their armor. Only high Sarugs wore armor, while the others were not allowed such heraldry. His blade was black, along with everything he wore.

The commander Sarug failed to eliminate

Carador with a swift strike, the consequences lead him to be engaged in battle.

The Sarug commander swung viciously at Carador, Carador quickly evading each swing. Carador in return, stroke back at his assassin, the Emerald-Star clashed with the enemy's blade. The fight in Farrow Forest occurred for not but a few minutes. The Sarug swung again, slashing Carador's left hand, it began to bleed. Nevertheless, a small flesh wound was not going to stop Carador. They moved around the campsite swinging and deflecting each other's strikes.

Carador quickly thought of a plan, he led the Sarug commander behind Azaful, and continued to clash blades with one another. Carador's plan had worked: Azaful neighed in fear, and it kicked with its hind legs at the Sarug, with enough power to force him into the air and crash into one of the trees.

The assassin groaned, picking himself back up. Sarugs are trained from spawning to remain ignorant in the face of dire fear or pain, whether it is as small as a cut, or as large as an amputation.

The Sarug again, was prepared to strike, and so was Carador. Their blades impacted, delivering such incredible force, that they began to lose their grip. They continued to battle on, moving all throughout the forest.

The assassin figured sword combat would lead to nothing, and as a substitute, he began to use his fists. Carador swung again, although the Sarug grabbed his wrist, preventing the strike. The Sarug punched Carador repeatedly, damaging his helmet increasingly, blow after blow. It reminded Carador of his brawl back at the bar in Faradown, although this was much worse, with more than a mug of ale at stake.

The brawny commander, still holding Carador, threw him forwards, Carador was sent to the Earth. Carador attempted to stand back up, although the Sarug was too quick, with fierce determination the enemy charged at Carador who was rising upwards to recover from the first blow. Instinctively, the Sarug flung out his arm, and Carador attempted to ward off another potential lethal attack. The impact from the Sarug spun his body into a backwards tumble, placing him face down to the ground.

Carador's head began to ache, he was ill

prepared to muster a defense, however, he was not going to give up; the memory of Arush'n'aug's treachery gave Carador the strength to stand back up. When he succeeded and was back upon his feet, the Sarug had grabbed a hold of his neck, to his luck the Sarug was not choking him, but prepared to throw him as an alternative. The strength of the Sarug had lifted Carador off upon the grassy ground. He swung his arm back and forced it forward, throwing Carador a distant from his camp.

When he impacted the Earth again, he began to roll down a hill, and at the bottom of the hill, was a lake, unluckily, jagged rocks surrounded it. Carador attempted to stop himself from rolling, although with no success, he reached the bottom of the hill, and hit his left wrist on one of the rocks, shattering the bone.

Carador groaned in pain, dropping the Emerald-Star in the lake, and grabbed his broken hand. The assassin located Carador at the base of the hill, his objective was now a sword swipe away from him. He slid down the hill to finish his evil deed.

Carador too, saw his enemy, and hastily reached in the lake with his broken hand to retrieve his sword. Although he hastily pulled out his hand, for the lakes' water had burned him, feeling as if he had placed his hand over a roaring fire. Carador swiftly eyed his hand, expecting to locate evidence of a burn, however, to his surprise, there was nothing of the sort, and in fact, the water had cured his broken wrist, and healed the flesh wound on the same hand. He moved his wrist back in forth, still baffled at the full response from his hand.

The Sarug suddenly appeared at Carador's feet with his blade held behind him. His dark eyes glared at Carador, ready to strike. Carador's eyebrows rose, he thought quickly, and he reached into the lake to grab his sword. Again, the miracle water stung his hand with the burning sensation, although he ignored it. With a swift action, he grabbed the Emerald-Star's hilt and brought the dripping blade out of the lake, the water splashing in all directions.

The assassin swung downwards, Carador blocked the swing, the swords barely clashed together as the Emerald-Star sliced the Sarug's blade in half, akin to an axe splitting a log.

"Huh?" Carador wondered to himself,

shocked that he had disarmed the opponent with nothing more than a parry.

The Sarug grunted as he dropped his broken sword, he was prepared to fight melee.

Carador swung his sword around, water drops from the lake dispatched from the blade and landed on the foe's worn black robe, the robe quickly began to burn, and smolder under his gray skin could be seen. The Sarug angrily groaned in pain.

Carador looked at his blade in concern. He lightly let his finger slide up the Emerald-Star, yet it felt normal to him, the moisture on his finger nothing odd to him.

The assassin extended his arm outwards to strike Carador, however, Carador dropped down to avoid the strike, and he hastily dipped his blade in the lake, far down enough until it reached the hilt. Carador swung the Emerald-Star across his face, releasing the blessed water from his blade all over the injured foe. Three droplets impacted his face burning through it like acid, the remainder contacted his clothing, arousing him in flames. The Sarug roared in pain, dancing around as a fireball, stumbled around, and threw himself into the lake, he did not get the desired effect as the water acted as fire, and it aroused the rest of him in more flames, scorching him alive, until he was nothing more.

Carador sighed in relief that the conflict was over. He assumed from the battle that the water from the mysterious lake was there to destroy evil, and aid the good, in its blessed splendor. He equipped his water flask, drank some, and poured the remainder out, for a compensation, he filled his flask with the lake water, hoping it would be of some use in future conflicts.

Although he was sore from battle, Carador still had the strength to climb up the cliff and reach his campsite.

Azaful neighed joyfully as he spotted his master still, struggling uphill. Carador stood up straight, stretched, and let out a gasp of relief.

"How about one more ride, Azaful?" Carador asked his steed, exhausted, as he began to stow away his supplies, and then he tied various bags to the saddle.

His horse hastily rose, sensing it was time to depart. Carador untied and skillfully mounted Azaful.

"Yeah, let's go," said Carador wearily placing the Emerald-Star back into its sheath.

Carador rode away, out of Farrow Forest, and onto the plains. It is a two-hour ride from Farrow Forest to Banlafar. Carador stared straight ahead. He could not see to clearly from the dusty earth, although he knew he was heading the right direction.

The plains did not last long as anticipated. There were no trees or villages in sight, only the dust and dirt all around him, the product of a thirsty Earth. He could barely see what was in advance of him, from all the loose dust piled up upon the Earth.

It was one dusty ride.

* * * * *

Carador shortly afterward departed from the dusty plains, until he could clearly see the golden gates of Banlafar that shone like a mystical setting sunset, ahead of him.

The ride had been exhausting for Carador, nevertheless, he approached the gate of Banlafar in great relief. Carador rode to the front gate, there was two elves guarding it. Carador rode closer to the entrance, until a guard stopped him.

"I am sorry, although I cannot allow you into Banlafar so armed, stranger," dictated one black haired elf, equipped with a sword and fully armored from the chest down. The other elf was staring intensely at Carador.

"By order of, Aros, my kinsman, and Captain of the Guard," The elf continued.

Carador dismounted from his horse, he stepped closer. Carador then detached his sword, hatchet and his hunting knife.

"Be careful with these, they come from a place far away from here, another land."

"And what business do you bring to Banlafar?" questioned the elf facing him.

"I seek council with Lord Arien. I am Carador son of Caradeer," Carador lied well. "Hero-knight, and ex-healer of Androuge," he preached. "I come on behalf of Lord Faraduel of Faradown, to request permission from Lord Arien for an important task," said Carador, his words working swiftly, this time speaking the truth.

"What important task do you speak of?" asked the elf curiously.

"The slaying of the mighty Arush'n'aug," Carador declared.

"You alone?" questioned the elf almost surprised.

"I highly doubt that, although if I must, then my answer is yes."

The elf chuckled shaking his head.

"One cannot slay Arush'n'aug alone, not even an army has accomplished such a deadly task," he declared promisingly.

"Yes, you are correct, although you must trust me, I am not going single-handedly," Carador snapped.

"Yes, for that is why you have come to Banlafar, to seek warriors to join you," assumed the elf.

"Not exactly, I am requesting a meeting from Lord Arien to summon the greatest fighters in all Earacill," corrected Carador.

"Ah, I understand," he said slightly taken aback.

"Yes, with them, we can, and will, slay

Arush'n'aug!" thundered Carador clenching his teeth.

"Every chance we get to kill Arush'n'aug must be encouraged. Best of luck to you!" roared the elf grinning.

The guard stepped back towards the gate, and opened it, with the assistance from the other guard.

"Thank you," replied Carador relieved, and he bowed. Carador approached and climbed back on his horse and slowly rode inside.

Once he was through the gate, all Banlafar was in view, the clear waterfalls in the distance, the homes, shops, and great halls. Banlafar was a stunning town. It had sparkling blue houses, silver roads, and white bridges. A blue river ran beneath every road.

Carador slowly rode inside. He looked around the town examining every aspect. He looked upwards, upon a hill where Count Arien's palace sat. Carador grinned and headed north upwards to Lord Arien. The hill was higher than it had appeared from afar, although it was not too steep as to wear Carador out. He reached the entrance of the palace. He dismounted his horse and walked to the entrance.

He entered the palace house and gave word of Faraduel of Faradown.

"My Lord, Arien," announced Carador casually gaining his attention.

Arien, who was sitting informally, looked up at Carador. He gazed upon Carador, his blue eyes twinkled in the sunlight coming through the roof of the house. Arien's house was a full sky blue, surrounded by ten windows on each side of the house. The sunlight was brighter coming into the palace windows, rather than it had been outside.

"I have come here on behave of Lord Faraduel of Faradown," attested Carador hotly.

"Lord Faraduel?" questioned Arien unexpectedly. "Why, he hasn't spoken to me for three years now," he continued puzzled. His long black hair seemed to rise, while he stood up from his throne.

Arien wore a silver crown that always seemed to shine even in the dark. His clothes were jade green, and he wore a beautiful crimson red shirt underneath his green gown. Arien has always been the Count of Banlafar, he makes up the senate in Earacill along with the King of Faradown: Faraduel, and the King of Anaron: Earathell.

Arien was once well befriended with former King Tharagor, even before they both traveled to Earacill. Arien himself was unsure if he genuinely wanted to embark upon the journey. Nevertheless, he joined Tharagor on his quest to find new land. When they had succeeded, Tharagor and Arien constructed Banlafar, giving Arien headship over the town, while Tharagor became the King of Anaron. Arien proclaims the laws in Earacill, all Earacill's councils had been held there, and he conducts them, to see if they would come about, in ordaining his decisions.

"Lord Faraduel has sent me here to inform you that Arush'n'aug has attacked Androuge again yesterday, on Seragone to be precise, its third strike. This brutality has to stop, my Lord!" roared Carador rolling his hand into a fist, cracking his knuckles with the same hand.

"If I could possibly gather together a legion of warriors, we could march to Aromer Mountain and slay that fire demon!" cried Carador.

"Carador, you of all people well know that many who have tried to slay Arush'n'aug have failed, what makes you think ten or fifteen people can slay it?" Arien asked calmly judging that Carador was out of his mind.

"I am not sure yet, although with time, I can build the perfect plan, with Earacill's greatest masterminds. I will slay it! I am certain of it," he proclaimed heroically.

Carador was dumbfounded, for he has no strategy as to how he was going to slay Arush'n'aug.

"Are swords too weak to harm a monstrous and vile creature with scales stronger than steel?" Carador thought to himself, the fog of doubt now enshrouding his thought.

"Would I need a ballista to fire upon it and bring it down? Or is nothing at all effective against it?"

"I presume I can form a legion for you, Carador," breathed Arien reaching over to the marble table in front of him, taking a goblet of water, and drank a small amount of it.

"I will begin writing numerous letters, and I shall send them to various cities and towns, the counts and kings can decide who to send. Do not expect the perfect army, Carador," announced Arien writing.

Carador nodded in acknowledgment.

"I hope you understand that what you are planning to do is pure suicide, only a handful have survived Arush'n'aug's attacks, and those who have are scarred for the rest of their lives, whether the wounds are of flesh or mind," he said looking up at Carador. "Life is a game without cheats, Carador."

"Do not doubt a Hero-knight of Androuge, my Lord. For I know all too well the wicked mechanism of the beast. It is I who I trust to hope, and it is that hope that will liberate our fears! Yes, I do understand that this will be a peril quest, however; one must accomplish this. Someone must stand up to the enemy, no matter how many times we fail. I believe I can do it, not for the respect of my peers, but for my people, my city, my kingdom, and all of Earacill!" cried Carador.

"Alright, Carador!" started Arien. "I will prepare a meeting tomorrow, at noon, when the sun reaches the summit of Mt. Stager. It will consist of all who respond to my letters. As I hope, Earacill's finest warriors will be present. We will see if your quest is to initiate," said Arien.

"Excellent!" cried Carador, gratefully nodding. "I shall wait tomorrow for your convention, farewell, Lord Arien!" Carador bowed and swiftly walked out of Arien's palace.

With a grin on his face, Carador headed out of the palace, he stood upon the high hill of Banlafar, looking outwards, his view had now fixed upon the entire town, enjoying the swift breeze that flowed through him. He untied Azaful, mounted him and galloped to one of Banlafar's stables east of Arien's palace.

Carador had now appeared back upon the silver roads. His errand was run, and now Carador had nothing more to do, he figured he deserved some free time and decided to explore the town of Banlafar for the remainder of the day.

He had never been here before, he had met Lord Arien from his visits previously to Faradown, and occasionally, Arien visited Androuge.

Carador quickly decided what would be best for everyone and himself. He decided to return to Faradown instead and inform Faraduel of Arien's approval on the meeting. Touring Banlafar would be a plan for another time.

Carador headed over to the stable where Azaful was kept. He patted his steed, untied him, and mounted Azaful. Carador grabbed hold of the reigns and ordered Azaful forward. He rode off riding through the streets, and then riding out of Banlafar.

* * * * *

An hour of riding had past, Carador could hardly see his sense of direction, however; his experience in travel was there to guide him when he rode through the plains before. Ahead of him he could faintly see what materialized as black figures, motionless. Carador dismissed these figures as a product of the fatigue on his mind, as he carried on.

More black figures appeared, and Carador was concerned if they were more Sarugs. He heard whistles in the air, so he glared up, eying the sky. Out of the orange sky came a wave of five black arrows. Three of them missed, although the fourth impacted Carador on the shoulder of his left arm, and the fifth struck Azaful's back, sending his

Carador's horse crashing to the ground and Carador flying off, to the same fate.

Azaful had not been severely hurt, as he remained low, to rest from exhaustion and his arrow wound until it would be safe to return to his master. Carador erected himself upwards instantly and drew his sword, ignoring the pain in his shoulder where the black-feathered arrow now took residence.

Around him, Sarugs appeared from within the dusty fields, surrounding him, it was an ambush. Carador angrily clenched his teeth, and plucked out the arrow from his shoulder, blood now freely flowing. He began aiming his sword towards his enemies in a three-hundred-and-sixty-degree rotation, as to intimate them.

The first Sarug made his move to strike, Carador slashed him down with great force. Then the others came, Carador was forced to fight them all at once.

Carador repeatedly swung his blade in every direction, recklessly slaying them, leaving them to the care of the cold ground.

He blocked numerous strikes from getting anywhere near his abdomen. The blade wasn't the only part of the sword he's using, Carador used the hilt to strike several across the face. The sword itself was not the only weapon, he made use of his own hands and feet in a fight.

The Emerald-Star, now covered in dark blood, swung in a constant pattern as to keep its enemies at bay. With a lucky strike, one Sarug from behind, managed to slash Carador's forearm, and blood spat from the wound. Carador roared loudly with great fury and tightened his grip upon the Emerald-Star causing the blade to glow green, he felt a surge of strength, his muscles tightened. The Sarugs took a step back, partially startled from the roar of their enemy, nevertheless, they showed no fear or mercy and continued to fight.

Countless enemy corpses dropped, unfortunately, their overall numbers seemed to remain, as more leaped into the attack. Slowly, Carador lost stamina and increasingly he felt the sting of new wounds emerging, eventually fewer Sarug bodies were dispatched, and slowly the Emerald-Star began losing its green glow, as Carador's grip was loosening.

Carador had again, been slashed behind his

right leg, causing him to land upon his knees. He began to feel lightheaded, his sight slowly becoming distorted, and he was no longer much of a threat. Sarugs moved closer, surrounding him.

That was the last sight Carador saw, as his legs gave out, and his body plummeted to the Earth, his eyes rolled back and his vision turned to darkness...

CHAPTER V

* * * * * * * * *

IMPRISONMENT

Carador awoke to the rotten smell of bodily fluids, dirt, and other less than desirable odors. He could hear shouting from a distance, he couldn't identify if they were cries of anger, pain, fear, or even perhaps euphoria. Carador opened his eyes, his vision was blurry, yet they adjusted themselves to make out a fellow with long black hair looking over him.

Carador's eyes opened wider, he staggered to get up, only to fall backwards, far enough until he hit a wall. Carador looked around him, he was in a prison cell, a quick visual scan, and he estimated the dimensions at ten feet by fifteen feet. The bars were forged from iron, each a foot apart, extending your arms out of them was possible, yet crawling out was not. The walls were constructed from stone, though they appeared poorly made, there were a great number of holes and cracks evident, which were just large enough for them to peak through. The cell bars, like the stonewalls of the jail, were weakened by age. It seems escape would be conquerable, although looks can be deceiving.

Carador rubbed his head, feeling a wound on his temple. He looked at his hand and groaned, for he seen it stained in blood. His shoulder felt inflamed from the former arrow that had penetrated it. He groaned attempting to conceal the open wound with his gray tattered undershirt, looking around himself for his water flask with the miracle water from the lake, it was nowhere to be found. In fact, Carador had been stripped of his weapons and armor, he was only clothed in his recreational clothes. Outside of the cell, stood two guards, they were Sarugs, both equipped with swords, one had a set of keys.

It came to Carador after much disorientation that he now was imprisoned, and that the fellow with the black hair, was an inmate as well.

"Who are you? Where am I?" Carador asked dazed.

"Not your enemy, if that's wh. suspecting," he replied darkly.

The man was an elf, Carador identified, he akin to Carador, had a wound on his head, above his left eyebrow. He wore a robe, which once appeared clean and fancy, but now, torn and tainted.

"Obviously not, why else would a Sarug be imprisoned? Refusing to do Saratrox's will?" he laughed. "Never in a lifetime have I heard of such a thing," replied Carador eyeing the jail cell more.

The elf grinned. "I am Arados of Anaron, archer of the North," announced the elf.

As a child, Arados was raised to enjoy life the fullest extent, proving his love for the Earth, not before his seventh winter, Arados began questing different regions and territories in his homeland, sometimes even getting himself lost deep within forests, or trespassing on forbidden land even without having the slightest idea. Even with the wilderness at his side, Arados became depressed, wanting to seek more and occasionally leaves his home when he is in a state of depression, or stress, wondering elsewhere to sketch the different plants and animals he would encounter, studying their behaviors, and becoming more acquainted with the wildlife.

In his teenage years, Arados had already perfected his gifted skill of archery. Over the years, it had become his obsession. He would use his handcrafted Yew bow every chance he got, whether it be for sport, or for subsistence.

Many years pass for Arados, having each day repeat its cycle and Arados became filled with restlessness and what he considered to be hopelessness. He yearned for new adventures, or even just the chance to return to his old childhood activities, of questing new land, and so Arados decided to follow in the footsteps of his idol, Tharagor, the first of his kind to make an extraordinary journey.

And so, Arados had set sail with a handful of other elves, out of Arcon Realm, and arrived upon Earacill in the year of 108 of the First Century. Arados traveled to where he would fit the most in, and he resided in Archara of the kingdom of Anaron. His first task was to prove his worth to the one elf he admired the most, and Arados was successful in proving worthy enough of his skill and he had become a high archer for King Tharagor, and a great addition to the soldiers of Anaron. Throughout the rest of the First Century, Arados fought alongside his fellow soldiers in all Anaron's battles, with his old Yew bow.

In the year 140, King Tharagor is slain during the great battle upon the plains of Camalon against Saratrox. Tharagor wielded a bow, a legendary bow known as Sky-Piercer. The bow was enchanted with miraculous powers. Arados had dreamed of owning that bow ever since he first witnessed King Tharagor use it in battle. After King Tharagor's death, Arados musters up the courage and makes a dangerous effort to the steal the priceless artifact, to keep for himself, a crime that was punishable by death. Sky-Piercer bared a close resemblance to his own Yew bow and he had switched Sky-Piercer with it, no one had ever noticed the difference.

"I am Caradorian Saladar," replied Carador leaving out his last name. "Hero-knight of Androuge," he added.

"Ah, nice meeting you, err- we might be here for a while," Arados assumed.

"How long have you been here?"

"Since last night, well I believe it was last night when I was ambushed by those Sarugs."

"You were ambushed by Sarugs?" said Carador raising a brow. "And they took you here?" he chuckled slightly. "Well I guess that's something we both have in common, we're both prisoners of war, because the same had happened to me. I was riding out of Farrow Forest when fifty or maybe even one hundred Sarugs ambushed me."

It came to Carador's attention what items he lost, as well as his task. "My sword!" barked Carador suddenly as he began searching around him for the Emerald-Star although it was nowhere to be seen. "They took my sword! And everything else of mine!" he shouted angrily, punching the stone wall next to him, only to receive great pain in his hand, he looked down and watched blood spill out of his knuckles.

"Yeah, they took everything, except the clothes on our backs," said Arados eyeing the two Sarugs angrily. "I lost my bow, arrows, Bansers, and food I packed for a trip I was on."

"Where were you heading?" asked Carador.

"From Anaron to Banlafar, I received a message from Lord Arien of Banlafar that King

Earathell gave me and asked me and others to join in a debate over Arush'n'aug," Arados replied.

"A message from the Count Arien? Did the letter mention in there anything about Arush'n'aug's current attack on Androuge?" Carador asked concerned.

"Yes, it stated that Arush'n'aug's attack on Androuge has called together a meeting in the courtyard of Banlafar to debate it. Why? Have you received the same letter?" asked Arados.

"I returned home from Faradown, Anlar, to be precise, and I saw my homeland, the capital of Androuge, scorched in flame, Arush'n'aug had attacked it greatly. After this incident, I rode to Banlafar and insisted Lord Arien to put an end to this terror. When he agreed, he told me that he would write to various cities and towns in the land, to call together Earacill's greatest warriors! You must be one of the few who would debate this along with myself," announced Carador.

Arados appeared shocked. "So, it was you wanting to slay Arush'n'aug, huh? King Earathell confirmed the message and sent me to join you."

"Small world, I guess," shrugged Carador.

"Wait, Arien's messages were sent out yesterday, so you must have received it later. Did you ride all yesterday? From Anaron to Banlafar is at least a day's ride."

"Well, I received the message around noon," informed Arados, scratching his scalp. "Yes, then my friend, Farond and I rode out of Archara, Anaron's capital in case you didn't know. So yes, I rode through the day and during nightfall, although on my way I was ambushed by Sarugs, they knocked me unconscious and the next thing I know, I am in a prison cell, I awoke several hours later, you were still unconscious."

"Ah," Carador understood. "So... Where is this Farond you speak of? He must have received the letter as well. Was he ambushed along with you, or did he manage to escape?" Carador asked desperately hoping freedom for him.

"No, Farond akin to you and I was captured. I believe he is being held in another cell," said Arados attempting to look out of the cell into another.

"Damn!" growled Carador. "If he did manage to escape the clutches of the Sarugs, he could have alerted others that you were captured, and possibly an army could come and break us out of Aussarok." A sudden thought flew into Carador's mind. "Wait! We are not in Aussarok are we?" Carador asked. "No, I don't think so," said Arados shaking his head. "I have peaked outside, and this is no Aussarok territory," Arados pointed out.

Carador slowly stood up and walked to the back of the cell and looked outside, the ground was not black, as Aussarok's is, it was grassy, with trees surrounding the area, yet it was difficult to make out where he was.

Carador sat back down on his side of the cell. "No, this is not Aussarok," he Carador relieved. "Although I cannot make out where exactly we are."

Arados let out a chuckle. "You know the ironic thing about this whole situation is, that my sister Farah in Anaron warned me not to peruse in this mission, and now for not listening, I'm in jail! Maybe I should heed her warning from now on."

Carador smiled, "Maybe it is best if you do not tell her about this, or you won't ever hear the end of it from her," he laughed.

Arados laughed cheekily. "What about you, Carador? Do you have any family? A wife?

Children?"

Carador shook his head. "With how our world is now, I feel it to be an unwise decision to raise a family. I am a Hero-knight of Androuge, I dedicate my life to my blade to protect our people. I cannot have the troubles of my family haunting my every move, especially with Saratrox and Arush'n'aug roaming the land," he took a breath. "Perhaps one day, when we live in harmony, I can retire my blade and settle down with a wife, yet not any time soon."

Arados nodded, "A wise decision my friend," he said taking a deep breath. Arados glanced over to the cell parallel to them for the first time and noticed two more inmates. "It looks like we are not alone in this," he said pointing to the cell.

Carador turned his head and he located the two inmates Arados spoke of, and sure enough, there they were, sitting jaded. The two were both dressed in black robes, not those of the Sarug's, yet those of Faradownian hunters. One had fiery red hair, and no facial hair, appearing to be in his late twenties.

Carador gave a quick glance down the halls,

assuring no Sarug jailers were present. "Psst!" he whispered to the cell across from him. This caught the two's attention. Carador quickly glanced around again. "Have you two been ambushed by Sarugs recently?" he whispered.

One nodded, having a hopeful look in his eye. "Yes, not two days ago I was riding to Banlafar when I was caught and arrested by Sarugs, I swear they came from nowhere," the man said.

Arados turned his attention to the inmate.

"What about you?" Carador asked to the other.

The other man did not respond verbally, yet slowly shook his head.

"He has been in here for at least a month now, he claims," said the inmate.

"Thirty-four days actually," he corrected. "The same has happened to me, as what has happened to you, only it had been thirty-four days ago," he said with a cold voice.

"So, we are all in this together, huh?" whispered Carador shaking his head. "How did they get to us so easily?" he mumbled to himself.

"Wait, so did you receive a letter from Lord Arien of Banlafar for a meeting?" asked Arados curiously joining in the conversation.

The inmate nodded. "Yes, how did you know?" he asked concerned.

Arados shook his head, "this is not coincidental, my friend. This must be some plot deprived by Saratrox or another," he sighed.

Carador's eyes caught sight of a Sarug jailer gradually walking towards them. "Wait! Quiet!" he informed, seizing the conversation and allowing the Sarug to keep his pace without drawing attention. Carador and Arados placed one hand on their foreheads to shield their faces, not wanting Sarug to stare them down. After a minute or so, the jailer passed out of sight.

"Hey!" Carador whispered back to the two. "What are your names?"

"I'm Rugsha, hunter of Faradown," he replied.

"D-Deltun," the other said weakly, and to their disposal, he passed out from exhaustion.

"Is he alright?" Arados worried.

"Yeah, he has been in and out of it for a while now," Rugsha replied, looking down at the unconscious

Deltun. Rugsha caught sight of another jailer walking towards them at a faster pace.

"Get him some water!" ordered Carador.

The third Sarug walked by Carador and Arados' cell. He stopped in front of them and threw what appeared to be meat into their cell. Carador caught it from the air and eyed it over. Arados caught his piece. The appearance of the meat ruined their appetite with its first impression. It was old, rotting away, the color of the aged meat was a dark gray, and larva had already overtaken. However, worse than the sight, was the stench of it. One whiff of the stale meat was enough to make even the hungriest man turn away from it.

"CHOW DOWN," said the Sarug snickering and walking off.

Carador sniffed the object, which he much regretted. Surprisingly, he bit a small amount of it as to taste it, hoping the appearance was only an illusion. The taste was so foul; he could not bear attempting another bite. Carador threw down the rotten meat and spat the aftertaste out of his mouth. Angrily, Carador stood up and walked towards the cell bars.

"Hey!" Carador shouted to the Sarug who had given him the rotten meal.

The Sarug stopped walking and turned around, snarling.

"You got any water?" Carador asked darkly, fearing no one.

The Sarug walked back to Carador, clenching his yellow teeth, he came close to his face.

"YOU'LL GET WATER WHEN WE GIVE YOU WATER! YOU GOT THAT?" he spat and stormed away. His voice was dark.

Carador clenched his own teeth.

"No use talking to them," said Arados. "They are as stubborn as a mule."

Carador turned around. "We will get out of here, Arados. I promise you," announced Carador.

"What do you plan to do?" asked Arados, sitting in his corner, tapping his fingers against the wall.

Carador sighed. "I do not know yet. But we will find something, I assure you..." Carador looked around their cell, from the rotten filthy floor, to the damaged walls, and at the black ceiling.

"There!" Carador pointed to the ceiling. At the right corner of the cell, a good portion of the ceiling was missing, not so much that looking out was possible, however; large enough that the top of the cell bars was visible.

"If we could break off a portion of one of those bars, we might be able to use it against the guards," estimated Carador.

The Sarug stood guard outside of their cell, Carador assumed their intelligence was low, not knowing what Carador was planning to do.

Carador walked over to the front of their cell, he looked up, getting a clearer picture of the gap. He began to climb on the bars, heading for the top. It was going well at first, it seemed as if the guard did not care. Carador's eyes were fixed on the ceiling and looked for nothing else. Unsuspectingly, the guard made his move. He drew his sword from its sheath, the sword sliced through the air.

"Carador watch-!" warned Arados. The Sarug was too quick, he walked up to Carador and brought the hilt of his sword to Carador's face. Carador was thrown off the bars and landed on his back on the ground before him, his nose began to bleed.

"Damn it!" groaned Carador wiping the warm blood off his nose.

The Sarug walked back to his guarding post and kept an eye on Carador.

Arados scratched his scalp in frustration. "I tried to warn you," explained Arados. "Unfortunately, he was too quick."

"You think?" growled Carador upset. "I'll try it again shortly, it can easily be broken off. We, or perhaps Rugsha, need to distract him."

"What do you plan to do?" asked Arados.

Carador breathed. "I am not sure yet, I may need your help though."

"Yeah, no problem, I'll help," nodded Arados.

"Rugsha," Carador alerted him.

Rugsha turned his attention to Carador. "Yes?"

"We will get out of here, I promise."

* * * * *

Carador and Arados sat in the cell for six hours. Carador was desperately thinking of an escape plan, while Arados was thinking of an escape route. Carador sat in his corner with his head down on his knees, growing impatient. Arados rested his head on the darkened wall with his eyes closed, canceling out all foul thoughts and senses. Rugsha awoke Deltun who regained much energy.

"Arados, we cannot remain in here, we have to figure a way out of here before it is too late. Arien is expecting us, we need to meet him as soon as we can."

"What do you propose to do?" questioned Arados, hoping he had an escape plan.

"We need to distract him," said Carador pointing to the Sarug outside of their cell. "But first, we need to acquire some form of weapon, like what I was trying at earlier," he said pointing to the metal pole sticking out of the ceiling. "We may need that, or something similar."

Well luckily for us, he doesn't stand guard there every hour," began Arados. "He'll patrol left and right, examining the other cells," he whispered.

"Yes, the truth you speak, Arados. I believe we will have to wait it out," Carador sighed.

"Wait! I got a better idea!" announced Arados.

Carador's eyes quickly fixed on him.

"Look," whispered Arados making sure the guard does not observe what he had to show Carador. Arados revealed a broken rod of his own, it was inches shy of three feet in length, and the ends of it appeared to be sharpened to a point.

Carador's eyes grew big. "Where did you get that?"

"I've had it, before you arrived here. I didn't tell you about it because, it wasn't finished, and what I mean by that is, I have been secretly sharpening this with the ground, hoping to use it against one of them."

"It looks sharpened enough to me! I got a plan," announced Carador.

"HEY! KEEP IT DOWN IN THERE!" shouted the Sarug on the other side.

"Sorry!" said Carador.

"That was close," breathed Arados.

"Yeah, but this will be closer..." said Carador darkly.

"D-don't do anything stupid, Carador!" Arados said with a worried tone.

Carador stopped in his tracks and looked back. "Leaving us in here to die is the only *stupid* thing I would do."

Carador slowly reached out and grabbed the metal rod Arados had made. "Hey boss!" shouted Carador standing up and walking towards the bars, holding the rod behind him. "Boss!" he shouted again. The Sarug heard him perfectly, nevertheless; he ignored Carador.

Frustratingly, Carador stormed around and grabbed his stale meat he was given to eat.

"Carador, what are you-" broke of Arados.

Carador carefully and accurately threw the meat between the bars, striking the Sarug in the face.

"*ARGH!*" he shouted angrily, wiping his gray, moldy flesh. "*YOU'RE DEAD!*" he stormed walking over to their cell, equipping the cell key with one hand.

Carador grinned as his plan worked.

"*YOUR BLOOD IS NOW FORFEIT! YOUR FLESH BELONGS TO ME!*" The guard stood inches close to the bars, about to open it, preparing for some vengeance.

Hastily, Carador revealed the metal rod, and gutted the guard in the abdomen. Arados jumped up, surprised that Carador's plan worked. The Sarug died quietly, thus attracting almost no attention. Rugsha, with an immensely surprised look at his face, almost let out a shrill of excitement.

Carador reached out with one hand and grasped the keys the corpse equipped. With his other hand: he kept the corpse upright against the bars.

"Arados! Take the rod! Hold him up," ordered Carador while hastily placing the cell keys into their cell lock.

Arados swiftly did as he was commanded.

From a distance, the dead guard did not appear lifeless, but to the contrary: he appeared if he was having a conversation with the inmates.

"Why are we holding him up?" asked Arados, bewildered by everything that was occurring so quickly.

"We cannot leave his corpse exposed! The guards will be onto us immediately."

"Right, right, I understand!" announced

Arados.

Carador unlocked the cell door, and opened it slowly, he carefully stepped out; the door remained ajar. He looked to his right: nothing, but and blank stonewall. He looked to his left: more Sarug guards.

Arados, whom was still holding up the dead guard, waited for Carador's command.

Carador looked back to him, with a last breath, Carador uttered, "Now!"

Arados' eyes widened at the command, he yanked his metal rod out from within the Sarug, and its corpse fell down with a loud thud, which attracted a lot of attention. The Sarugs from down the hall quickly turned around and noticed Carador's presence outside of where they had allowed it.

"HEY! STOP!" they shouted storming down the hall at great speed, drawing their weapons.

Carador and Arados, as well, ran down the hall to confront their enemies. Carador remained unarmed, whereas, Arados armed himself only with the handmade rod. The first two Sarugs confronted them. The first violently swung his sword, Carador quickly ducked out of the way. In return, Carador gave him a hard jab in his gut. The other Sarug behind him, attempted to stab him, he retaliated and headbutted his face, sending him downwards.

The other prisoners including Rugsha and Deltun in their cells shouted Carador and Arados on, cheering and whistling as they might all have a chance of escape.

Other Sarugs stepped in to seize the riot. Arados aided Carador and impaled a few more of them, having them drop their weapons in the process as their corpses fell to the ground. Quickly, Arados looked down and equipped one of their swords.

"Carador!" shouted Arados.

Carador quickly turned around.

Arados threw the rod towards him since he was now equipped with a sword. Carador caught it, now using steel in the replacement of fists.

Carador used the rod like a knife, and began to stab them, or mercilessly slit their throats or other vital bodily functions. Arados gladly helped with the cause and took various amounts of them down easing their retreat.

The path was clear for them. They began to sprint, but then came to quick halt.

"Wait! We need to free Rugsha, Deltun, and all the others!" pointed Carador.

"We were captured riding to Banlafar!" shouted one of the prisoners. "Sarugs ambushed us everywhere! They wounded my brother, I do not know how long he will last!"

Carador investigated the cell where the utter had occurred. The cell apprehended five prisoners.

"Hold on!" shouted Arados, preparing his sword. He brought his blade behind him, and swung downwards, against the lock on the cell bars. His sword recoiled from the swing, and the lock remained intact. Arados clenched his teeth, upon his failure of freeing them.

"He's got the keys!" shouted a familiar voice to Arados behind him.

Arados quickly turned around, at the voice, and in the cell behind him, was his friend, Farond.

"He's got the keys!" Farond announced again, pointing to one of the Sarug corpses.

"Err, right, Farond. Glad to see you made it!" replied Arados reaching down and removed the key ring.

"Yeah, for now," sighed Farond.

Carador stood guard for the reinforcements, which were sure to come.

Arados hastily placed the keys into the cell lock, and the door became ajar.

"Hurry, more will be coming!" shouted Carador gesturing for them to get out.

Arados ran to the opposite side of where the prisoner with his brother was kept.

Footsteps were approaching from the end of the hall, some of them yelling, their gruff, deep voices could be easily made out as Sarugs.

"Hurry, Arados!" yelled Carador looking from down the hall to Arados fidgeting which key was the correct one.

"Aha!" cried Arados with a grin, as one of the keys was inserted into the lock and unlocked it.

"Rugsha! Deltun, we're coming!" Carador cried, aggressively slashing down another jailer. "Arados throw me the keys!" he ordered.

Arados seized fighting quick enough to hurl the cell keys over to Carador. He caught them and forced the keys into the lock.

"Hurry! Let's move!" shouted Carador ordering them out.

"Great job on the escape," Rugsha said, "I'll help out now."

The three sprinted down the hall where the riot continued.

"Hurry let's go!" Carador roared ordering the host through the pile of Sarug corpses.

"What about my brother?" one freed prisoner asked anxiously.

Carador quickly turned his head back and forth, to what was more important: Escape, or someone's life. Carador looked down at the prisoner's brother. His eyes were shut, and he was heavily breathing. Carador noticed a stab wound in his abdomen. "Not to worry, I can heal him," announced Carador.

The prisoner's eyes widened.

Carador quickly knelt in front of him and reached out his hand over the wound.

White static shock formed from his fingertips, and traveled to his palm, and then vanished into thin air.

Carador groaned. "Come on!" he shouted, hearing the Sarugs get closer.

Again, the white lightening formed from his

fingertips and traveled into his palm, only this time, the static formed into a bright white orb, and traveled into the wound, and vanished. The wound stitched itself closed, and the patient was able to breathe easily again, nevertheless, he barely had the strength to stand up, let alone fight.

"Thank you!" said the brother of the wounded one, as he helped his brother up.

"Yes, now we must hurry, get him out of here!" said Carador. "And you!" Carador pointed to the other three. "Can you fight?"

"Gladly!" one with a dark robe announced. His name was Teradorn.

"Yes!" roared another. This one was a dwarf, known as Dalan.

"Against this scum?" Spat one of them. "Humph, of course!" the brawny barbarian, Harken roared. His size was much greater than the others.

Harken was bald, he had a short beard and wore clothes that he seemed to grow out of.

"Good! We must fight them off if we want to escape! Now let's go!" ordered Carador.

The fifteen prisoners rushed down the hall, to

their only exit, unfortunately, their exit happened to be the same place the reinforcements came.

Carador and Arados went first, for they were the only ones armed. The company shouted in anger, as loud as possible to damage the enemy's morale, and with that the escapees rushed down the hall at great speed.

They became face to face with their enemies, the Sarugs drew their swords, hoping to stop the riot. To the company, it was only intimidation to continue.

Arados ran ahead of the others, quickly, he performed a violent swing, knocking the sword out of the first Sarug's hand. Along with that, Carador tackled the next one, both were sent to the floor. Carador violently punched him in the face, assuring the Sarug would not get back up. The other thirteen behind them, were easily overpowering them.

Without weapons, they are forced to kill their enemies in any way they could. Farond grabbed one from behind, and repeatedly smashed his face into a wall. Dalan, due to his lack of height, managed to trip his opponents, and finish them off on the ground.

"This way!" shouted Teradorn, the one robed in dark, as he pointed forwards to a promising exit.

The crowd took the weapons from the pile of Sarug corpses, now each of them armed. It was an action that will surly lead them to freedom.

They rushed down the hall with great speed, racing the remainder of guards sure to come. A war horn was blown from the exterior of the prison; it was sure to warn of the escaped prisoners.

"Now they all know!" shouted a prisoner.

"Hurry let's keep a move on!" shouted Farond.

They continued to run down the hall, until they were left with two options: Left or right.

"Left! The exit is that way!" shouted the prisoner with the former wounded brother. They were moments away from turning left until their decision was cut off.

"No wait!" roared Arados. "Look!" he pointed to a wooden handcrafted sign above the right path, with the words *"Armory"* etched into it. "We all had weapons and personal belongings that we lost when we were taken here, they must be held in there!

Come on!" he cried, as he ran down the right path. The others followed.

The path was short, and moments later, they arrived into a large square room, surrounded by various weapons, armor, and other traditional belongings.

"Take what's yours, and hurry!" shouted Carador. Carador quickly glanced around, searching for his sword and armor.

The other prisoners ran forward, and quickly located their weapons. They dropped their current swords, the swords of the Sarugs, and replaced them with weapons they knew.

Carador located his armor and other personal belongings, strangely enough, his sword was out of place. He looked around seeing if one of the others had stolen it, although he saw nothing. He figured it would be a waste of valuable time to stand there and look around when he could be armoring himself up.

The burning sensation in his shoulder quickly reminded him to recover his flask, so he can heal himself. He did exactly that, Carador hastily grabbed his flask and poured three droplets over the wound, burning him on impact, he groaned from the pain.

However, his groaning quickly seized as his wound began to heal itself. He grinned and now being in a healthy condition to fight, he quickly moved towards his armor, and grabbed his breastplate, quickly applying it. Along with that, he slipped on his gauntlet's, tightening them, and began applying his greaves.

A Sarug entered the room, armed with a great sword. The foe sprinted towards the first opponent he saw, Carador was his victim. Carador was only half applied with his greaves, when he heard a foul roar behind him, and with quick reflexes, he wheeled around, safely securely his sword in front of him as to shield his face. The large foe swung his great sword forward, and Carador was barely able to withhold it, he eyed the enemy's weapon, it looked familiar, because it was his very own Emerald-Star.

The foe was a head Sarug, like the one Carador first confronted in the forest. The enemies roar alerted everyone in the room to his presence, they prepared themselves, willing to fight.

"That's my sword!" roared Carador, releasing his current sword from the lock of the Emerald-Stars.

Carador growled, while performing some violent swings towards the commander, although his blocks were deflected. The thought of him using a blunt weapon against his prized possession pained him emotionally.

The allies came from behind and slashed at the commander, it had lost its focus on Carador, and fixed his attention on the irritation, which was occurring behind him. The enormous foe growled, and turned behind him, grabbing the closest opponent to him, the unfortunate Helldar was grabbed by his collar and with a quick thrust, was thrown forward, crashing into shelves of armor and weaponry, showering down upon him. This diversion gave Carador a clean shot, he swung forward, and amputated the large Sarug's arm. The Emerald-Star came crashing to the ground, with the arm still attached. Helldar quickly emerged from the pile of armor and weapons, luckily, none had injured him.

The ferocious opponent roared in anger, and with his intact arm, he clenched Carador's neck, and lifted him off the ground. His grip tightened around

Carador's neck, virtually crushing it. Carador began to panic because of the loss of air, while kicking around.

The death grip of the commander Sarug was loosened, his hand released Carador, and Carador fell back to the ground. He looked up at his opponent, the Sarug was still. Carador watched the Sarug fall to his knees, and then onto his face, the enormous figure fell with a loud thud, shaking the contents of the armory, and catching the prisoners by surprise.

Carador noticed a white feathered arrow sticking half way out of the Sarug's skull. Carador quickly turned around, only to see Arados, with a recently fired bow in his hands. Arados managed to give Carador a quick nod, before he recovered the remainder of his equipment, Carador grinned in acknowledgment.

"What was that?" Rugsha asked, sliding one hand through his hair.

"A Sarug commander, one of Saratrox's finest," breathed Carador, standing back up while retrieving his rightfully owned sword. He gripped the blade tight, it glowed greener the harder he grasped it. He felt a rush of energy flow through him. Carador slowly released his grip, and the blade turned back into silver. Carador returned to finish applying the rest of his armor.

"I have never seen one of th-" broke of Rugsha, as three black-feathered arrows unsuspectingly struck him, and he dropped to the floor.

"Rugsha!" cried Deltun angrily and attempted to make his way over to him.

"Watch out!" yelled Arados noticing more reinforcement Sarugs storming in. These ones were armed with bows and didn't think twice before firing.

"Take cover!" yelled Carador, eyeing a volley of seven arrows soaring through the air. The company swiftly ran in different directions, avoiding the arrows, some leaped against the wall.

Behind the seven archers, more guards armed with swords besieged the armory.

"Arados! Throw me those!" yelled Farond whom alone was surprisingly still unarmed.

Arados wheeled around and looked for what

Farond was shouting for. Quickly, Arados located two twin twelve-inch knives that he knew belonged to Farond. He quickly grabbed the knives and threw them to Farond, who managed to impressively catch them, both on their hilts.

Farond twirled his knives, and turned around, stabbing the closest Sarug to him, twice. He worked on the other ones as well, slashing them down. His body count can rise in a matter of seconds, Farond was a magnificent fighter.

Farond was an elf with long brown hair. He wore a dark blue robe and underneath his robe was a red shirt. Farond never creates a boundary for himself, he fights usually alone. He was born in Arcon Realm in 6842.

Farond is the son of Farradol, a soldier of a once great elven city in Arcon Realm. Farond was one of first elves to arrive in Earacill, in its foundation in the first year. He was a great warrior back in Arcon Realm, he traveled along with the first elves to Earacill, after he grew tired of Arcon Realm, and wanted to become an explorer, and travel to new lands to observe what there is to see and learn about the different parts of the world, his lifelong dreams were quickly shattered as he now is trapped in Earacill with the threat of Saratrox present, his life goal now is to destroy Saratrox.

Carador rushed over to the prisoner brothers, to his surprise, they were twins.

"How's your brother?" asked Carador aiding them, in defensive stance.

"His strength is failing, I don't think he can help us, I need to protect him," he said.

"Here use this!" said Carador aiming the hilt of his sword to the weakened brother.

"What's it for?" he breathed looking suspiciously at it.

"Just grasp it if you want to survive!" ordered Carador.

He did as he was commanded and grasped the hilt. The power of the Emerald-Star rejuvenated his stamina. He felt if no trouble ever surrounded him.

More arrows soared across the room, Carador and the brothers avoided them, while the others were fighting them off. It was noticeable to the company that Rugsha, whom was struck, had died, for he was unresponsive.

"Hey! Wha' happened?" the healed brother asked astonished.

"My sword has the power to restore one's stamina, as you have witnessed," said Carador focusing on the enemies as he saw one break through and head towards him, he swung his sword forward and slashed him across the chest.

"Anyway, thank you, err- my name's Selldar and this is my twin brother, Helldar," he pointed out. "Now it's my time, time for a little revenge...," Selldar stated seriously, focusing on the enemies.

The lone dwarf that Carador had seen during the breakout was armed with a battle-axe, and aggressively hacking down the Sarug Archers. "Arrghh! You want more!" Dalan, the dwarf roared, forcing his axe into another's gut. He may be short, nevertheless, he was full of spirit.

Dalan was a brawny dwarf. His weapon of choice is a legendary battle-axe he received in placement over his old war hammer. Dalan wears a helmet, which did not conceal his rugged face. He bears an unkept, long dark brown, greasy beard. Dalan lives with the rest of the dwarven community in Earacill, within the Manor Mines. The only settlement constructed by the first dwarfs in the year 300.

Dalan was born in 2651 and was known to be the youngest dwarf ever to become a warrior. He is the son to Harten the Fierce, a famous miner for his expeditions in the mines. Dalan would train for weeks, then months, learning everything about the art of war. His friends had nicknamed him: *The God of War*, as he was unstoppable to anyone. He was awarded a grand battle-axe for his skill by the dwarf's in the Manor Mines, which he still uses today.

Arados notched another arrow, firing it upon the last archer, piercing him in the forehead.

The exit was clear, at least for a while.

"Hurry! Grab the rest of your possessions, we must leave now!" yelled Farond looking out of the armory, searching for more Sarugs.

Carador applied the rest of his armor, and lastly equipped his helmet. He recovered the remainder of his equipment, everything that he had brought with him in the beginning, had now been retrieved.

"Check them," ordered Arados, pointing to

the injured fellow prisoners on the ground.

Teradorn checked the four fallen prisoner's pulses, they were unresponsive, including Rugsha. "Bless these souls, they did not fall in vain..." He whispered.

Teradorn, the son of Tarador, was born in 2695 in the kingdom of Faradown. He lived with his father throughout his childhood, one day Teradorn's father had robbed a market, he was being pursued by guards ordering him to stop, Tarador was cornered in a busy location, to avoid being caught, Tarador equipped a knife from behind, it was concealed from the guards. As the guards came closer to arrest him, Tarador quickly revealed the knife and attacked the four guards with it, killing them. Witnesses saw the crime Tarador committed and they reported it all throughout Faradown.

When Teradorn heard of the murders his father committed, at the age of fourteen, he ran away from his home and began living the remainder of his adolescent years living on his own, and hunting his own food, he never once purchased food from stores.

At the age of eighteen, Teradorn became one of Earacill's most renowned hunters, his trademark was his ability to hunt with only his sword. Teradorn was capable of sneaking upon animals from behind and stealthily taking them down. He was given the nickname: *The Phantom Hunter*. Teradorn never took his name seriously, although the citizens, who knew his ability, believed it.

Teradorn returned to Faradown and lived alone. He hopes he will never see his father again, nor does he know if he is still alive, he was never caught.

"Rugsha..." Carador said quietly down to a fallen friend. "We must depart now!" ordered Carador continuing.

The others nodded in acknowledgment.

"Hurry this way!" Arados pointed to the reverse direction of the armory, running.

They closely followed him, staying together like a pack of wolves. Once they were out of the armory, they stayed on the escape path, which shortly led them to the exit, marked off by torches, and a locked gate.

Arados, ahead of the group, grabbed on the gate's bars and attempted to open the gate, yet he was not achieving boldly.

"Hello, what's all this, then?" asked Selldar, sliding one hand through his hair.

"They blocked us off! Damned cowards," said Arados angrily trying harder to break open the gate, still no luck.

Carador gave a good kick at the lock, only forcing the gate to move back and forth from the recoil. Carador gave another kick, with the same effect. Carador stormed around, looking for another method, and he saw it.

He raised his head up and looked up to one of the prisoner he freed, which stood a striking seven feet tall.

"You! What's your name?" Carador pointed to him.

"Harken!" he barked.

"Alright, Harken see if you can break that open with your axe!" he said grinning looking at his massive weapon.

"Great idea, Carador," said Arados.

"Gladly!" the immense man roared, stepping boldly in front of the gate. He took his mighty weapon behind him.

"Get back!" ordered Carador to the others,

preparing for the impact that the mighty weapon which was about to occur. They each took a large step back.

Harken took a strong swing at the gate, visually fracturing it. He took another swing, and with this one: the gate broke open. Escape was now a step away.

"Good job, Harken!" cheered one of them.

"Right, now let's get out of here already!" stormed Helldar. "And Selldar, don't do anything stupid to get us caught!" his twin brother warned.

"I don't!" confessed Selldar.

"Let's hope you don't!" replied Helldar.

"I don't, Helldar!" cried Selldar trying to get the point across.

"I'm just saying I hope you don't, because you always do!"

"I do not!" he whined.

"Yes! You do!"

"But I-" Selldar cut off, being interrupted by Carador.

"Hey! Enough with the sibling rivalry!" He barked.

"Sorry we ju-" broke off Helldar, as he heard

the familiar alarm go off again.

The company looked around, panicked yet determined.

"Now look what you did, Helldar!" scoffed Selldar.

"Me? I didn't do anything! You're the loud one!" They argued some more.

"Enough!" barked Deltun. Deltun looked worse than any other of the prisoners, only for the fact that he had been imprisoned far longer than any of the others, over a month, being tormented in the process. "How long are you guys going to go at it?" Deltun barked. "You two just can't al-" His sentence was cut short as he covered his mouth with both hands and turned his sentence into a severe case of coughing. Some of the worst sounding any of them ever heard.

"Hey, all you alright?" asked Arados concerned.

"I'm fine!" snapped Deltun partially still coughing. "I just inhaled something foul!" he lied noticeably.

They stared down at him, as he tried to cover up his cough.

"The name's Deltun if you were wondering," he announced to the others, changing the subject.

"Err- Deltun, how long actually have you been kept in there?" Carador asked. "Thirty-four days would not do such damage to you so fast," he said.

"Never mind, that's not important," he snapped. "Let's just go!" he ended walking off alone.

"Hey! Wait up!" yelled Selldar catching up to him.

"What was that all about?" asked Helldar.

"There's something unpleasant about him... Some shadow surrounds his judgment. I don't trust him, be mindful of him, Carador. He may betray us," warned Arados seriously to Carador as he watched Deltun walk ahead of the others.

"Either that or he's traumatized by something, or someone," said Carador.

"Hey!" began Farond.

The others looked at him.

"When we were captured, they took our steeds, well at least I know they took mine. Where do you suppose they're held? That's if, the Sarugs didn't kill them," he feared.

Carador's mind quickly fixed on Azaful, and his personal feelings for him returned.

"They can't be far from here! Search around this Godforsaken prison!" ordered Carador. "Be on your guard!" he added.

Two search teams broke out, half of the group headed west around the wall, the team consisted of: Farond, Dalan, Harken, and three other escapees, while Arados, Helldar, Selldar, Teradorn, and two other escapees headed east. Carador ran up ahead to catch up with Deltun.

"Deltun!" shouted Carador catching up to him.

Deltun gradually looked behind him.

"Deltun!" he said again appearing next to him. "Our friends are searching for our horses; did you have one in need of rescue?"

"No..." Deltun replied shaking his head and walked on.

"Don't you have anything?" asked Carador. "I did not see you acquire anything in the armory."

"Only my sword, which is all I need in my life. I live alone, I wonder alone, I have no family, no home, where I go and what I do is up to me, I have allegiance to no one."

"No allegiance? I can give you some," said Carador.

Deltun glared darkly at Carador.

"Join me Deltun, have allegiance to me," praised Carador grabbing a hold of Deltun's arm.

Deltun eyed Carador intensely.

"Join me on the quest to slay Arush'n'aug! You don't have much to enjoy in life, you can join me and commit something fulfilling. Didn't you ever want to do something extraordinary in your life before you see too many seasons? Don't you want to go down in the history books for something memorable? Don't you want to be a part of something grand? Something that you may never get to be a part of again?"

"No, thanks for the offer," Deltun breathed. "I don't fight," he lied.

"You can fight, Deltun, I saw you handle those Sarugs back in there, you were a confident fighter!"

"What I was doing was protecting myself! As you were protecting yourself! As they protected themselves!"

"Yeah! We were! We joined together, to over throw the enemy, together! And that's exactly what we did, there's no reason we can't join!" cried Carador.

"What does it matter?" asked Deltun. "I don't even know your name."

"The name's C-"

"It doesn't matter what your name is!" interrupted Deltun holding his hand in front of him, cutting him off.

"I only work with myself, and for myself, and if you want to group up with your little friends, then go ahead! There's your legendary legion of: Arush'n'aug slayers!"

"So, it's all about you, huh Deltun? Does no one else in the world matter to you? You have no sympathy for others? No feelings or concern for the safety and well-being of others?"

"No. Goodbye, Slayer," Deltun ended walking away, into the trees that surrounded them.

Carador breathed in anger at Deltun's stubbornness. He knew Deltun would have been of great service to him on his quest, nevertheless, faith has decided other whys. Carador unhappily turned around and headed back to the prison to catch up with the others in search of his steed.

From within the trees, Deltun's dreadful cough returned, Carador could hear it, it still concerned him.

Carador rushed back and joined up with Arados' team.

"Where were you?" asked Arados.

Carador sighed. "I was trying to help Deltun, persuade him to join us, but I failed, he is now gone."

"Maybe it was better for him to get away from this all, God knows how long he was kept a prisoner in there."

"Yeah, you're right," Carador smiled.

They approached a corner of the prison and Teradorn cautiously peaked around at the other corner, he spotted a Sarug. Foolishly, Selldar walked on, past the corner, coming in clear view of the Sarug. Teradorn's eyes grew larger than usual, as Selldar's presence was in view of both him and the Sarug, luckily the Sarug had not seen him. Teradorn reached out and grabbed Selldar by the collar and threw him back towards him, slamming him into the wall.

"What the hell do you think you're doing!" whispered Teradorn angrily. "There is a Sarug right there! We need to assassinate them! We can't be seen or more will come!"

"Sorry!" apologized Selldar placing his hands in front of him, feeling threatened.

Teradorn sighed, releasing Selldar. "Hey you, archer!" He now pointed to Arados.

"The name's Arados," he replied.

"Err- Arados, take him out," Teradorn ordered, pointing to the target.

Arados notched an arrow, and swiftly peaked around the corner. He silently drew his bowstring back and released. The projectile spiraled in the air and impaled the Sarug in the neck, he fell silently.

"Now let's go!" announced Arados, as the path was clear.

The group moved ahead, they remained quite in case there were more.

"Look!" announced Selldar pointing to where the Sarug was guarding. He was guarding the stable.

"We found the stable, hurry let's free the horses," said Selldar.

They headed into the stable and approached the first horse they saw. All the steeds were chained up. The chains were not a sturdy built, as their swords easily cut through them, the horses were set free.

"Belor, glad to see you're unharmed," said Arados stroking his steed.

They were each overlooking their horses, making sure there were no physical wounds on them.

"Azaful, how are you?" asked Carador packing his equipment from the armory in the saddle pocket which remained intact.

"We have company!" cried Arados, as he spotted another wave of Sarugs running from around the corner.

The others quickly turned an eye and fixed their attention on them.

"Watch out!" warned Helldar, as he set off with his sword drawn.

The others quickly followed. They were yet again engaged in a sword fight.

Unfortunately for Teradorn, a Sarug had jumped upon his back and attempted to strangle him.

"Ah! Get him off me!" Teradorn roared while uncontrollably prancing around attempting to free himself.

"Hang on, Teradorn!" cried Farond, slashing down two more Sarugs.

"Archers! Arados, deal with them!" Carador ordered.

With quick hand movement, Arados notched his bow and fired upon the Sarug archers before they could even return fire.

"Well done!" Farond spoke quickly.

The enraged Teradorn was desperately attempting to rid himself of the Sarug nuisance, roaring about, while trying every method to free himself.

The enemy number quickly began to drop with their success.

"Help Teradorn!" ordered Carador.

"ARGH, GET OFF OF ME!" roared Teradorn. Luckily for him, he managed to grab a hold on the back of the Sarug's robe, and with an aggressive action, he threw him forward, and the Sarug landed on his back with a loud thud. Fuming with anger,

Teradorn lifted his leg and stomped down on the Sarug's neck, breaking it, a loud crack confirmed this. The crowd cringed at the dreadful sound of the neck breaking.

Teradorn breathed heavily, looking down at his enemy. He managed to crack a smile. "Glad that's over," he chuckled slightly.

"Err- right," said Arados dumbfounded, scratching his scalp.

"Hurry now! Let's leave this forgotten place!" said Carador, heading back to the stable.

Carador, as well as the other eleven, mounted their steeds and rode out of the stable and away from the prison in general.

"I don't think I have ever fought that much in one day," laughed Selldar. "It's got to be a new record.

"So according to the land texture and the scenery surrounding us," began Arados looking around. "We're in Farrow Forest! This whole jail must have been secretly constructed deep within Farrow Forest!" laughed Arados.

"Never would have thought," said Carador shaking his head.

"So, which way is south then? South to Banlafar?" asked one of them.

Arados looked up to the sky, "We're heading south now! The sun always sets towards the south!" said Arados pointing up to the cloudy sky.

"It's roughly a two-hour ride to Banlafar," said Carador remembering his ride from yesterday.

"Excellent! I can't believe we actually escaped!" cheered Selldar.

"That will warn them to ever try an ambush again on us!" roared Dalan.

"Yes! A swift ride to Banlafar, and this mess will be all but over," said Carador. "And waiting for us will be a roaring fire, freshly picked fruit, and swan-feathered pillows at the inn while we watch the moon ascend," said Carador relieving everyone of stress and pain, replacing it with peaceful thoughts they came close to never enjoying again.

They managed to ride faster, wanting peace and silence as soon as possible.

* * * * *

Two hours had come and gone, and the legion

of prisoners arrived at Banlafar, the guards at the entrance opened the gate, remembering Carador. With a bold stride, they entered Banlafar, their hearts filled with grace they had a successful breakout.

Carador, ahead of the company, commanded the legion to halt.

"I will talk with Lord Arien, and I will tell him everything that has occurred since yesterday. While I do this," he stopped sounding demanding. "You guys enjoy yourself at the bar, you deserve this, and the drinks are on me!" he announced.

The crowd roared with euphoria, causing their horses to neigh with surprise.

"Meet us at *the Blue Dolphin*, Carador!" said Dalan joyfully.

"I shall," nodded Carador in acknowledgment. "I will return," he announced as he dispatched from the crowd and rode to Arien's palace.

The Banlafarians acknowledged the company. They respected any warriors, protecting their homes and lands. The company dismounted their horses and entered the Blue Dolphin bar behind them.

Carador approached the familiar palace visited the day before. Without any hesitation, he stepped inside, and quickly made his way to Arien, to explain everything.

"Carador!" cried Arien quickly standing up, upon his presence. "Where were you? What has happened?" he asked eagerly.

"I was ambushed by Sarugs on my way back to Faradown after my stay here. Several others and I were held captive in a hidden prison within Farrow Forest. We managed to break out of the cursed place, and we hastily rode back here, the prisoners I had freed, were of the exact ones who received your letters, Saratrox or someone must have known who you summoned, each of them was ambushed by Sarugs, just like me, and we were taken prisoner!" Carador announced short of breath, quickly recovering.

"So, you are saying that the ones you freed were those who received my letters?" Arien asked hoping he heard correctly.

"Yes, one of them is Arados of Anaron, an archer," said Carador.

"Yes, yes, I am familiar of Arados, he is one of

Anaron's elite archers, a master of the art." He said. "He is with you?"

"Yes, the ones who managed to escape all are, they are down at the Blue Dolphin, I will meet them in there later."

"Shall I still hold a grand council? Or have you informed them of the plan? Will they go with you?"

"Yes, the majority of them told me that they accepted the task, which is why they were ambushed, they were heading here!"

"Good, Carador, go to them, give them my order that they can continue on the quest.

"I shall!" cried Carador as he swiftly wheeled around to rush out.

"Wait, Carador!" interrupted Arien.

Carador faced Arien. "Yes, my Lord?"

"Here take this with you," he continued as he walked over to Carador and handed him a rolled-up sheet of parchment.

"What is it?" questioned Carador taking the roll and staring at it.

"It's a map of Aromer Mountain, there will be a labyrinth towards the entrance of the mountain.

You will not be able to get past it without this map."

"No one has entered Aromer before, who made this? How did you obtain it?"

"Aussarok has. Sarugs have tunneled and crafted pathways as well as stairs through the mountain years ago. It's no threat to them. You didn't think it was a dragon's doing, did you?" Arien laughed.

"Well, no! It appears that I have been oblivious to this knowledge apparently."

"To answer your next question, spies from Anaron ambushed a battalion of Sarugs in possession of a copy a few decades ago. This copy was taken, and more were made, and distributed out to nearby cities. One of these now belongs to you. Make use of it when you unsure of which way to go."

"Alright, I understand," confirmed Carador looking back down at the concealed map and placed it in his pocket. "Thank you."

"Excellent, Carador, and remember that underestimating Arush'n'aug could lead to you and your companion's death," stated Arien wisely.

Carador nodded. "Arush'n'aug will not be underestimated by myself, nor do I believe my companions will underestimate it either."

Arien smiled. "I am looking forward to you as the King of Androuge, bring back the dynasty to Androuge, and it shall reunite with Anaron and Faradown, bringing the fall of Aussarok into place, and reuniting *the Three Kingdoms*."

Carador nodded in acknowledgment. "There would be nothing more I would like to see than Aussarok fall to the armies of Earacill," announced Carador grinning.

"Yes Carador, bringing down Arush'n'aug is part one to Aussarok's defeat."

"Because it will reunite *the Three Kingdoms*?"

"And because Arush'n'aug is now a pawn of Saratrox and Aussarok, it is their greatest warrior."

"I understand," he nodded. "Arush'n'aug is Saratrox's General, its most feared warrior, Arush'n'aug's death would do us a great part. Wait... How can Aussarok seduce Arush'n'aug to their will? If we could accomplish such as thing, then we can use Arush'n'aug to destroy Aussarok."

Arien sighed. "Saratrox had committed the dark act. He had the power to seduce anyone he desired to follow his twisted will. Thousands of innocent lives were lost due to Saratrox."

"That's heresy!" he exclaimed throwing his fist down upon Arien's table, causing the contents upon the table to tremble. Arien looked up at Carador. "Forgive me, Saratrox's actions anger me ever so, since Seragone's attack."

"Very well, may I continue?"

"Yes, of course, my lord."

"Saratrox expects not for us to know, however, Saratrox was once given a crown, and with that crown he was able to corrupt any form of life to serve him. However, Saratrox's crown had betrayed him and almost withered him. The crown would first corrupt those around it, then later he who wields it. With Saratrox's near death experience, he had destroyed the crown and hid the shards deep within the Cave of Anlaw. If we could retrieve those shards, and use them against Saratrox, we then could destroy Saratrox forever!"

"Yes, soon we will recover those shards! Wait, why didn't Saratrox simply have them melted down?"

"We believe that, it's to bait us to enter the Cave of Anlaw in search for them, in our process, we would be attacked and killed by the dark forces within, there are such foul creatures within that none of us can imagine would ever exist. Many have tried to retrieve it, nevertheless, they were killed in the process, we need warriors that have the willpower to survive the Cave of Anlaw, and successfully retrieve the shards.

"I understand," exclaimed Carador, thinking.

"You know well he is no longer a living life form, Saratrox is now a living phantom, a ghost. He will never stop his attacks until all Earacill belongs to him. Saratrox will have no trouble destroying us all, this land along with us. We've seen it before when Saratrox had destroyed our former home worlds of Arcon and Legion Realm, we are next in line for destruction, unless we act now and wisely."

"Ah," groaned Carador in grief. "So, all the attacks performed by Arush'n'aug are from Saratrox's commands. Killing Saratrox would release Arush'n'aug. Although even before Aussarok's imperial nation came, Arush'n'aug was still an enemy of ours," he breathed.

"That's right."

"Why must I slay Arush'n'aug before

Saratrox?" said Carador thinking strongly about it.

"If all the armies in Earacill joined together and attacked Aussarok, as we once have. Arush'n'aug would come and aid Saratrox, we cannot fight both Saratrox and Arush'n'aug at once! It is impossible to succeed. We both have learned this from the defeat of our fore battles that were fought, whether we were involved in them or not," announced Arien.

"I understand, I must slay Arush'n'aug before Saratrox. I will look to it," said Carador thinking strongly about it.

"Good, we shall bring peace to Earacill!" He spoke sternly.

"Yes. Farewell Arien! We shall meet again. I swear to you," ended Carador, and he turned his back on Arien, and walked off.

* * * * *

Carador walked back to the Blue Dolphin to meet with his friends and give them word of Arien's approval. With a swift stride, leaving his horse behind, mind you, Carador approached the entrance of the bar. To Carador's eyes, the Blue Dolphin was a much cleanser and stronger built bar than the one he entered in Anlar.

With a breath of relief of all he has been through already, Carador entered the bar.

"You call yourself a drinker?" was the first thing Carador heard, from a familiar voice. "You can't even finish one!" roared the dwarf, Dalan, to Teradorn.

Carador smiled at the sight of his friends together.

"What are you talking about? Watch this!" roared Teradorn taking his half-drunken ale and gulped the rest down in seconds. "Ha!" he cried wiping his mouth and letting out an atrocious burp.

"Keep it going, Teradorn!" yelled Helldar to him, cheering him on.

Carador switched off from Teradorn and Dalan's heavy drinking, to Farond and Arados, who were target practicing with knives.

"Almost, Arados. You want to keep the knife leveled to your eye, and throw using your wrist," advised Farond.

Arados took Farond's advice and threw the

knife, planting a few inches shy from the bullseye.

"Ha! That was brilliant! A couple more of those shots and you might actually beat me!" laughed Farond.

"All in due time, Farond. All in due time."

"Here watch again," said Farond as he precisely aimed and with a quick chuck, he through his knife, landing dead center on the target.

"Amazing!" astonished Arados. Farond looked to Arados and smiled, then looked back to his target.

Without warning, a third knife broke through the air from behind them, and perfectly striking the hilt of Farond's knife. Farond alerted, quickly looked from the knife within the knife to whom had thrown it.

"Carador!" cried Farond, running towards him. "You made it! Did everything go well with Lord Arien?"

"Yes, Farond, I told him everything that had happened, and he has given us permission to head to Aromer Mountain, and slay Arush'n'aug," informed Carador giving Farond a hard hit on the shoulder.

"Great, Carador," interrupted Arados. "I am

grateful everything is going to plan," he nodded.

Carador grinned.

"Hey, Carador's here!" yelled out Helldar to the heavy drinkers.

"Hey! You're finally here! We've been waiting!" said a drunken Teradorn. "Come on! I challenge you to a drink off!"

"You, bartender!" shouted Dalan. "Bring over five more ales!" he ordered rudely.

"More drinks? And just who is going to pay for all these?" he said, sounding furious.

"I'll cover it," announced Carador walking over. "The drinks are on me!" he said pulling out several Bansers, which was more than enough of the actual cost.

The company roared, raising ales to him, with ale spilling out, not that they cared.

The bartender's eyes widened at the amount of them.

"What, just five ales? I'll make it ten!" he laughed, and with a stupid grin on his face prepared more mugs.

"Yeah!" they all roared some more. Carador walked over to Teradorn and Dalan, who both were wasted out of their minds.

"It's about time, hero," burped Teradorn.

Carador sat down without a second thought.

"My bets are on Teradorn!" announced Selldar, slamming several Bansers on the table.

"Well, mine are on Carador," said Farond, joining in on the crowd, and placed his wager.

The others joined in on the bet to whomever they bet on. The bartender came around with the ten ales he promised, laying them out on the table around them.

"Ha! This is a joke!" burped Dalan, drowning himself in a second ale. "This fellow couldn't even finish three," he said uncontrollably, referring to Teradorn.

"That's because I called Carador over!" he butted in and gulped down the third ale. "Let's do this, hero," said Teradorn cockily.

"Touché, Teradorn," said Carador lifting his mug, and hitting Teradorn's mug.

"Go! Go! Go! Go! Go!" all of them roared, as Carador and Teradorn brought their lips to their ales and chugged to an unstoppable point until their ales were emptied. Carador was the first to slam the ale on the table, followed by Teradorn seconds later.

The crowd erupted in applause as they witnessed the drink off. Giving Carador pats on the back.

"Luckily I already had three before that!" blubbered Teradorn. "You're still sober!"

Without letting Teradorn have another drink, Carador quickly grabbed another ale, and chugged it down in seconds, followed by another right after.

"There! So, have I Teradorn, now we are equal," Carador smirked, holding back the possibility of hurling.

"Again!" ordered Teradorn, clenching tightly another ale.

Carador too, equipped a second pint of ale, bringing it close to his mouth.

"Ready?" began Helldar, raising his hand. "Go!" he shouted, lowering his hand.

As soon as the command was ordered, Teradorn and Carador chugged their fourth ale, empty. Teradorn slammed his mug on the table, unintentionally cracking it.

"Ha! Burped Teradorn, thinking he won, he

saw Carador sitting there with an empty ale, grinning. Teradorn appeared dumbfounded. "Damn it!" he cried slamming his mug on the table, as it shattered in pieces. "Best two out of three!" he demanded.

Carador raised an eyebrow, feeling a massive rush of alcohol traveling to his mind.

"You got it!" he cried, picking up another.

Teradorn did the same.

"Ready?" repeated Helldar, raising his hand.

"Go!" he ordered dropping his hand.

With that, Teradorn forced the ale down his throat with so much force, that his body couldn't handle the amount of beer following through his esophagus, and the ale was forced back out. Teradorn chocked, and the ale spewed all over the table and the floor, while Teradorn coughed uncontrollably. Helldar and Selldar rushed over to him, patting his back hard to clear his throat.

"Yeah! There we go, Teradorn," laughed Dalan, who was still sober enough to witness the whole event.

"Damn, you know I was close too," breathed

Teradorn, spitting out some of the remainder ale.

"Never challenge a Hero-knight of An-," Carador attempted to say, but coughed in between the sentence. "Never shallenge a Hero, to a shrink off," he said cockily, his mind was uneasy, as he was unable to speak correctly.

"Yeah Carador!" some of the ones who bet on him, said.

"You guys- you guys keep that money, you deserve it," said Carador.

"Alright!" they shouted, taking the money, not giving Carador time to change his mind.

"Let's get out of here, go home, and sleep...," Carador said weakly, almost passing out.

"Right behind you all the way," said Arados, helping him up. "We'll drop you off at the nearest Inn."

With a few more coughs and slur remarks, Carador and his friends left the Blue Dolphin, and headed to a nearby Inn, where they would stay the night.

There was an Inn close by to both the Blue Dolphin, and Arien's palace. In no time at all they reached the Inn, they made reservations to stay one night, and each headed to their own room. Carador, Teradorn, and Dalan, the drunkest of the crowd, fell asleep the quickest. While the others, either under the influence, or ones that had no ale at all, prepared themselves for their quest, which was to begin tomorrow.

PART II

* * * * * *

THE JOURNEY BEGINS

"Earacill is gifted with eight heroes.
Each from different corners of the land.
Each with a different personality.
They are the peacemakers of Earacill.
They are the Sons of Freedom..."

CHAPTER VI

* * * * * * * * * *

THE ROAD TO AROMER MOUNTAIN

Carador awoke the next morning without remembering anything from the night before, it was as if he never had a drink at all.

As they planned, Carador and his legion left Banlafar on the first of December. They headed right away to Aromer Mountain, with no pauses to impede them. They will travel long and dangerous paths to get to the summit of Aromer Mountain and slay the wretched beast.

Carador and some of his companions left their horses behind, because not everyone had horse to ride. Walking would be far safer, if worse comes to worst, they would need to conceal themselves.

"Sons of Earacill!" began Carador. "Listen up, from here on we will head directly to Aromer Mountain, we stop nowhere, everything you want, we have with us now, and stopping will only impede our journey. Our successful breakout has already gotten us to know one another, nevertheless, some of you may not know your allies as well as you should, I advise we all get to know one another more, we will be in his together for a while, I suggest we make the best of it. The eight of us can bring down Arush'n'aug once and for all! If our tactics surpass, our victory is certain!" Carador continued giving optimism to the men.

"Lord Carador," advised Teradorn. "I will follow you to the end of our journey, my allegiance to you will not waver," affirmed Teradorn only letting Carador hear. "I owe you my life, as we all do, for rescuing us from that accursed place I am forever in your debt."

"I know this Teradorn, I expect nothing more from you," replied Carador. "I hope the others have such devotion."

"Forgive me for my foolish behavior last night, it was the drinks, I was not myself," apologized Teradorn.

"Neither was I, it is only normal, Teradorn."

"Come, soldiers of Earacill, we must make haste!" directed Carador to his companions. The eight started sprinting away from Banlafar and heading towards a new path. They all caught up with Carador who was further ahead.

"So, who votes that our clan has a team name?" asked Selldar.

The others looked at him.

"You know, if we succeed in this journey, people should remember us somehow, a name that will be written in the history books.

"Okay, Selldar," began his brother. "Humor me, what would you choose?"

"Uhm, well, how about the Dragon Slayers?"

"No, that sounds ridiculous," said Teradorn blankly.

"Oh, well then, how about..." he paused, thinking.

"Soldiers of Slay?" interrupted Farond.

"Close, something more heroic though," said Arados. "How about *the Sons of Freedom*?" he exclaimed. "I mean it states that we "free" our people from Arush'n'aug, and we are all "sons.""

"Sure, I like it," shrugged Carador.

"Then it's official!" said Arados. "We are *the Sons of Freedom!*"

The others smiled, some nodding in acknowledgment.

"We all deserve freedom nonetheless," said Helldar.

"So, from my experiences of entering the realm of Aussarok long ago, I know that Aromer Mountain is left of it. Aussarok is veiled from the Mountain," said Carador as if he was entranced.

"My brother and I have never trodden on this path before," explained Helldar to Carador.

"Then let Lord Carador lead the way!" Roared Harken. His voice was so strong it seemed it could be heard a mile away. Harken was at least twice the size of anyone in the company.

"Uh, so Harken, are you a Half-Giant by any chance?" questioned Arados curiously.

Harken's face turned dark red, full of embarrassment, and a bit of anger. **"DO NOT JUDGE ME BY MY SIZE!"** Boomed Harken, his voice was so effective that it caused Arados to lose his stance in fright.

Harken was a colossal sized man; however, he was no giant.

"Alright! Alright!" the archer trembled nervously. "Easy now, I can clearly see your size problem brings some embarrassment to you," blurted Arados without realizing what poor choice of words he had uttered. "Wait, I should not have said that," explained Arados talking quietly to himself. He chucked nervously, "uh, Harken, what I meant to say is-"

Arados was unable to finish his sentence, as Harken swung his arm right towards Arados. Arados' eyes bulged, and he hastily leaped out of the way of Harken's attack, barely missing him.

Harken glared angrily at Arados, then turning around, continuing to walk to their location. Harken disposition was already far less than a friendly to Arados. Harken loathes being teased or asked about his size.

"Wow, Harken's size, and loud mouth will alert everyone in Earacill to his presence," Selldar sniggered to Helldar. Helldar, who different then his brother, has enough sympathy to respect his fellow man, could not help but spew out a quick laugh.

Harken, however, knew of the insults, nevertheless, instead of becoming enraged and causing a scene, he lightly grunted, walked forward, and tried to ignore their childish behavior.

Carador noticed a hill ahead of him, in front of that hill stood the foundations of the Ruins of Caracross, Androuge's once great and fortified Stronghold that now sits in ruin. Taking this route would shorten the company's duration of travel.

Carador ran upon the hill, the others followed.

"Perfect! We can cross through here!" yelled out Selldar.

"No, we cannot cross down there. Yes, it may be the ancient Stronghold of Androuge: Caracross, however, Arush'n'aug patrols these Ruins quite often, crossing through it would make us visibly noticeable to it, we wouldn't know if it were close we would then surely be discovered. The dragon patrols the structure looking for survivors, or trespassers, nevertheless, we have the wit to outsmart it and not cross down there!" snapped Carador, ignoring the fear that burned his heart.

"I agree, we must travel on the safest path," said Farond scratching his chin.

"Come, we must go this way instead!" announced Carador, as he faced towards the opening of the Fields of Camalon, which lay directly ahead. There was nothing to see, except the waves of heat rising from the ground into the horizon.

They began to sprint on the grounds of the Camalon Fields, away from the Ruins of Caracross.

"I hate running!" seethed Dalan furiously to Arados. "We dwarfs fight, kill, mine, and eat for a living. I'm not meant for trekking in such a way, it is not within our blood!" he breathed heavily.

"Don't worry, Dalan, you will keep up," Arados replied nodding.

"We must be swift and silent through these fields!" advised Teradorn. "Arush'n'aug's presence can appear at any time! Its senses are well tuned."

"Camalon, should not last us for too long," said Carador. "If we're lucky, Arush'n'aug will not patrol this area in that time!" Carador finished speaking, and everyone doubled their pace.

"Hey Arados, Farond, uhh, those are your names, right?" asked Selldar.

"Yes," they replied blankly.

"And you both are elves, right?" asked Selldar already knowing the answer.

Arados and Farond eyed Selldar, puzzled.

"So, I guess you two must be really old since you are immortal, or at least that's what I've been told," started Selldar.

Arados nodded in agreement.

"So, do you two know from where Arush'n'aug came from? If it has existed here before time, or if it was newly created, born, or even perhaps- I shudder to think, being spawned?" he ran on. "I mean it's obviously older than me, and I have known about it all my life," he said almost chuckling.

"Yes, I have the answer to that question, Selldar," began Arados. "I'll explain its origin to you. During March of the second year, in the First Century, Earacill had its first earthquake in the southwestern realm, which is where Aromer lays now. That earthquake, crumbled Mt. Farshard,

Aromer Mountain, the former home of the Phoenix bird."

"One year later a miraculous thing had occurred on the grounds of where Mt. Farshard had once stood. It rose again out of its ashes. The magic of the Phoenix birds had enchanted the ashes with their power for it to rise again. Although Mt. Farshard never looked the same, it was a price to pay. It had lost its beauty since the Phoenix's were now extinct. We could not go on calling Mt. Farshard by its name. So, we elves had renamed it to: Aromer Mountain, or the Dark Mountain, as some may call it."

"Aromer Mountain in return had attempted to resurrect the Phoenix's, and bring them back to life, although the plan had backfired. The integrity and purity in the mountain had disappeared as the ashes of the Phoenix's rose into Arush'n'aug."

"Anyway, Arush'n'aug is, well, the offspring of Aromer Mountain. I know, it's hard to believe or even comprehend at first. Arush'n'aug has been around ever since. Of course, since the mountain is evil, so is Arush'n'aug," finished Arados and Farond who had both shared the story with the group.

"And no one has ever tried to slay Arush'n'aug or destroy Aromer Mountain?" questioned Selldar blissfully forgetting the numerous battles in the past.

"No, many have tried to accomplish both, though all have failed," Arados sighed. The company lowered their heads in despair. Arados spoke again, regaining their attention. "However!" barked Arados. "A few managed to win a number of the battles and actually wounded Arush'n'aug, unfortunately none have ever gone so far as to slay it."

"I don't understand why the mere eight of us are on this quest, when over hundreds have failed?" asked Selldar disheartened. "I think I may have agreed to this prematurely, not considering all the facts."

"Because, we are considered Earacill's greatest warriors! We each make up about a hundred Militiamen, so using basic math, we're the manpower of eight hundred Militiamen," said Farond with his usual naive confidence. "In addition, due to our group size, we have the advantage of stealth and speed to strike!"

"Thank you for elaborating, I understand now, and feeling optimistic!"

Farond grinned at Selldar, laying a firm hand on his back.

"Look trees ahead!" shouted Arados pointing. Out in the distance, a meadow of a couple dozen trees were visible, around fifty, with yellow leaves and light brown colored bark.

"We should seek refuge in there for a while," he suggested. "We can recover our stamina."

"Yes, Arush'n'aug may come anytime!" advised Helldar. "I agree with Arados, let us be quick."

"Yeah, but even if we do hide in the trees, Arush'n'aug would easily spot Harken?" joked Selldar one time too many.

Harken's face turned so red and hot he appeared as a human fireball. Harken smacked Selldar in the chin, with excessive force, launching him a good five feet in the air, and another five feet away from them. Selldar's body quickly hit the ground. He was unconscious.

"Selldar!" yelled Helldar with raised eyebrows. The Paladin quickly came to his brother's aid.

"Did you have to hit him that hard, Harken?" barked Carador clenching his teeth eying Harken. "You nearly killed him!"

"And next time I will!" roared the monstrous Harken.

"Harken! We must stay together! We must respect each other. Or our task will never be accomplished!" fumed Arados.

"If you cause the death of me, I will forever curse you in the underworld!" threatened Dalan gesturing his axe at Harken.

Helldar stood back up he did not look too pleased.

Harken sighed, cooling down, with a succession of deep breathes.

"You know, Harken," breathed Helldar. "Selldar is an assassin, a mercenary. He was not tasked to this quest, it was out of sheer will. He despises Arush'n'aug and Saratrox no less than you and I. Despite our different career paths, Selldar is travelling with me because we are brothers, he feels obligated to protect me. You might not notice, although Selldar is quite careless with his vocabulary, and sometimes acts before thinking. Despite his flaws, his loyalty is unmatched, he would sacrifice himself for those closest to him. If you get to know him well enough, I assure you will befriend him," Helldar finished by taking a seat on the dirt, laying Selldar down beside him. Selldar had sustained a massively bleeding lip.

"Hurry, everyone," announced Carador to the company. "We must not forget about Arush'n'aug, its presence can arrive at any time. We must get to the trees," he continued while looking at Selldar, a sense of anxiety was evident on his brow's low position.

"I think we better go right now," whispered Arados to them, stunned.

"Why?" five of them asked simultaneously, other than Arados, Carador, and the lifeless Selldar.

"Arush'n'aug is coming our way. Right now!" shouted Arados pointing to the sky. His exceptional eyesight had not failed him. Farond ran next to Arados and used his similar gift of eyesight to determine its current location.

"Run! Hurry!" roared Arados waving his hands to alert the others.

Helldar quickly sprung up and carried Selldar, with a weak hold on him. They ran at full sprint, as fast as they could to the shady meadow which lied a quarter mile away. Helldar's pace drastically dropped as he was now encumbered with Selldar. Harken whom was in front of Helldar stopped and ran back towards him.

"Give him to me!" roared Harken grabbing Selldar off Helldar's back.

"Run!" roared Harken, and Helldar took off behind the others.

Arush'n'aug was now in full pursuit, and with a few more steps, Arados and Carador would be in the safety of the trees, they were closely followed by Farond and Dalan who both took a leap of faith and landed in the covered ground.

Teradorn came next jumping into the trees and landed a little further than the others.

"Helldar, Harken hurry!" yelled Carador. Helldar now ran faster than he ever had. This was solely because he had never been in such peril. He quickly performed a high dive and landed in a shaded patch, almost crashing into one of the trees in the process.

"Harken! Run!" yelled Arados. To their demise, Arush'n'aug had appeared above the trees, unfortunately, it spotted Harken. Harken took Selldar off his back and carried him in his arms. He threw Selldar into the trees and Helldar and Dalan caught him, almost sending them to the ground.

Harken leaped, almost landing in the trees until, Arush'n'aug snatched him by the legs with its massive jaw and devoured him whole. Harken's axe lay flat on the Earth.

The incredible beast was so large, it took an entire four seconds before the whole thing could pass their sight. The simple force of it passing knocked the company down.

"No!" yelled Arados hastily jumping upwards, as he ran out of the trees, he notched his bow with two arrows, mysteriously they turned green, quite a spectacle. He began shooting madly at Arush'n'aug. He pierced Arush'n'aug with six arrows, in its neck before it swung back around towards Arados, who continued to shoot. The great dragon noticed the lodged projectiles.

"Arados!" yelled Carador, fearing Arados would be seen.

As Arados notched another arrow and took aim, Carador grabbed him from behind and jerked him back into the trees. Arush'n'aug had just missed him, as furious and commanding the beast was, it lacked the basic wit to be truly unstoppable. Its common sense was poor, as it became confused.

Arush'n'aug flew over the trees, and then headed away from the company, back west, to Aromer Mountain. Again, as it flew over, a quick burst of wind sent everyone to the ground, except for Arados and Farond: who both flew in the air, striking trees correspondingly. Since they were elves, they did not weigh much.

Soon enough, everyone dashed away from the trees out of sight.

Selldar had recovered from his injury and was active enough to speak. "Where is Harken?" he asked looking around himself, seeing Harken misplaced.

"He did not make it, Selldar," said Helldar shaking his head in grief. "He risked his life to save yours, even though he was not the fondest of you."

Selldar hung his head low in disbelieve. "I was so cruel to him," he looked as if he was withholding sobbing.

"Hasten! We must continue on with our duty, we will grieve for Harken's loss later," said Carador.

"Agreed," said Helldar sadly, his face fixed on the Earth.

The company ran further through the fields. They conserved energy by keeping a steady run, electing not to sprint until sometime later. They were eager for vengeance.

"When is dinner?" asked Dalan eagerly.

"As soon as we get out of the fields, we can eat," said Arados his stomach roaring in hunger.

With haste they ran through Camalon for about another forty-five minutes at the least.

"Camalon will take forever to pass," said Dalan out of breath seeing his situation as hopeless.

"No, Dalan, not that long, we're almost out," said Arados, his pace becoming slower with time.

"Yes!" roared Dalan excitedly.

"Once we are at the Great Lake we can drink

its pure water," spat Arados, breathing heavily in anticipation.

"Ha! You're starting to sound like my common sense, which, mind you, has been absent from my mind, obviously starting when I accepted this dreadful quest!" Dalan laughed.

"Well, you are the one asking the questions, perhaps you'd prefer if I ignored them?" replied Arados with a bit of arrogance to his voice.

"No, no, don't mistake my demeanor as ungrateful, I do appreciate it," he replied.

"Alright," replied Arados with satisfaction.

* * * * *

About a half hour later, they arrived at the lake. It was dusk now, and everyone was far past exhaustion.

They collapsed in front of the lake, looking as if they were going to fall into slumber, but instead they began drinking hastily. Selldar and Helldar were of the only two, to not drown themselves in needed water, they were ambitious to dive into the revitalizing water, for a refreshing swim.

"Hey, don't go swimming too far! The lakes currents may pull you out to sea!" yelled out Arados between deep gulps of water.

"Don't worry!" yelled Selldar back to Arados, swimming about happily.

"I too have the desire to go for a refreshing swim," said Teradorn happily, as he removed his sword and all his other belongings, doing a front flip into lake with his robes still worn.

"Wait for me!" yelled Dalan excitedly, while removing his helmet, armor and weapons, as he did a cannonball in the lake causing a small yet affective wave that took everyone underwater. It soaked Farond, Carador and Arados, who remained on land, preparing camp. This was much to their annoyance.

"Hey, Farond," began Carador currently drying his armor and hair. "Has it ever come to your attention that the Great Lake is actually a river?" He scanned across the smooth surface of the water, as it spread out, far as he could see.

"Yes, it originally was a lake, you see about the same time Earacill was founded, an enormous landslide occurred that crushed the opposite banks together to form the river. So, across this river, rests an island. This lake was once connected to both the North and South sides, however; they split, and now formed the island of Sarchara. It's what separates us from Aromer Mountain."

"So why wasn't the Great Lake renamed to: The Great River?"

"Because the Great Lake made history to Earacill, it has sort of become a natural landmark."

"I ponder the idea of why I was never taught that," replied Carador nodding in intrigue. "Thanks for the information."

Teradorn, Selldar, Helldar and Dalan began to play a game in the water they had quickly invented.

"Hey, what's the matter with Arados?" asked Farond pointing towards him."

"Arados, what is it?" asked Carador eagerly, looking up from his current task.

"There is-" broke of Arados foreboding. "There is a disturbance in the West, over the Great Lake," said Arados who sat deadly still, his voice as solid as stone.

Arados' eyes grew unusually wide.

"Arush'n'aug has come!" yelled Arados

spotting a glimpse of a black silhouette appear across the dark sky. "It is coming! Our way!" continued Arados.

Everyone residing within the water forfeit their merriment, electing to flee.

"The trees are out of our reach! There are only the wide-open lands and this here water, none of which will suffice as shelter!" said Carador. He looked around quickly for a plan, and then stopped, his vision fixed on the Great Lake.

"Into the water and stay submerged!" yelled Carador to everyone.

With a quick thrust, Carador threw off his helmet along with some armor, which he had enough time to remove, he quickly concealing them with a cover. He, along with the others, quickly ran to the edge of the lake, each gathering a sharp breath, then diving underwater.

Farond and Arados quickly followed.

By the time Arush'n'aug had flown over them, the water ceased to ripple, and was calm once again. It took Arush'n'aug ten seconds for its massive figure to disappear.

Everybody emerged from the water gasping

for air. They had been underwater for about a minute.

They returned to shore, taking their seats, or more so, collapsing on the shore.

"Where will we camp tonight? If we sleep in the open Arush'n'aug will surely see us!" said Dalan.

"There is only one thing we can do then," replied Carador. "We'll have to turn back and make camp at the grove."

"Sounds good, I presume," breathed Teradorn gathering his belongings.

"Why did leave there after using it as our initial refuge?" asked Dalan impatiently.

"Hmm, maybe because your lust for food and water got the best of us!" interrupted Arados loudly. "We planned on resting after Harken's sinister death, but your incessant complaining had forced us to tend to your whining!"

After a few chuckles, the company headed back to the Camalon fields.

"Hurry! As we know, Arush'n'aug may return at any time! It tends to attack with no warning!" said Arados.

The Sons of Freedom fled back to the meadow,

which would take another hour or so.

"If Arush'n'aug comes every two hours," began Selldar. "Then by the time we arrive, only one hour would have passed, we anticipate another hour before it returns."

"Right, but should we slow our pace, it would theoretically take two hours to reach the grove of trees and no doubt Arush'n'aug would see us," reasoned Arados.

"I'm not certain Arush'n'aug's appearance is that linear," said Teradorn.

"Not for two-thousand-seven-hundred-seven years, have I fought Arush'n'aug, I am still waiting to avenge my father whom Arush'n'aug killed in its attack on Anaron," said Farond. His usually calm voice was broken with a sense of rage hidden in his tone.

"And I'm certain that you will get the opportunity soon, my friend," said Carador placing one hand on his shoulder, giving him a reassuring grin.

Minutes later they arrived back to the trees where they were to rest, for the remainder of the day.

"Now then, let's set up our camp," said

Carador.

"I'll cut down a tree for a fire," said Dalan standing up, pulling out his axe. With a quick swing, he struck one of the hefty trees.

"I will start the fire," said Teradorn equipping some tinder from within his robes.

"And I shall cook the food," said Carador pulling out some raw salmon and some chicken."

"My thoughts have been preoccupied all day, I have forgotten to ask, but do any of you feel fatigued from today's travels?" asked Carador hoping to get a positive reply.

"Greatly is an understatement, stated Helldar as he and Selldar both raised their hands simultaneously only to have them fall back down to their sides.

"Sort of," said Teradorn standing, stretching his arms outwards.

"Here, firmly grasp the hilt of my sword," said Carador extending his arm out with his sword held tight.

Selldar did not understand, but he grabbed a hold on it anyway. The sword regained Selldar's strength.

"Wow!" said Selldar perplexed. "I have forgotten all about that! Hey, Helldar, remember this?" he said motioning for his brother.

Helldar reached over and grabbed the handle. With yet another glow, Helldar's stamina increased.

Dalan had finished cutting down one of the trees and began hacking at it as to procure logs. By the time the tree was cut into ten separate pieces, Dalan pushed them together and Teradorn started striking his tinder in the center, setting off a spark, which evolved into a faint smoke, which later rose into a roaring fire.

Carador equipped a long branch from the ground, and stuck the chicken and the meat on it, and stetted it over the fire, slowly cooking it.

"So, Helldar, you're a Paladin if I'm not mistaken, right?" asked Carador while focusing on his kebab.

"Yes," replied Helldar.

"And Paladins generally serve in castles. Which gets me wondering which castle you reside from?"

"I am from Anlar, in Faradown."

"Anlar..." said Carador thinking about that

name. "So of course, you would know King Faraduel."

"Yes, I am his Captain."

"Faraduel is closest living person to me, although we are not related, we have known each other since we were young," said Carador.

"I was at Anlar three nights ago, I convinced my old friend, Lord Faraduel, for permission to arrange this quest, after explaining the tragedy that has fallen upon Seragone, and all of Androuge."

"I know, I was there when you gave that speech about Arush'n'aug. Faraduel wanted me to go to the council, so I went."

Carador could not recall seeing the Paladin, but he elected to trust his companion. "Ah! The foods cooked everyone," said Carador while passing each of them a piece of cooked fish or chicken.

"Arados, where are you from?" asked Teradorn ripping apart his salmon, taking a bite.

"Ie armm fonn Asharan," said Arados, his mouth was so full of fish it was surprising he could muster the words. The others looked at him in confusion.

Arados took a big swallow. "Sorry, this salmon is so appetizing, I have forgotten my manners!" said Arados embarrassed. "I was attempting to say, that I am from Anaron, Farond and I both are."

"I am from Faradown," said Teradorn to everyone.

"And I am from the Manor Mines," said Dalan proudly. "The finest mines in all Earacill!" he boasted.

"The only mines in all Earacill," said Arados rolling his eyes, much to the annoyance of Dalan. Dalan developed a foolish look on his face.

"And I am from Seragone in Androuge," stated Carador. The City of Silver Knights."

CHAPTER VII

* * * * * * * * * *

THE GREAT LAKE

An hour had past, and everyone had finished their meal. Most of them were now sleeping peacefully fully concealed within the trees.

Teradorn, Arados, Helldar, Selldar and Dalan were sleeping. Carador, awake, was reading another page of Tharagor's journal.

Day 4

Today I had my going away party, in the town square of my hometown. It was a heartfelt day, full of comings and goings, sorrow and even comedy at some points. Some people were never going to forgive me for taking their friends away, however, it was of their own decision to come with me. Their presence in my journey is by no means arbitrary.

"I am not forcing anyone to come with me, it is their own decision. Citizens please do not fill me with misery and woe I do not deserve!" I cried out desperately at one point.

"Because of your trip, Tharagor, we will never see them again! They are some of our closest friends and you have absolutely no right to take them away from us!"

"People, why do you not listen? It is not my right or decision at all that they want to come along with me on my journey. It is of their own decision. Please if you disagree, talk to them about it. This trip was originally supposed to be me departing alone!"

"He's correct!" yelled one of the townsmen. "It is not of his choosing to take them along with him. It is their own decision!

"Yes!" I exclaimed, relieved that someone had taken my side.

"Arien! Why have you decided to go along with Tharagor?" the townsmen asked. But I did not want to stay around for that any longer. I talked with many of the town's citizens about my travel plans and where I would go.

Later that day I packed my final bags and was ready for my maiden voyage down south tomorrow...

-Tharagor

Carador was seconds away from closing the book when Farond interrupted him.

"What are you reading?" asked Farond eyeing the leather book.

"It's the journal that Tharagor wrote on his way to discover Earacill. It tells all about why he left his homeland, and how he succeeded, the most authentic part? Every word is written by Tharagor himself. I began to read it because I don't know too much about the history of the founding of these lands," replied Carador.

"Ah, I have heard of it, although I have never gotten around reading it. I'll look at it someday."

"Yes, it's quite historical... Did you know that Lord Arien and King Tharagor were once the closest of friends, and that they set sail together and founded Earacill?" asked Carador.

Farond nodded, "I have heard stories of that, although I never got a chance to ask any of them personally about it," said Farond eying the book.

"I actually had come to light of that, just today, who knew?" he laughed. "Well goodnight, Farond, sleep hearty, we few will need to be well rested for tomorrow."

"Very well, goodnight, my friend" said Farond with a slight smile.

Carador placed the book away in a sheltered location next to one of the trees, there, he sat down and rested his back upon and closed his eyes.

* * * * *

The company awoke the next morning revitalized, the water from the Great Lake had all but extinguished their fatigue.

Carador was the first to wake, or so he thought. Arados was examining further on to see if Arush'n'aug had come around. He stood tall, scanning the tree lines with his exceptional sight.

Carador walked over to Arados. "Do you sense anything?" he asked in a whisper.

"Arush'n'aug flew past us twice during nightfall. You can tell by the disturbances in the sand," alleged Arados pointing to the waves in the terrain.

"Are you certain that they're not from prior passing?"

"No, the disturbance in the sand is too fresh. If you look elsewhere the waves in the sand aren't quite as deep," pointed out Arados.

"Well, that settles it then," said Carador.

Arados looked at him.

"We have to leave and get to the Great Lake now before Arush'n'aug returns. Hurry let's wake the others." They went back into the trees and woke Farond, Selldar, Helldar, Teradorn, and Dalan whom alone was infuriated, with having to awake, premature to his content.

"Quickly, we must get going," said Carador.

"How will we get across the lake?" said Dalan yawning.

"Hey, Dalan is correct," began Arados. "How can we get over the lake if there is no bridge or boat to transport us?"

"I know!" said Dalan instantly awake. "We can assemble our own raft." He said running towards one of the trees and started hacking away at its base.

"Well, it's the only way," said Carador agreeing with Dalan as he started hewing away on a separate tree with one of Dalan's hatchets.

Dalan joined him.

"If only Harken was still here," Carador sighed. "His size and strength could probably take down these trees with a swing or two."

Carador cut down two trees, and Dalan cut down three. They then skinned the branches of the trees and brought the five logs together.

"Now what can hold them together?" asked Dalan looking at Carador and then the others.

"Hmm," growled Carador his mind occupied with a possible solution. "I might know, Arados, pass me your bow."

Arados tossed Carador his bow, in which Carador bent the bow into a sharper arch then it already was. He then pulled the bowstring out. Arados opened his mouth to utter a complaint, although he closed it again as he saw what Carador was doing to utilize the string.

"I'll need another string," said Carador quietly to himself. "Arados, do you have another bow string by any chance?"

"Yes," said Arados, running back to the trees to retrieve his pack.

Carador looked around himself before turning to his companions for the answer. "Does anyone have any string or rope of any sort? We can use that to hold the logs together."

"Yeah, I do," said Selldar drawing out around ten feet of white, nylon rope, and tossed it to Carador.

"Thanks."

Arados came back with a spare bowstring. "Here, Carador," he said as he passed the string to Carador. "You never know when I might come in handy."

"Now, I'll have to tie the five logs together, using your bowstrings," said Carador looking at Arados. "And your rope," he continued switching his eyes over to Selldar. "So now we got ourselves transportation over the lake!"

"Well thought out, Carador," complemented Teradorn.

Carador took the two bowstrings and tied them together. He wrapped the two strings around one end of the logs, and he used Selldar's nylon to tie the logs together on the opposite end.

"Alright, the raft is set, prepare your belongings, for we're going to drift across the Great Lake."

Selldar, Helldar and Teradorn went back to the trees and retrieved their belongings.

"Quickly now, help us lift this up," said Arados while he and Carador both were struggling with holding the raft upright. Teradorn, Farond, Selldar and Helldar, helped them hold up the raft. Because of Dalan's height, he could not help them.

"Dalan, go forward, and scout ahead for Arush'n'aug, if it is coming," said Arados. "Since of course you can't reach.

Farond refrained himself from a sudden outburst of laughter. Dalan did as he was told.

* * * * *

It took them longer than before to reach the Great Lake, as they were now in the process of carrying a raft, resulting in them to lose a lot of speed.

"Careful," warned Arados, as the company lowered it slowly into the water.

"Now then, let's get a move on," said Carador.

Arados walked onto the raft following behind him was Carador, Teradorn, Selldar, Helldar, Farond, and last came Dalan who gave the raft a push to get it on course.

"What is the duration of our ride from here to the other side?" asked Carador while he and Arados equipped one rafting stick they crafted themselves.

"Approximately twenty minutes," said Arados looking straight ahead to the other side, which was a half a mile away.

"Time is against us, Arush'n'aug as we know, could come at any time," said Arados looking ahead.

"Right, let's move out," said Dalan.

Carador and Arados started paddling across the lake on the raft, Carador on the left side and Arados on the right. The raft then slowly started to move away from the shore

"So, who will be paddling it after Carador and I?" asked Arados.

"You will be doing the whole way, and

slaying the dragon yourself," said Dalan laughing comically," while he was lying down on the raft enjoying himself.

"Well then I believe you won't be needing this anymore," threatened Arados snatching Dalan's axe from his side, and threatened to throw it overboard.

Immediately, Dalan leaped forward with a quick cry of, "No!" and snatched his axe out of Arados hand, almost launching himself in the river.

Arados stood and laughed.

"Fine, Teradorn and I will paddle the raft next," he breathed. "I was not being serious anyway."

"What?" interrupted Teradorn, coming out of his nap as soon as his name was mentioned.

"Very well, I'll join Dalan," said Teradorn, closing his eyes again.

"Look onward!" pointed out Selldar. "There are rocks, they are sure to impede us." Ahead of them lie twenty to thirty surfaced rocks, blocking their path.

"Carador, Arados, turn the raft southwards down the river, until the obstruction ends," barked

Farond.

Carador and Arados immediately, started paddling in a different direction, eventually turning the raft.

"Okay, we should be in the clear for now," breathed Carador. "Good sighting, Selldar." But Carador spoke to soon, there was one rock directly in front of them, which they failed to dodge. The raft impacted against the rock in the center, which in turn split the centermost log in two. There, unfortunately, lied Arados' unstrung bow of the ancient King of Anaron, Tharagor, it had fallen through the crack in the raft, and was now out of sight.

Arados noticed this almost immediately, and without a moment's hesitation, he dropped his paddle, almost allowing it roll to off, and land in the river as well. At the last second, he jumped towards the back of the raft, dunking his head and arms into the water, nearly falling in. The loyal companions: Teradorn, Helldar, and Selldar managed to reach for Arados' feet and pulled him back up, there in Arados' grasp, was his bow.

"Do you care that much about your bow?"

laughed Teradorn, his heavy breathing was apparent.

Arados looked at Teradorn confused. "What? You think I would uncaringly allow my bow to drift away? That be madness!"

"Well, that is not exactly what I meant," Teradorn chuckled.

"This is no mere bow, Teradorn, this is, *Sky-Piercer*, the legendary bow of King Tharagor. I've only confessed to few; however, I stole it after his death in 2045. I have altered its appearance quite a bit, becoming unrecognizable. The bow, I believe," he said with a slight pause, scratching his chin, "received its name from its fabled ability, to shoot farther than any other for its time. It has the power to set arrows, in position, to be shot, aflame, or inject the loaded arrow with venom. The fire and poison flow through Sky-Piercer, then through its string, and injects into the back of the arrow, and moves rapidly to the arrowhead. I desired a new bow at the time more than anything, having my old one break from much usage, unfortunately. I was living in poverty and lacked the means to purchase my own.

Personally, I believe it to be the best bow in all of Earacill!" he laughed.

"Well, that makes sense to me," said Teradorn tiredly. "Wait a minute... you said the year 2045? That was over seven hundred years ago!" He choked being suddenly awake. "Just how old are you?"

Arados chuckled at the question, and violently shook his head, as to expel a great deal of water from his silky black hair. "Teradorn, remember we elves are immortal, we cannot die from age alone. I am three-thousand eight-hundred-sixty-five years old, and I would not be caught surprised if Farond is any older than I."

Farond laughed. "I am four-thousand two-hundred-thirty-five years."

"See?" said Arados raising a brow.

Teradorn sighed, "I wish I could live to be that old," his voice full of disdain and self-pity.

"It sets arrows on fire?" cried Selldar a little late in the conversation.

Arados and Teradorn quickly glanced over at him.

Selldar's eyes were big and fixed on Sky-Piercer. "Can you shoot an arrow on fire into the sky? I want to see how high it can go!" Selldar yelled excitedly.

"No Selldar!" yelled Arados angrily. "Even if there is the slightest chance Arush'n'aug will notice it, I will not jeopardize our quest over such a meaningless action! Not to mention I would be wasting an arrow, which is dwindled as it is," he said rolling his eyes.

"Sure... but what if you were to recover it when it comes down?" he asked vacantly.

"Selldar!" roared Arados angrily at him.

"Alright!" cried Selldar apologetically, and disappointed.

"I-I believe Dalan and I shall maintain the raft now," interrupted Teradorn while standing up, to ease the tension of the company.

"Yes, I agree," said Arados looking away from Selldar to Teradorn.

Teradorn took Arados' position and Dalan took Carador's.

"That's nothing," laughed Farond standing up.

The seven looked upon him.

"My knives, properly known as the *Twin-*

Vipers have the famed ability absorb fire!" he announced revealing them to those who had taken interest. "The perfect weapon to challenge any foe that prefers the substance, such as Arush'n'aug," he stated boldly.

Arados nodded. "Not bad, Farond, not bad at all," he said as he watched Farond sheath them.

"Speaking of weapons," said Dalan beginning his own conversation. "If you want legendary," said Dalan while chewing some sort of meat he had brought along with him. "You should see this axe in action," he bragged grasping his axe high with one hand. "The perfectly polished razor-sharp blade will cut perfectly through the dragon, like a knife cuts through butter!" he laughed spitting chunks of meat into the river, much to the disgust of those to witness it.

Arados, Carador, Teradorn, Farond Helldar, and Selldar all looked upon one another shaking their heads, chuckling all the while.

"Its leather grip would make it impossible for you to lose grasp of it in battle," continued Dalan. "And its light weight is perfect for any battle you choose to fight! Ha!" laughed Dalan with his perpetual enthusiasm.

"Although, Dalan, my friend, I believe yours can't be sold in stores for a hundred-thousand Bansers!" replied Carador with a smirk of his own.

"Aye, I don't believe any blade can be sold at such a high price!" nodded Dalan, placing his axe back on the log.

"Then I believe that you are unaware of the Emerald-Star!" announced Carador removing the Emerald-Star from its sheath, holding it high to the sky with one hand. The sun's reflection complemented of its stainless silver-blue blade, blinding everyone. The blade gave off a sharp sting of metal, as it was drawn.

"Carador, conceal your blade, it could attract Arush'n'aug," said Farond with one hand over his eyes, blocking the white light.

Carador placed the Emerald-Star back in its sheath, coincidentally restoring the company's vision.

"My sword, the Emerald-Star, was forged by the greatest blacksmiths of all, in the Cave of Anlaw," he began reciting what knowledge he knew of his blade.

"Its blade glows Emerald green when one is filled with fury, for more strength. The hilt regains your strength when weak, something quite handy, if I do say so myself," he said running his fingers across the blade. "The inscription carved into it says: The Emerald-Star, the sword of leadership, as you can see here."

"Tharagor's blade!" asked Arados astonished remembering the famous name, whilst furiously working to dry his unstrung bow. "That sword has been lost for the past one thousand years!"

"Yes, I believe it was Tharagor's and his kin after."

"The first King of Anaron? The first King of Earacill?" asked Arados still in shock.

"Yeah," said Carador repeating himself. "Isn't that funny, Arados? We both own one of Tharagor's weapons," he chuckled sitting back down.

"Yeah, I guess you're right!" he laughed. "We make quite a legendary team then!"

"How did you get it?" asked Teradorn calmly staring at the hilt of the sword.

"I bought it in *The Sword and the Shield*, an armory in Anlar, Morler the merchant there, sold it to me. He told me that he found in lying in the Camalon Fields in the year 275, about a hundred years after Tharagor's son, Morather, fell during his own quest to slay Arush'n'aug. That's when Morler found it and took it for himself, and after all these years of having it in his possession, he decides to sell it to me. I'm convinced he was waiting for the right customer to come along. He knows more about me than I thought," he said intentionally leaving out the details of his heritage.

Thinking about it more now, Carador concluded the Emerald-Star's page in Morler's book was cloaked, in the same manner the weapons on display were when he first entered the store. Otherwise, the sword would have been sold centuries ago.

Teradorn looked sadly and blankly at his own blade, it possessed no powers to it, nor had it garnered any prestige of its own.

"You say grasping the hilt upon your sword regains strength?" asked Teradorn. He took his eyes off the hilt and now looked upon Carador.

"Yes," said Carador blankly, slightly annoyed at having to repeat himself.

"That will definitely come useful in th," said Teradorn confidently.

"What do you mean?" asked Carador, partially already knowing the answer.

"Look ahead," pointed out Teradorn.

Carador turned his head away from Teradorn and looked onward, towards their destination. The land ahead of them produced a thick cloud of smoke.

"Once we pass the Great Lake, we will be forced to tread through the Dead Land," said Teradorn. "The Dead Land will wear us down in no time at all, the humidity of the

Earth there will expel us. We will be cooked faster than a fish upon a grill."

Carador eyed the land intensely, watching the smoke build up. Knowing Teradorn was speaking the truth.

"Although, Carador," Teradorn continued. "If we use the sword's power against it, we should be able to manage the path," replied Teradorn looking ahead.

"Who said anything about letting you use its power?" said Carador darkly staring at him.

Fear crept across Teradorn's face.

"I merely jest with you, Teradorn!" said Carador laughing.

Teradorn gave out a quick laugh as well and continued to paddle harder.

"Teradorn is right, the land ahead will threaten our process, this is for sure," Arados grimly stated.

"Well, it's only a little way further, let's keep moving before we become Arush'n'aug's meal," said Dalan, thoughts of Harken plaguing his immediate thought.

The thought of Arush'n'aug's inevitable return prompted Teradorn and Dalan to put more force into their work and reach the shore quicker.

"We're coming up, only a few more feet!" barked Farond watching the destination of the Earth tighten as the raft was approaching. "Teradorn, Dalan, slow down! We're coming in too fast!" warned Arados. "Be careful now as we make our approach," he spoke as they began slowing down. "Slow down."

Their raft came to a halt, and jerked, causing Arados and Farond to plunge forward then downwards onto the shore. The raft had successfully come to a complete stop on the other side of the Great Lake. Teradorn and Dalan with a lack of grace, mind you, were the first to depart only to be quickly followed by: Arados, Carador, Selldar, Helldar, and Farond lastly.

Carador and Teradorn pulled the raft onshore, and began to disassemble it, they untied the logs and returned Arados' bowstrings to him. Arados gladly took them back with a quick snatch, and restrung his bow, and tested it for strength and integrity.

They began walking southwest, approaching the Dead Land, where nothing but death would await them. There wasn't anything for their eyes to designate, other than the sharp rocks, and steam rising from the dead Earth. Aromer Mountain was cloaked by the thick smoke. Their eyes began to water from the steam that blocked all long-range sight.

"Come, Aromer Mountain is not too far from here," announced Carador.

With a last deep breath, the seven companions walked bravely onward into the Dead Land, until death may take thee.

CHAPTER VIII

* * * * * * * * * *

THE DEAD LAND

One hour had come and gone since the company's arrival upon the Dead Land from the Great Lake. The seven dragon slayers traveled slowly and wearily across the Dead Land. They were unable to travel at the pace they had planned. The Dead Land's atmosphere reminded the companions of their worst memories, which slowed their steps down to an even slower pace.

"These rocks are razor sharp!" said Dalan weakly, as they treaded across the dark land's sharp rocks. Their feet had been repetitively cut and burned, leaving a thin, barely visible blood trail behind them.

"That is why we must move faster, Dalan," said Arados quietly. "Come on," he continued, struggling to help Dalan move faster.

Arados attempted to move faster, however, his strength reached its limit and had failed him, causing him to fall to the Earth. Arados' hands were burnt and felt if they were lit ablaze, luckily their appearance did not change. Arados pushed himself back up, although he began to slowly fall back to the scorching Earth.

"Here use this," Carador muttered while he drew his sword slowly from its sheath and handed it downwards to Arados.

Arados slowly reached one arm in the air and clutched the hilt. The Emerald-Star gave Arados instant strength causing him to stand upright, full of renewed vigor. They would have to tread faster, or death was sure to welcome them.

"Here, Teradorn, take it," said Arados noticing Teradorn moving weakly.

Teradorn cracked a smile and took a hold of the hilt and with his new-found power, his face renewed its healthy color, and he walked in his powerful stride.

Teradorn passed on the sword, this time to Dalan, whom passed it to Helldar and then to Selldar, who passed it to Farond, and back to Carador. They had made a chain reaction, of divine healing. None of them had the slightest intention of losing a companion to this cursed land.

Teradorn opened his water flask and snapped his neck back in anticipation. A few drops of water fell out of the flask and hit the Earth, evaporating instantly. The seven continued to walk through the empty land, they became disheartened, as well as exhausted.

Arush'n'aug would soon be informed about their immediate arrival upon its territory.

Arados handed the sword back again to Dalan, only this time, the sword did not glow, nor did Dalan feel any rejuvenation.

"Carador, I think the sword's power has extinguished. It's not enchanting me with strength anymore."

"What! That is the only thing preventing us from death right now!" said Carador horror struck. "We must have worn it out!"

"We must quicken our pace then!" coughed

Dalan.

Desperately, they attempted to move much quicker, nevertheless, the Dead Land was too strong, and it sapped their energy, quicker than they could restore it. Teradorn dropped to the Earth, exhausted, and needed to force himself back up, after much strain, he was able to accomplish this and move on.

"This journey will be our doom!" cried Teradorn weakly trying to stand back up. "I told myself from the start. I said it would be impossible," he said weakly. "We sent ourselves to our doom, I knew it from the start."

"We all risked our lives on this journey. My risk is no greater than yours!" said Carador.

Arados helped Carador to stand back up, and Dalan helped Teradorn. "Our time is not yet," wheezed Carador attempting to open his flask for water, though his hands were much too weak now to move, he took the flask up to his mouth and pulled off the cap with his teeth, and drank some, the cool liquid sustaining him, as he swallowed hard. He then closed the cap as to ration the remaining drops. "Think of the Dead Land as the wall to Aromer Mountain, and every wall must be scaled to succeed."

In the rear, Selldar plunged downwards and started crawling, however, he was quickly helped back up by his loyal brother.

"We will make it through this, I promise you, as long as we don't stop moving," said Carador to Teradorn.

Teradorn nodded his head weakly and tried with all his might to walk faster, being wary of plunging downward again.

They trudged on, diligently watching over each other.

* * * * *

Thus far, all seven of *the Sons of Freedom* knew to one another that getting across, and out of the Dead Land was a task which would not end in their triumph. They fell upon their hands and knees, slowly crawling their way across the Dead Land.

"Carador," said Farond slowly. "Remember how my blades can absorb fire? I do not know if they can absorb heat, but if they can, it might just give us a chance."

"Well, pierce it into the ground and see what happens!" cried Carador, causing the company to look up, at the sight of hope.

Farond drew out one of his twelve-inched curved knives and with the remainder of his strength, he pierced it into the Earth. Several moments past and when nothing occurred to their avail, the company turned their heads in despair.

Suddenly, the heat surrounding their location began to vanish from the Earth, the ground was now cool, it no longer burnt at the touch; the company cheered in praise of Farond.

"Once I remove my knife from the ground, the heat will slowly return," said Farond slightly stronger.

"Alright," began Carador. "Let's use this time to recover much of our former strength," said Carador sitting down, he grasped the Emerald-Star tight, to no avail, no hope for them.

Teradorn lied carefully on his back to rest, hoping the sharp rocks of the Dead Land would not cut him.

"Now if only we had something to clear this smoke!" said Arados angrily trying to wave it off, with his hands meagerly moving about. "Then we would have visibility of Aromer Mountain and see how close we are."

"Yes, that would indeed be useful," said Farond with a slightly stuffy nose.

"Come on, let's continue, the sooner we get away from here, the better," exclaimed Arados slightly coughing.

"No, we should use this precious time to recover, and cover our wounds," said Carador.

Teradorn nodded. "Yes, I agree."

The group rested for few minutes and managed to rebuild some of their strength and heal their wounds.

"Now that we've recovered we should continue, and continue fast," said Carador.

"We shall!" nodded Farond. "I will remove my blade from within the Dead Land," he said forewarning everyone. The company rose up and took the proper precautions as they were about to sprint.

Farond removed his knife from within the ground, and with that he yelled, "Run!"

The crowd dashed onwards with the strength

they had recovered, as fast as their burned and bleeding legs would carry them.

The burning sensation on their feet started to return slowly but most noticeably.

"Run, and do not halt for any reason!" yelled Farond warning them on.

The travelers did as they were told, they sprinted for another good five minutes and without noticing, the Dead Land had come to an end, they continued to dash while congested. They located a cave in front of them, with living and vibrant green grass inside, and surrounding the small rock cave.

Not caring at the blessed site of grass and heatless ground, the seven wearily headed for the cave. They were fortunate to be alive, some praising Aruanor that they successfully reached a rest spot to fully recover.

Once they resided inside, they sat down, and poured cold water on their feet to cool them, which at the same time stopped the previously intense bleeding. They then wrapped their feet with various cloths, which they had brought with them or were wearing at the time.

They were so parched from their travels that

they fell asleep, not wanting to, even before darkness would overcome the land. The heavy-eyed *Sons of Freedom* fell asleep blissfully unaware that they were next to their desired destination.

CHAPTER IX

* * * * * * * * *

AROMER MOUNTAIN

The next morning began after darkness dissolved into the thick air of Aromer Mountain, and light returned to Earth. It was not by chance that there was a patch of vibrant grass surrounding the companionship. There were no former ashes of Mt. Farshard that had been concealed there, allowing the land to remained flourish and prosper.

A great screech and a movement that shook the land had awoken the company from sleep. The earsplitting screech nearly shook them, mid slumber.

Sleep in Sarchara Island, and Aromer Mountain could never be peaceful, the land exposed thick air, in which case made each one of their noses stuffy and clogged, making breathing difficult as well.

"Ah! That would have had to be my best night of sleep I've ever had! It was much needed!" Dalan yawned.

Contrary to Dalan, Teradorn awoke disgruntled. "That damned beast has awoken me, my rest is not yet complete," he spat angrily as he lied back down, Carador, however, had suspended Teradorn from any further sleep by shaking his shoulder.

"No, not now, Teradorn, Arush'n'aug has left its post, now is our chance to infiltrate the mountain. Later you shall receive your well-deserved rest," smiled Carador.

"What is the hour?" asked Arados stretching.

"No way of telling in Aromer Mountain," said Farond tying his bootstrap. "Although I'd say it's not yet noon," he said looking straight upwards.

Helldar and Selldar both gave out a big yawn and wiped their watery eyes. Arados couldn't help but let out a laugh at the sight. "Do you two do everything together?"

"Huh? What do you mean, Arados?" asked Selldar concerned.

"What I mean is, you both are twins, so you

obviously tend to look similar, although, you two are completely different people educational and character wise. Uhm- I mean no offense, Selldar," Arados chuckled.

"None taken," Selldar stated with a mood in his tone.

"You both do the same facial and hand expressions," said Arados half laughing and half yawning.

"Ah! Well we are twins, as you had stated, our minds are un unison, I guess," said Helldar.

"I believe so," finished Arados.

"Well," started Carador, while moving some of his belongings around. "Arush'n'aug will not be back for an hour or two, so I believe it is safe for us to have some breakfast."

"Ha! Just what was on my mind," said Dalan excitedly and happily. Arados looked at Farond, who looked back at Arados and the both shook their heads.

"You sure enjoy a meal don't you, Dalan?" asked Arados.

"Well of course! I am a dwarf, and we dwarfs eat, mine, and kill for a living," stated Dalan proudly.

"Carador shared his food with us one night ago. I shall cook my breakfast today," said Arados while bringing out some sausages from his pack.

"Well, we have no trees to cut down this time to build us a fire, so how can we cook the sausages?" asked Dalan eagerly.

"Relax, Dalan, we will use the heat from the rocks in the Dead Land to cook our food."

"Aye, no doubt that would work," said Dalan in great relief.

Arados walked and headed back to the Dead Land and placed seven sausages in a pan and laid the pan upon a rock. It took slightly longer for the pan to heat up and the sausages to be cooked, for there was no fire, only heat, and enough of it. "So, Arush'n'aug has left its post about ten minutes ago, it will most likely return here in two hours or so. We have just enough time to eat, pack up, and infiltrate Aromer Mountain," explained Teradorn.

"Right," agreed Farond looking to the others.

"Has anyone ever actually entered Aromer Mountain? I'm curious to know what is inside of it," said Selldar bluntly.

"With the exception of Sarugs, no, no one has ever essentially entered the mountain, we shall be the first. And I am most certain that it will be dark, hot, and perhaps flames about, assuming from the steam vents," said Carador pointing at Aromer Mountain. "It'll be all but miserable. I hope you've prepared yourselves."

"If you are wondering about great battles that took place here against Arush'n'aug, those were held around the base of the mountain." Added Teradorn. "As you can imagine, the Dead Land did not give them the advantage."

"Ah! I understand, " said Selldar.

Carador and Selldar examined the sheer size of Aromer Mountain. It's surface, like that of the Dead Land's, was blistering. The mountain had around fifty smoke holes spread throughout its outer surface, relieving built-up pressure from the inside. On the summit of Aromer Mountain, sits six large black spikes, taking the appearance of a scimitar, sticking outwards and curving upwards towards the sky. It was modeled after the former crown of the dark ruler of Aussarok: Saratrox.

"Where do you suppose they got the name

Aromer from?" asked Carador to Selldar, looking up at the rugged mountain.

"Where did they get Androuge from?" said Selldar abruptly cutting off Carador, while trying to sound smart. "It's nothing more than a name someone thought of, Aromer was a made-up name as well, you know?" replied Selldar cockily.

"No," said Carador shaking his head. "The name, Androuge, came from the creator of the city, Earicadal. He named it after his ship, in which he sailed across Legion Realm to arrive here. He and numerous others constructed the city."

"Ah, I am sorry for giving you false details," Selldar apologized. "Anyway, I don't believe Aromer holds any meaning, it's possible it directly relates to Arush'n'aug, or Saratrox?" finished Selldar.

"Ah! Arados is coming back with our food," said Carador, locating Arados walking back with cooked sausages.

"So," began Arados. "We only have seven sausages here, so one per person, unless of course you don't want one, then you can offer yours to Dalan," he laughed. Everyone excluding Dalan snickered.

Arados tossed them each one sausage.

"They may taste different from your common sausages, they were not cooked by flame," said Arados. They each took a bite, and each developed different expression on their faces.

"One sausage each is certainly not enough to satisfy us," said Teradorn bleakly. "Therefore, I shall cook us a steak, it should last us for the remainder of the day," he finished.

Dalan's jaw dropped at the sound of the words, as it became apparent that he would object to such a proposal.

Teradorn walked away from the host, shoving the rest of his sausage into his mouth, and laid a large piece of steak on a flat surfaced rock, towards the dead lands. The tantalizing scent of the steak was detected by the company, whom promptly began to drool at the thought of it, having not eaten such a meal in a few days.

"Well, while Teradorn is back their fixing us a steak...," said Arados breaking the heavenly induced silence.

"Yes?" asked Carador, Farond, and Helldar.

"Shall we duel? I have not practiced fighting with anyone in a long time," said Arados. "I fear my combat skills are sure to become dull."

"Aye, I agree!" said Dalan heartily. The act of fighting always pleases Dalan.

"Carador! I request a duel!" Yelled Arados.

They eyed each other, both smirking, only to draw their weapons the next moment.

Carador struck downwards at Arados, as for Arados, he shielded himself with his bow, towards his forehead, and blocked the Emerald-Star from striking him.

Arados plunged Sky-Piercer upwards as to keep Carador's Emerald-Star away from him. Carador swung his sword upwards then downwards. Arados blocked both attacks. The others started cheering them on, either favoring Carador or Arados, the crowds favor shifted as more lethal blows were exchanged. Arados removed the head of an arrow and fired it upon his opponent. Carador easily deflected it, with no damage to the arrow.

Arados sprung forward at Carador with his bow aiming at him parallel to a spear, attempting to stab him with the front of his sharpened bow.

Carador leaped from the upcoming impact.

They swung and blocked each other's hits some more, coming close to body contact with each other.

"What form of wood is your bow made from?" belted Carador moving nimbly as to avoid another strike.

"Just Oak... and reinforced with Triton!" exclaimed Arados, still fighting.

Carador laughed. "No wonder your bow does not get damaged," laughed Carador.

Arados nodded mid swing.

Selldar and Helldar began to duel each other. Dalan and Farond decided to join in the skirmishes as well. The weapons clanged on contact, delivering earsplitting screeches each time, occasionally sparks flew out of them as well.

Teradorn started his walk back to the company and serve them the steak he had prepared, until he noticed the company dueling.

"Hey! Our breakfast is finished!" yelled out Teradorn.

The others continued to duel.

"Our steak is finished!" yelled out Teradorn

again.

This time they responded with suspending their fight instantly, losing interest upon proving themselves worthy fighters, and walking towards Teradorn.

In one of Teradorn's hand was the steak and in the other was his sword. He threw the steak upwards into the air, filling the bewildered spectators with terror to waste the steak. Teradorn then swung his sword upwards, cutting the steak into two, then across, cutting it into fourths, then downwards, into eighths. Teradorn then placed his sword back into its sheath and caught the falling sections of steak.

He tossed them each a slice and tossed the remaining two slices to Dalan.

"Enjoy!" beamed Teradorn biting into his portion.

"Why, do you give me two?" said Dalan in a reply as if he already knew the answer.

"Well, according to you, you are the one who loves to eat," Teradorn grinned, biting into his portion.

"Aye that is true!" he laughed heartily.

"Although I am not rude, and I would only prefer only like our friends," said Dalan half expecting the reply he was to receive.

"You go ahead and eat both, you will not be considered rude in any way by any of us," said Teradorn.

"No thank you, I prefer only one," said Dalan hoping not to provoke an argument.

"It is alright, truly, just take both," stated Teradorn again, with a mustered calm voice.

"No, I will only have one," said Dalan, his voice rising.

"Have both of them!" spat Teradorn. "Why waste it?"

Carador and the other five were looking at one another in slowly and surely escalating conversation, suspecting to what was going to happen next.

"No! I am only eating one!" said Dalan angrily closely placing his hand on his axe.

"I insist, Dalan!" roared Teradorn with a harsh look on his face.

"No!" Boomed Dalan drawing out one axe, his face was turning red as he began to sweat with anger.

"I'm not asking, Dalan!" Boomed Teradorn even louder and drawing out his sword, pointing it at Dalan.

"You would threaten a dwarf? Then you are even more foolish then I first figured you to be!" And with those last words Teradorn and Dalan drew their weapons upon each other, both eager to make a move.

Carador, Arados, Farond, Helldar, and Selldar quickly intervened, preventing any bloodshed.

Carador, Arados, and Farond grabbed Dalan. Helldar and Selldar held back Teradorn.

"Teradorn, Dalan, no!" yelled both Carador and Arados.

"We need to stick together! Such a petty squabble will impede us from completing our mission! Let's not have our differences interfere with our duty," said Arados angrily.

"If the dwarf would have accepted my token of friendship, and not have been so stubborn, this would have been avoided!" fumed Teradorn, breathing heavily.

"I told you thrice! I do not want to appear

rude in front of the others and receive more then what was being served!" explained Dalan furiously brushing off dirt of his clothing.

"You stated that you love to eat, so I figured I could give you the remaining portion of the steak because you adore eating more than any of us here!" exclaimed Teradorn slightly calmer, breathing in a rapid succession.

"Actually," began Selldar raising his hand half way in the air. "I love to eat a lot too."

"Shut up, Selldar!" yelled everyone except Teradorn and Dalan, who still were exchanging harsh looks.

"Sorry!" said Selldar taken aback, quickly lowering his hand and keeping his head down.

"Listen, Dalan, it was unwise for both of us to start a fight over something so simple. I am tolerable to the fact that you are not comfortable in taking the piece," breathed Teradorn. "The last thing I want is for this great company, we the greatest warriors, our moment of glory, and our chance to destroy Arush'n'aug, to fail!" said Teradorn looking from Dalan to everyone now.

"The legendary seven *Sons of Freedom* will and

shall bring Arush'n'aug down from power! And finally bring down one of our greatest threats, forever! Arush'n'aug will never again be feared in these lands! Aussarok's tyranny will be no more! Today our dream! Our people's dream! Will become reality!"

"We are *the Sons of Freedom*!" "We are *the Sons of Freedom*!" he roared again. "WE ARE *THE SONS OF FREEDOM*!" finished Teradorn drawing his sword from its sheath and raised it to the sun.

All seven of them roared in agreement as they raised their weapons to the sun, clanging together.

"Now let's kill some dragon scum!" roared Teradorn, as he was first to race off in the direction of Aromer Mountain. The other six ran after him, following his spirit.

They began their climb of the mountain, the height of the mountain was far higher than that of the Dead Land, and only this time they had to touch the heat of the earth with their hands. It did not last them long, only for they dropped themselves back downward not knowing how it would be possible to ascent the mountain without their flesh melting from their hands.

With one touch of the mountainside, they

screamed as their hands had erupted in fiery pain.

Carador shook his burnt hand, taking a calming breath, and tried again. He slowly placed one hand on the mountain and released it immediately, groaning in pain.

"How will we be able to get inside?" asked Selldar blankly.

This question irritated Carador. "We'll knock on the front gate and ask Arush'n'aug to let us in. Does that answer your question?" he said wiping his hand on his armor-plated thigh and then blew on his hand, to no avail. Selldar remained silent.

"The only way up..." Carador said quietly to himself looking around. "Farond, I have a plan, throw me your knives!"

Farond nodded, and drew his knives from within their sheaths, and carefully tossed them to Carador, fearing Carador might grasp them improperly and harm himself.

"The only way we can get up there, is to use these knives!" said Carador looking at them. "If we use them as ice picks we can scale the mountain, and they absorb heat! We will have an easy way up," said Carador excitedly.

"Yes, that will work, the only problem, there is only one set of knives, we're going to have to take turns, and travel one at a time," said Farond.

"Yes, that is true, so we will have to go up one at a time," said Carador.

And with that Carador forced one knife into the mountain by his neck. And he pierced the other above him, and thus he started to climb, relieved the twin knives seemed to absorb the heat around him.

"So how high will we have to climb?" yelled Helldar up to Carador, catching Carador gain elevation.

"We may have to climb to the summit! Although I am not sure!" yelled Carador still climbing.

He climbed some more until he reached a flat surface with a dark entrance ahead. Carador pulled himself upwards onto the surface.

"Well, the climbing ends here!" yelled Carador downwards to the others. He was one hundred feet upwards from the land. Carador pulled out both knives, and threw them back down, having experience with throwing knives. They landed a couple feet in front of Farond.

"Hey! Watch your aim!" he feared.

Farond took his knives from the Dead Land and thrust them into the dark surface of the mountain as he began to climb upwards, not with a great pace though.

"Farond! Pierce your knives into the impressions Carador has already made! It should be easier," yelled Arados up to Farond.

Farond took Arados' advice, he looked for the holes that were already present, and he climbed the mountain far faster than before.

Soon Farond appeared at the top with Carador, and Farond did the same, throwing his own knives back down to the others. Carador and Farond sat down, waiting for the rest to get up with them.

A minute or so later Arados appeared in front of Farond and Carador.

"Welcome!" they both beamed. "If you want to go any farther ahead, then Carador and I, then I must say that you are an old fool! Ahead of here lies the entrance to the dragon's lair. In the dragon's lair lies the evil dragon: Arush'n'aug, the largest and most malicious dragon in the world!" explained Farond jokingly.

"Then I shall be the first to slay this Arush'n'aug!" smiled Arados heroically, attempting to keep a straight face, the same went for Farond and Carador. Arados, Carador, and Farond started to laugh, as they helped Arados upwards.

Arados followed the chain reaction: climb Aromer Mountain, throw Farond's knives back down, and wait for the others. After Arados' arrival, came Teradorn, followed by Dalan, then Helldar, and last Selldar.

"Here are your knives, Farond," breathed Selldar handing Farond the Twin-Vipers back. Farond twirled his knives at a fast pace and began to juggle them with fancy swordplay, and then placed his knives back into their sheaths.

"Whoa! How do you do that?" asked Selldar astonished. Farond replied only with a smile.

"Well, here we stand, prepared to enter Aromer Mountain: lair of Arush'n'aug. Remember no matter what happens in there, we will not come out until we confront Arush'n'aug and slay it! We must first make it to the summit where we will confront it," said Carador with a deathly serious tone.

With Carador's speech, they entered one at a time, Carador first, followed by Teradorn, Arados, Dalan, Farond, Selldar, and Helldar.

The only sight in front of the seven now: was darkness.

* * * * *

Two flames ignited in the haunting entrance of the mountain, the flames stood upon two torches in which Teradorn and Helldar grasped. The seven wielded their weapons in a guard formation no one had ever entered Aromer Mountain before, there are only a few points of history that are known, convening the dark cave. The company wasn't sure if they were traveling the correct way, or so they thought,

"So! Left, or right?" asked Dalan curiously as they came to a stop and looked at two paths, on the left and right.

"Right," assumed Carador.

"How can you be sure?" asked Teradorn eagerly.

"I think we should split up," said Farond.

AROMER MOUNTAIN

"Three of us on the left side, and four of us on the right side."

"No!" cried Carador. "We have to stick together. What if one party is ambushed? We wouldn't know."

"Yes, however, if we do end up going the wrong way, we can simply go back and take the left path," said Arados quickly.

"Aye! Right it is then!" said Carador. And they walked on, hoping they were wandering on the correct path."

"Why do all "evil" caves must look the same, what is the connection?" asked Selldar.

The other six suspected something ignorant to slip from Selldar's mouth.

"I mean, even in stories when characters journey somewhere as haunting as a cave, the appearance is always misty and dark. Sure, this mountain is somewhat evil, but it looks the same as it would in a tale."

"That's a well brought out statement, Selldar," said Arados surprised it was not an ignorant question.

Selldar grew a smile on his face, being greeted with praise, opposed to the usual group disdain.

"Well, it's very possible. I believe that this is one of the few caves in all Earacill, and people had visualized an evil cave from this wicked mountain," said Arados.

"Yes, you may be correct, only one flaw..." began Helldar. "We are the first people to enter this mountain!" he said strongly.

"True, however, this isn't the only cave, the Cave of Anlaw is a cave, hence the name, and soldiers have entered that numerous times to search for the shards of Saratrox's crown," added Carador.

"Ah! I believe that is the most logical explanation about evil caves," said Arados.

"You fail to mention the Manor Mines, it is truly a legendary cave!" announced Dalan.

"You don't suppose we'd have to enter the Cave of Anlaw and search for the shards, do you?" asked Helldar.

"If this mission is a success, I would make continue my journey, and gladly search for the shards," said Carador.

"Yes, I would too," agreed Arados.

"And myself," added Teradorn.

"And I," agreed Farond.

"Aye, any chance to rid Saratrox and his minions, I would gladly accept," said Dalan.

"You can count me in!" announced Helldar.

"I suppose I would go too," added Selldar.

"Then let's plan on it," announced Carador looking to them all. "If this mission is a success, then our next mission would be retrieving those shards!"

"Yes! Let's enter that evil cave of Anlaw and succeed with that mission!" said Selldar boldly.

"Evil caves..." Teradorn chuckled. "It sounds so humorous, like a tale you would tell your son or daughter. Can't we use a more improvised word? Perhaps "wicked" or "malicious"? I don't know."

Arados chuckled. "I agree that our vocabulary is poor. Have you considered writing, Teradorn? You can write a tale about our quest, or other ones you may partake on, or perhaps even a biography! You would become quite the author," said Arados.

"Well, maybe someday, when I have seen too many winters that is," replied Teradorn with a quick laugh.

Farond smiled. "I'll be looking forward to reading it!"

"Speaking of which, what does Anlaw mean anyway?" asked Helldar.

"It's Androugen for "death" so you can call it the Cave of Death," Carador replied, being fluent in his own home language.

More they treaded on, taking turns, hoping they would not encounter another fork in their path.

"Great!" growled Carador. Frustrated, he abruptly stopped in his tracks, the others right behind him.

They looked blankly at the dead end of their path.

"I believe left would be the correct way, let's go back and take it," Selldar stated blankly.

"Obviously, Selldar!" yelled his brother, motioning as if to strike him. "Of course, we're going to have to take the left path!"

"Alright! I'm sorry! It's just that, I don't want to be the quiet one, you know?" the Assassin replied with grief.

"You're the ignorant and annoying one! Think twice before you speak!"

Selldar remained silent his head bowed.

Heading in the reverse direction, they treaded until they arrived at the entrance of Aromer Mountain.

"And left it is!" cried Teradorn while he and the others took the left path.

A memory flew into Carador's mind. "Hold your ground!" cried Carador.

The company froze themselves in their tracks instantly, at Carador's command, and quickly shielded themselves in case Carador was to reveal a previously unseen danger.

"What is it?" asked Arados eagerly.

"Before we departed from Banlafar one night ago, Arien gave me this map," stated Carador pulling the rolled map out of his pocket. "He told me to use it only in Aromer Mountain, if we became lost."

"What? A map detailing Aromer Mountain?" asked Teradorn in surprise, lowering his weapon.

"No, not exactly, Teradorn. It is a map to find our way around this labyrinth. Arien told me to use it when we would get lost towards the entrance of the mountain. I am highly sure he was talking about here," he finished

"Yes! No more wandering," said Selldar happily.

"Wait, but that doesn't make any sense," said Arados.

The others looked at him.

"If we are the first people to enter this mountain, then how could and illustrated map exist? Is there something Arien failed to mention to you?"

"No, Lord Arien explained it was illustrated by Sarugs. Spies from Anaron, I believe, ambushed a group of them in possession of a copy, and stole it. Arien gave me this copy."

"Well, let's take a look at it," said Farond taking an eager glance at it.

Carador unrolled the map and laid it out for all to view and Behold! Displayed out in front of them, lay the paths that surrounded them.

"Alright, here is the entrance of the mountain," said Carador motioning to it. "Yes, we do take the left path," he continued moving his finger from the entrance over the left path.

"Then let's get on with it!" roared Dalan, who was more than eager to be through with the journey.

Carador rolled the map back up, and kept it in his hand, along with his sword.

The company treaded forth onto the darkness of Aromer Mountain. They continued until they came to a stop, with two options: left or right. Carador unrolled the map and examined.

"Left," he said simply.

Farther and farther they walked through the dark paths of Aromer Mountain, following their map as they traveled throughout it, wishing their saunter would soon end.

"Well, we are here now," said Carador while pointing towards the end of the cave. "We make a right, then another, a left, and take the second path on the right, and then we should get out, I hope," he continued while pointing out his destinations. They walked on, following the guided directions as their only hope.

To keep himself entertained, Arados began to sing his own poem:

> *"Through and through the mountain we go.*
> *Deeper and deeper the darkness grows.*
> *Left or right our path unknown.*

> *Our directions will be shown.*
> *Arush'n'aug's reign will come to a stop.*
> *The Three Kingdoms will be on top!*
> *Aussarok will soon be withered.*
> *Earacill will be at complete.*
> *The Lord Saratrox will meet his defeat.*
> *Androuge will have a great new king.*
> *Peace to all the land, he shall bring."*

Sang Arados, he made a slight pause as he consulted the map, and then continued down the path.

Selldar grinned after hearing Arados' song, and began singing a song for himself:

> *"Arush'n'aug will meet his doom.*
> *Oh, so very, very soon.*
> *The seven of us will slay the beast!*
> *And soon we all shall have a feast.*
> *And then we-"*

"Ah forget it!" broke of Selldar. "I can't sing, nor can I do justice with my lyrics," he said embarrassed.

"It was fine, Selldar," said Arados, supporting him. "Sing what comes from your heart how you truly feel, the rest will take care of itself," he said placing one hand on Selldar's shoulder.

"Alright, next time," he breathed giving a couple nods.

"Look!" cried out Carador as he thrust his arm to motion forward.

The others turned their heads, facing to where Carador was pointing. In their sight was one long, slender, pathway to the exit.

"That has to be the exit!" cried Arados with glee.

"Yes, and according to the map, this is the exit," said Carador.

"Then let us move!" roared Dalan as he started striding faster than usual, ahead of the others.

They walked through the path and then reached the exit. They found themselves in a dimly lit room, the only light was a faint red one. The room was silent, not much to see. It had ten pillars within the center, five on each side, reaching the top of the mountain. In the center of the pillars, stood a rock formation in the shape of a table. The room was high, on the other side of it stood spiral stairs, which lead up the side of the mountain and ended at the summit. You could faintly see light from the top, the rest was darkness. It was heated, although not to the point of being unbearable.

"Be on your guard," said Carador taking one-step in gingerly.

"It's so hot," breathed Helldar sweating.

"What do you expect from the den of a fire dragon?" spat Selldar cockily.

"Exactly this," admitted Helldar shaking his head.

Farond chuckled. "I never knew Aromer Mountain was so empty," said Farond looking about the vast area.

"Well, the dragon is large. It probably comes in here," said Arados.

"Aye, most likely," said Farond.

"Well, that's it?" asked Dalan. "We climb these stairs and we'll get formally acquainted with Arush'n'aug?"

"No, it cannot be that simple!" said Carador slightly annoyed. "Even if we are to reach the summit, we may still not face the beast right when we arrive," stated Carador, he and the others looked up.

"Alright, that's it then! Let's get on the stairs," said Teradorn as they moved on.

They walked slowly and cautiously through the

unfamiliar mountain, a small amount of light was shown in from the summit. There however, was enough light for them to walk about through the mountain.

"Hey, do you hear something?" asked Selldar and stopped walking.

"No?" said Teradorn raising a brow. The others shrugged and looked at each other. A flap followed by a burst of wind came down from above.

"Yes!" cried Arados quickly grabbing his bow and notched it with an arrow, aiming it upwards. "I see nothing!"

Another flap of a wing was heard from the east. The seven turned their heads east. Carador, Teradorn, Helldar and Selldar brought their swords into their grasps. Arados aimed Sky-Piercer at whichever direction the noise was emitting from.

"It's probably just a bird," said Selldar.

"Oh yeah? A bird in Aromer Mountain? It's nearly impossible for any living thing to survive in here, let alone a bird," said Farond focusing keenly on the sound.

"See! I knew it. It wasn't going to be that easy, we have an enemy, I assume," said Carador rather angrily. He looked at his sword. It was translucent silver. A worried frown appeared on his face. "Why isn't it green?" Carador asked rhetorically.

"What?" asked Arados while trying to focus on the sound.

"The Emerald-Star is not green, normally it is supposed to glow green when I am filled with anticipation or anger."

"Well, are you angry?" asked Arados sensibly.

"Err- well kind of," said Carador trying all he could to illuminate the blade.

The flap of wings was heard again, although nothing was to be seen.

"Maybe it's broken," said Selldar not paying the closest attention to Carador, but on the sound akin to the others.

"Or maybe you're not in the correct state," said Arados quickly turned his eyes upon the

Emerald-Star then back on the flaps. "And I am starting to believe that this is not Arush'n'aug."

"Not Arush'n'aug? What else has wings and lives in Aromer Mountain?" asked Helldar.

"I am not sure, at all," he added.

A breath of fire came from the south side of the mountain rolling down in a wave of bright orange, coming upon Teradorn.

"Whoa!" cried Teradorn failing to spot the flame coming, although he quickly avoided it, with a lucky roll. "Never mind! This definitely has to be Arush'n'aug if it can emit fire!" cried Arados ducking, thinking he had spotted a shadow in the shape of a dragon soar above him.

Carador clenched his teeth in anger because his sword refused to pursue its function. "Well, then kill it! Kill it now!" yelled Carador, and he sprung forward as he followed the shadowy figure.

Arados shot one poisoned arrow towards the dragon, impaling it in the right side. Arados grinned and pulled another arrow out of his leather quiver.

The dragon came back around, retaliating by blowing a burst of fire back at Arados. With that strike it was clear now that it was a dragon. It however, was not Arush'n'aug, but a smaller black dragon, an offspring of Arush'n'aug.

Dalan growled and swung his axe and striking the dragon on the same side where Arados' arrow had stuck. The young dragon lost a small amount of blood, gushing from its side, landing on the rock floor.

Now the dragon came for Carador, whom was eager to use his Emerald-Star for the first time. The dragon came head on to Carador.

"Watch out, Carador!" cried Arados firing another arrow in its back.

Carador stabbed the dragon in the stomach letting his sword go deep into it. A large amount of black blood came pouring out, the dragon let out a nasty squeal.

Teradorn ran to hide behind a pillar. Not with the intention of becoming a coward but rather waiting for the dragon to come back around towards him.

The dragon blew some small amount of fire at Farond. Farond stood idle.

"Farond, move!" yelled Carador and Helldar to him.

Farond grinned and quickly placed his two knives in front of him. The dragon's fire evaporated within his blades.

"Right! Your knives absorb fire," cried out Carador. The others smiled.

"Teradorn! It's coming upon you," yelled Arados.

The dragon came upon Teradorn, whom behind the pillar, quickly exposed himself and he swung his sword across the dragon's breast. The dragon lost its control and crashed through one of the ten pillars.

"Rubble! Watch your ground, Selldar," yelled Carador watching the rubble.

Selldar look up, and quickly rolled out of the way of the falling rocks.

The dragon flew besides Helldar. Helldar thought too fast and he hurled his sword into the dragon's back, yet the dragon flew on. "That was foolish," yelled the unarmed Helldar hastily searching for cover, almost chuckling.

The young dragon came from behind Dalan and it grabbed a hold of Dalan by his shoulders and brought him into the air.

"Ahhh! Release me," yelled Dalan in anger taking his axe and hacked away at the dragon's leg, dispatching the limb, in a bloody mess. Dalan dropped ten feet to the ground on his front side. He quickly stood back up and shook his head in anger.

The dragon began losing stability and couldn't fly too high anymore. Farond took advantage of the dragon's new-found weakness and jumped onto its black scaly back. Arados quickly shot one fire arrow into the dragon's neck. Farond moved towards its head and brought his two knives to the neck, one on each side, he then sliced and brought them to the opposite sides of its neck. The now decapitated dragon fell to the earth, Farond along with it. He landed upon his feet, prideful.

"Wow, nice kill, Farond," said Selldar full of pride. Farond nodded while grinning.

"I hope you all know that was not Arush'n'aug!" breathed Arados, his brow low and voice serious.

"Yes, I figured as much when I noticed the size," said Teradorn.

"I agree," said Carador staring at the decapitated dragon head.

"Also, Arush'n'aug was far larger! When we saw it that is," said Helldar drawing his sword within the dragon's idle corpse.

"Aye," said Arados.

Farond was breathing heavily, he was exhausted. Carador turned the hilt of his sword towards Farond. Farond brought his eyes upon it, knowing quickly what its intention was. He grabbed a hold of the hilt and his exhaustion vanished.

"I'll never get tired of that power," Farond chuckled with glee. "And I am fortunate that it works again."

"You in need of strength?" asked Carador to all of them.

"No, but it's always good to have as much stamina as you can!" said Arados grasped a hold of the sword. The others did so as well.

"Well, we should continue on, up the mountain, I believe," said Carador observing the spiral stairs.

"Yes, let's go," said Teradorn as they headed up the first sets of steps, walking to gain a higher elevation up the mountain.

"Does it make any sense?" asked Helldar. The others looked at him. "Think about it, this is the home to Arush'n'aug, a dragon. So why exactly are their stairs? I mean it is not likely Arush'n'aug can walk upstairs. I find it odd."

"Plenty of things in this world are non-sensible... I mean look at..." said Farond thinking. "Take Saratrox as an example, he once had a crown that could seduce all life to obey his every command. Whether it was to murder, rampage, steal, or contradict their very being, it could be made so. How can a crown do that? It seems like a tale told in a book, and yet, it's real, it happens whether we want it to or not. I guess that even the most surreal and unrealistic events may come to be the present, a horrifying reality."

"Ah, you are truly correct, Farond."

"Either that or Saratrox built them, or better yet, his Sarugs built it for him," stated Arados.

"Yeah, probably that," chuckled Farond.

"Forty-four. Forty-five. Forty-Six," counted Selldar randomly.

Teradorn and Farond looked at Selldar.

"What?" Teradorn asked.

"Oh, I am just counting how many steps there happen to be in Aromer Mountain," he said smiling.

Teradorn laughed. "Very well, Selldar, you do you."

"We will wait for Arush'n'aug at the summit of the mountain. It will be pleasantly surprised," said Carador with a hint of arrogance in the warrior's low voice.

"Are we certain it is not there now?" asked Arados.

"When we had awoken, Arush'n'aug had left us alone. We have had no sign of its return."

"Where has it gone off to?" asked Helldar.

"To destroy another city?" said Teradorn asked himself.

"No, most likely to Aussarok," said Carador possibly blankly.

"Aussarok? What evil deeds could it possibly commit there?" Teradorn asked. "To destroy it, is what I would hope for."

"Saratrox and Arush'n'aug will communicate, probably in unison for Androuge's destruction."

Carador remembered his home, withered in ruin. The scar on his heart burned with pain.

"Yes, Androuge's destruction," he said angrily, thinking deep on the dark memory.

"I am sorry for your loss, Carador," said Teradorn fixated on the steps. "Don't forget why you are, why we all are; justice for Androuge and to see the end of Arush'n'aug's reign come forth."

Carador grinned. "Soon it will be done. We shall not alter. We shall not fail."

"Hey look down!" belted Selldar. "The chamber appears so small, and yet it was there where we fought and killed an actual dragon!" said Selldar, while looking downwards. The others did so as well.

"Very much so, Selldar, although look ahead. The light at the end of the stairs, it must be the summit of this dreadful mountain."

"Aye!" roared Dalan.

"Come on! The sooner we slay Arush'n'aug, the more lives spared his wicked wrath!" he said as they ran the remainder of the stairs.

"Careful! Watch your path, it would be a mess for one of us to slip and fall off these stairs into the chamber from whence we came," chimed Arados.

With ten remaining steps they approached the top. They wore a look of relief on their faces, although the relief soon turned to despair.

"I knew it was too good to be true." Carador sighed. In front of them lay another path turning into a spiral, leading to the peak of the mountain.

"The way is not much more, I assure, Carador," stated Arados.

"Well, let's get this over with!" said Dalan bored weary of climbing as he was.

"Patience, Dalan! Your time will come, we will confront Arush'n'aug in due time," admitted Farond.

"Good! And when I do, I will force my axe into its throat!"

"Well, let's get a move on then," said Carador as they continued to walk on.

"So, Selldar, how many steps were there?" asked Teradorn only allowing Selldar to hear.

"Oh, well I counted one hundred forty-five."

"Alright, that seems reasonable."

"Ugh, never tell me the answer to those sorts of questions," said Helldar, apparently listening in on the conversation. "I don't want to be reminded of what dreadful events I had passed."

"Right, sorry, Helldar," said his brother.

"Wait, this makes no sense," interrupted Arados.

"What doesn't?" asked Carador puzzled, standing next to Arados.

"There are spiders up ahead!"

"What, in Aromer Mountain? The only place in Earacill with giant spiders would probably be the Cave of Anlaw."

"Well, no time for debate, kill them!" roared Arados.

"I hate spiders, they terrify me," said Teradorn, nearly shivering at the thought.

"Do you have Arachnophobia, Teradorn?" asked Selldar.

"Yes! Please kill them and get it over with," said Teradorn uneasily.

They sprinted towards the spiders, and approached them face on, the spiders were at the companion's knees in height. They were black, with two red stripes going straight down the thorax. Their eyes bore into the company, lodging a profound fear into their uneasy minds.

One of the ten stood upon its legs, it hissed wickedly.

"Do not threaten me!" snarled Carador and retaliated with a swift slash towards the spider's underside from its left thorax to its right neckline. A streak of dark green blood extracted from the spider and splattered against the mountainside.

Arados fired a projectile, piercing one of the spider's numerous eyes.

Dalan roared and brought his battle-axe behind him, and with as much strength as he could acquire, he swung the axe forward, brutally impaling another spider. More blood erupted from the spider, and spewed across their vision, covering Dalan's axe from the blade to the hilt.

"That's not going to come off easy!" grunted Dalan angrily and almost laughed as he glanced down on his blood-soaked axe.

Farond went forth and stabbed two spiders in their black round carapace with his knives at a downward angle. Like Dalan's axe, Farond's silver knives had now stained dark green.

"My turn for a kill, finally," said Selldar with a grin, he missed out on the only chance to fight the former dragon in the chamber down below. He swung his sword forward at one, emancipating its cephalothorax from its opisthosoma.

Teradorn came and he slashed at the seventh spider beginning at the head and exiting at the other side, the spider collapsed in two separate pieces. The remaining three spiders scurried away, down the mountain's walls.

"Leave them, hurry up the mountain," ordered Carador.

Obeying the order, the seven dashed farther up the mountain. Dalan and Farond wiped away the emerald colored blood off their clothes and weapons.

The seven dragon slayers ran a few more yards through the spiraling mountain. And they soon found themselves on the summit of Aromer Mountain.

"Well that was easier than expected," breathed Carador. "I guess we're here, right where we want to be!" announced Carador with a sound of relief to his voice.

Arados chuckled, shaking his head with a grin. "We're the first people ever," he said almost gloomily.

In front of the seven lay the summit of Aromer Mountain. Above them stood six, fifty-foot-tall spikes scratching the sky, surrounding the top of the mountain. The summit was Arush'n'aug's resting place. It was empty, and the ground was rough, yet cool.

"We made it to the top Aromer Mountain, Arush'n'aug will defiantly not be expecting us here," said Carador as he walked forward and looked out from the summit of the mountain, they glanced the horizon, only for their vision to be blocked by the smoke rising off the Dead Land in the distance.

"So, what do we do now?" shrugged Farond. "You know, until Arush'n'aug comes?"

"We wait," said Carador short and simple.

* * * * *

The company waited for roughly an hour and Arush'n'aug had yet to come, patiently they waited for another ten minutes before the seven sensed something was near as the Earth below them shook with a violent force.

"It is here," Carador announced calmly and focused on what he well knew was about to appear in front of them.

"It has come..."

CHAPTER X

* * * * * * * * * *

AN UNEXPECTED ARRIVAL

The company stood motionless, and silent. Their fiercest opponent to date was about to challenge them. It would be the beginning of the end, for either Saratrox and Aussarok, or the citizens of Earacill. It is now all in the hands of seven brave heroes.

A great lash of breaking wind, from Arush'n'aug's lengthy wings, could be heard below. And with that, the Great Black Dragon, appeared in front of the seven. Its devilish fiery eyes glazed heavily into Carador's enraged and contempt ones.

For a few seconds, yet what felt eternal, they gazed into each other's, waiting in anticipation to see who was prepared to conjure the first strike.

Then it had occurred. Arush'n'aug let out a heavy battle cry as to bring *the Sons of Freedom* into submission, to no effect on their sturdy hearts. Arush'n'aug had warned them, to its return, they did not abdicate. Arush'n'aug let out a different battle cry, and with it, a great flame extracted from the throat of the dragon, rapidly advancing on the companions.

"Watch out!" cried Carador tense.

Carador and five others quickly abandoned their current position to evade the raging flame. Farond stood there, focused. He swiftly placed his Twin-Vipers into the position of an "X." To his result, Arush'n'aug's flame began to vanish into the Farond's blades. The six others drew themselves upright and moved to aid their companion.

Arush'n'aug continually used its evil gift of fire. More and more, the flames evaporated into Farond's knives, so much, that it was quickly tiring Farond out. The Twin-Vipers had absorbed such a great amount of heat that it began to extract out of the knives, in a straight line reaching the sky above. More fire dispersed into the knives, and were extracted from their tips, reaching a tremendous height in the sky.

"Fallback, Farond, your knives can't hold such

a large amount of fire!" cried Arados. "You will be incinerated!"

Farond quickly contemplated his own death and he attempted to back away, slowly, nevertheless, he was stuck in the direct line of fire.

Arush'n'aug suspended its fire, for it was breathless. This was the right moment for Carador and his fellow dragon slayers to pull Farond out of the line of attack. His knives were bright red, incredibly hot, and smoking. Farond quickly recovered his strength and got back into fighting position, in hopes of his knives holding their integrity.

Arush'n'aug flew upwards, circling his mountain, and the companions. They followed its flight plan, prepared for any of its sudden attacks. The horrid creature circled them from above, with that, it blew another great burst of flame downwards. The seven had to think quickly, they swiftly evaded the oncoming fire bolt, which had struck the center of the mountain, quickly leaving behind a great smoldering mark, like a meteor strike. The companions were each sent towards different sides of the mountain, staring bewildered at the smoke.

"Be careful! That fire can instantly evaporate you!" cried Selldar.

"Oh yeah?" yelled Helldar sarcastically to his brother's outburst.

Arush'n'aug continued to circle them, glaring cruelly at its opponents. It soared down towards them with its jaw shut.

"Careful! It's doubtful that it will breathe fire upon us this time, watch your back!" cried Arados as he observed Arush'n'aug shutting its massive jaw.

Arush'n'aug landed on the side of Aromer Mountain, it revealed one of its scaly razor-sharp claws, with it, Arush'n'aug attempted to slash at the seven, luckily for them: it missed. Arush'n'aug roared menacingly at them. It then tried another strategy. Arush'n'aug hastily spun around and came towards the seven: was its lengthy spiked tail. Carador, Arados, Farond, Selldar, and Helldar each rather jumped or ducked away from the enemy's tail, although Teradorn and Dalan were struck by it and flew several feet, impacting their backs on the walls of Aromer Mountain. The others looked shocked as their friends were struck down. They were, however, not injured severely as they were able to get themselves back up.

Arados equipped himself with an arrow and shot upon Arush'n'aug's dark and repulsive skull, with no effect. The ill-fated arrow was deflected off Arush'n'aug's head.

Arados grinned angrily, clenching his teeth. "My bow is all but effective against Arush'n'aug!" snarled Arados angrily clenching his teeth. He equipped another arrow from inside his quiver, notched it, and shot with fury towards Arush'n'aug, striking it within the abdomen. His aim was true, as an arrow slid into the beast's stomach.

"Excellent!" cried Arados loudly, relieved.

"Arados, your arrows can also pierce Arush'n'aug's neck! Remember Harken's death?" cried out Carador to him while focusing on Arush'n'aug's next strikes.

"Yes! Yes, I do!" replied Arados.

Selldar looked down in grief, remembering the loss of him, however, he quickly brought back his attention to the present as the beast circled around.

Arush'n'aug slashed again with its lethal claws, coming inches to Teradorn's flesh, slightly tearing his black robe around his torso.

Arush'n'aug had enough toying with them, it rose from the mountain and flew directly overhead, the seven watched its plan. With its great scaly claws, Arush'n'aug clutched Arados, Carador, Helldar, and Selldar and dove down its mountain preparing to drop them from a great height.

"No!" cried Farond. He quickly thought, and devised a strategy, which was quite a foolish technique, while at the same time, it was an extremely brave one. He sprinted and jumped off the mountain, following Arush'n'aug's path down. Slowly and carefully Farond controlled himself to land perfectly on the dragons back. He landed on its mark, keeping his balance. He slashed and hacked at Arush'n'aug, barely scratching the surface of its thick armored scales. Farond conjured a plan, he swiftly jabbed his Twin-Vipers under Arush'n'aug's scales, easily piercing the flesh. This was an affective attack on the dragon. In return, Arush'n'aug turned on its side to do away with the pest.

Farond carefully kept his balance and began stabbing it repeatedly in the same position.

Arush'n'aug had attained a few bloody scratches, drops of black blood extracted from under its scales. With this opportunity, Farond used all his strength, and he shoved one of the Twin-Vipers in its wound.

Arush'n'aug shrieked loudly, and dropped the four that it remained grasping, they fell to the Earth. The unpleasant fall was not at a great high to injury the company greatly, nevertheless, they still slightly struggled to stand back up. Arush'n'aug quickly and greatly whipped its neck as to throw Farond off, he lost his balance and stumbled off the dragon. He too crashed to the earth along with his four friends on the patch of grass from whence they came.

Teradorn, Dalan, Helldar, and Selldar stood at the summit of Aromer Mountain as they witnessed their fellow companions taken down by Arush'n'aug.

"Come on! We have to get back down there!" yelled Teradorn to the three others.

"All this way for nothing!" Dalan scoffed. "Well, we must return where we started then," barked Dalan furiously.

"Right, let's hurry, Carador and the others are

counting on us," said Helldar while he and the others rushed back into the mountain, and back down it.

The others hastily picked themselves up. They faced up at the dragon, enraged. They rearmed each other. The merciless Arush'n'aug joined them at the foot of the mountain.

"Careful, you three! It's much harder to go down these steps than it was going up them," said Teradorn to Dalan as they placed their backs against the wall of the mountain, and went down the spiral stairs on their backs, at a rather quick pace.

"Are the others alright?" asked Selldar with great concern.

"Their fall was of little likeness to kill, nevertheless, Arush'n'aug may have slain them already!" said Teradorn surprised. "Come on! They need us."

They stepped off the last stair and ran through the chamber where their former foe lay slain.

"Oh no! Carador has the map detailing our direction through here!" cried Helldar. "If we enter ourselves, we will surly get lost without the proper directions!"

"Well... not if you have a good memory!" interjected Selldar somewhat cockily.

The other three looked at him in surprise and confusion.

"I remember..." said Selldar thinking and looking straight ahead. "We go down this path, and I do believe our path followed the order of: Left, Left, Right, Right, Right, and Left. Wait no! It was: Left, Left, Right, Right, Left, Right," he beamed with confidence.

"Are you sure, Selldar?" asked his brother somewhat gingerly.

"Yes, yes! I remember the map," he cried running ahead of the others, down the lengthy pathway, coming to a stop at the end of it, with the options of left or right.

"Now then, the last direction we had taken was the right one, so easily enough, we have to take the opposite direction."

They took the left path.

"Yes! Great, Selldar, you are not as foolish as I figured," chuckled Dalan smiling.

Selldar grinned.

"Hurry! The others don't have much time remaining!" feared Teradorn.

* * * * *

"Arados watch out!" cried Carador locating Arush'n'aug's claw attempting to strike Arados.

Farond walked next to Arados' side and slashed at the dragon's claw with great ferocity.

Arush'n'aug struck again and impacted Farond with the back of its claw, sending him down.

Carador and Arados gritted their teeth in anger and positioned themselves to conjure another lethal attack. Farond picked himself up and got into his fighting position.

"We won't be able to hold off Arush'n'aug much longer!" cried Arados hastily whilst fixating his sight upon all the dragon's strikes.

"Where are the others?" asked Farond, still oblivious of the companion's position.

"Still on the summit of Aromer Mountain," said Carador blocking and slashing some more. "Arush'n'aug did not pull them down with us, they must find their way back out," he feared.

Arados notched his bow with an arrow and fired the projectile into Arush'n'aug's abdomen. Arush'n'aug blew a flurry of fire towards them, and Farond utilized his knives again to absorb the approaching flame.

* * * * *

"Okay, this one was... right, so we'll go the opposite: left," said Selldar quickly, they were on their third tunnel. "Faster!" ordered Selldar, feeling a sense of cockiness as he took off running further through the caves.

"We're at the last three, and I remember them to be: left, left, and right. So, we go, right, right, left!" he announced, grinning almost foolishly.

The four ran as fast as they could manage through the paths that Selldar had designated before them. They rushed through the remaining three paths, hoping it was not too late for their friends.

"There. The entrance!" cried Teradorn pointing ahead to exit of the mountain. The light outside the mountain was gray, because of the menacing smoke surrounding the land.

"Yes, Great Selldar, you have led us out," said Helldar proud of his brother.

"Now let's hurry! We may already be too late."

They successfully exited Aromer Mountain and were back at the ledge that they had once climbed. The four looked ahead of them, then downwards, their eyes fixed upon the site of the great dragon fighting with three small figures.

"They're alive!" cried Selldar. "They're alive!"

"Alright, we must get down to their aid, but how?" asked Helldar in panic, scratching his scalp rather roughly.

"I know! Selldar, do you still have that nylon rope? The rope you used to make the raft?" asked Teradorn hastily.

"Yes, I do!" said Selldar quickly reaching into his robe and pulling out all his nylon rope, passing it to Teradorn.

"Perfect!" cried Teradorn as he began to fiddle with it. Teradorn made a loop at one end. He ran to the edge but put the loop around a rock and tightened it with a sharp tug.

"We'll climb down Aromer Mountain using this nylon rope," announced Teradorn throwing the rope down the edge of the mountain. He then grabbed a hold of the rope and jumped off the edge, sliding smoothly down. The others quickly followed his path and grabbed the rope and slid down the mountain.

The rope ran out ten feet before the earth. Teradorn let go of the rope and landed on the black earth with a: thump, the other four soon after.

They ran as fast as they could to aid their friends, they were in immediate need of it.

Carador and Farond continued fighting off the dragon, Arados was on one knee.

"Carador, Arados!" yelled Teradorn while he, Dalan, Helldar, and Selldar ran next to his side swinging defensively at the aggressive beast.

"You got out? How?" Carador asked surprised.

"We'll explain later, Carador, Farond, rest a bit, we will watch your back!" yelled Helldar.

"No, we're all in this together!" cried Carador continuing the fight along with the others.

Arados stood back up, with a slight burn on his shoulder, it was not going to affect his fight with Arush'n'aug. He drew another arrow and fired with immense precision under a black scale in the dragon's skull, piercing it.

Arush'n'aug shrieked with anger and pain. It quickly blew smaller amounts of flame, burning Carador's helmet, which heated greatly, with a strong burning sensation within it.

Arush'n'aug ceased omitting the hellish blaze. Carador yelled in pain and quickly grabbed his helmet and threw it down, permanently. Arush'n'aug slashed at Carador, throwing him to the ground.

Arush'n'aug shrieked again and placed one of its sharp claws over Carador's body, it was not crushing his body, although Carador was incapacitated.

"No!" cried Farond running forth to cause a diversion. With all his strength he slashed repeatedly with his Twin-Vipers at the dragon's chest, scarring the breast of Arush'n'aug with countless cuts over it. Arush'n'aug roared, looked down and blew more fire at Farond. Farond only had time to use one knife to evaporate the fire. Farond struggled to repel the fire, he lost his strength and fell to the earth. Arush'n'aug had seized its fire, although it remained crushing Carador.

The sound of hooves, and roaring men appeared from the smoke of the Dead Land, and along with that, three spears, spears of Faradown soared through the air above them and impacted Arush'n'aug. One spear in the chest, another in the back, and the last in the shoulder.

Arush'n'aug shrieked with great pain and flew high into the sky, releasing Carador, giving time for Farond to pull himself back up.

Out of the rising, gray smoke of the Dead Land, came the King of Faradown, along with a couple hundred Faradownian horsemen of Faradown.

Carador stood back up, brushed off the dirt on his armor, and wiped sweat off his forehead.

The seven turned around and greeted Faraduel, with much relief.

"My Lord Faraduel!" said Carador graciously. "You've arrived, with no warning."

"Yes Carador, we have come to aid you. Seven people cannot slay a beast as great as Arush'n'aug, no matter how courageous they are. We come now, to permanently destroy Arush'n'aug! We shall avenge our forefathers who fell to the beast!" announced Faraduel heroically.

"Yes!" roared Dalan with joy. "A long-expected task, which will leave us with sympathy and help lead our people to freedom!"

Arush'n'aug recovered, it soared back down towards its enemies.

"Watch out! Here it comes again!" cried out Helldar.

Faraduel, and all the soldiers in the surrounding, glazed upon Arush'n'aug. Arados was prepared, as always, and took a shot Arush'n'aug's neck. Arush'n'aug flew down at their height level, preparing to strike back.

"Gordoff, Hanel!" the king yelled out to his two Faradownian Champions, who he had lost in the crowd of horsemen.

"Wait, what?" Carador quickly asked being unaware that Faraduel had not even called for him.

Out of the Dead Land rode two riders. They were both armed with bows, Gordoff on the left side, and Hanel on the left. They individually armed their bows and aimed upon Arush'n'aug.

"Fire!" yelled Faraduel dropping his hand, giving the command.

Gordoff first shot his bow, Hanel seconds afterwards, followed by a wave of allied arrows from within the Dead Land. Most of the arrows fired, pierced Arush'n'aug, the others were either over or undershot.

Arush'n'aug shrieked, with pain and anguish, it came at them blowing great amounts of fire, precisely where the concealed riders were hiding. Cries of death were heard within the Dead Land. The Great Black Dragon soared into the Dead Land. For a few seconds it vanished, although it reappeared again with a handful of soldiers within its claws. Arush'n'aug dropped them from a great height, high enough to easily kill them.

"Volley!" shouted Lord Faraduel.

Again, roughly fifty arrows soared through the air striking Arush'n'aug. The dragon shrieked yet again, however this time, Arush'n'aug flew away from the battle, and away from Aromer Mountain.

"It's retreating!" yelled Selldar.

"We have to go after it! Who knows where it will go. We must draw it away from Faradown or Anaron if that is where it is heading!"

"We have come this far, our journey must not end here," explained Farond coiling his knives and placing them back into their sheaths.

"No. No Arush'n'aug is wiser than that, I think? I assume it will head to Aussarok," said Carador in grief, as he watched the Emerald-Star lose its familiar glow, returning to its normal silver hue.

"Well that's it then," started Farond. "We don't have the strength to fight Aussarok, let alone enter Saratrox's territory at this time."

"So that's it? Our journey comes to an end here?" seethed Teradorn holding in his rage. "We fight Arush'n'aug and succeed. We injure it, and then it retreats... FOR AID FROM SARATROX!" thundered Teradorn infuriated as he threw his sword down into the black earth and laid his hand on his forehead.

The others looked down in failure, and misery.

"Wait. We don't know for sure if it fled to Aussarok. Maybe it's hiding out in the mountains or somewhere," said Helldar.

"Yeah? And what difference will that make when it retreats? We will still have to hunt it down," spat Teradorn still angry. "And why wouldn't it go to Aussarok?" he asked rudely.

"It may need to recover its strength in isolation, and the Ruins of Caracross is the most logical place. There is a possibility it won't go to Aussarok until later hours."

"That's always a possibility?" Teradorn sighed.

"It may need to recover its strength in isolation, and the Ruins of Caracross is the most logical place.

"Well if that's the case, then where should we look for it?" asked Dalan rudely.

"The Ruins of Caracross. As Faraduel had stated, Arush'n'aug destroyed Caracross, and it was abandoned years ago. It probably claims it to be his. That's where we should look!" said Carador.

"Yes, the Ruins of Caracross once belonged to Androuge. In the process Arush'n'aug fought the army of Androuge there and destroyed it. It claims it as its second home, we shall ride there. We will move out, and hunt down Arush'n'aug!" exclaimed Lord Faraduel.

Faraduel equipped a war horn and blew into it. It was the signal to move out.

"Wait. We need horseback," said Helldar reminding everyone.

"Yes, of course!" said Faraduel agreeing with Helldar. "Hanel! Bring seven horses forward."

"Yes, my Lord," said Hanel, and he rode back into the Dead Land, disappearing in the thick smog.

"Hmm, the horses don't seem affected by the Dead Land," said Carador contemplating.

"No, all they required was strengthened horseshoes that can withstand heat," pointed out Faraduel.

"Ah, clever thinking, my old friend," said Carador smiling.

Hanel rode out of the Dead Land, holding with him seven harnesses with horses loyally attached to them.

"May they serve you well, now we must ride, and hunt down Arush'n'aug," stated Faraduel.

The six mounted their given horses and followed Faradown's king.

"Ha, you seem to be riding that well, Dalan," said Arados grinning.

"What? You think because I am a dwarf I can't ride a horse? No matter how ill-mannered they act, I can tame them!" he said trying to prove a valid point.

Lord Faraduel blew his horn again, longer than the first time. He along with the seven dragon slayers rode through the Dead Land. It was not painful to ride at all through it, while mounted on horseback, though their vision was less than perfect in the perpetuated smog filled environment.

On foot, the Dead Land seemed endless, having the land drain your strength, and allowing your body inescapable rest. On horseback, however, the ride was quick, or at least it seemed fast to them.

And before they knew it, they were out, of the wicked region.

"Ah! A hasty ride, without much soreness!" cried Dalan relieved though cracking his spine.

"How my Lord?" started Carador. "How did you pass the Great Lake without a boat?"

"The Southern Bridge, Carador... did you not take it?" replied Lord Faraduel.

"Southern Bridge? Is that new? Carador asked, never hearing the name.

"Yes! It was constructed not too long ago; the news of its development is still new, and most have not been informed of it yet. The Northern and Southern Bridge connect us to Sarchara Island."

"Ugh, I now learn of this?" he replied shaking his head. "Right then, let's make haste!" agreed Carador on the brim of his nose. They could have taken the bridge instead of building the raft.

The companions rode forth, past the Dead Land, now with the company or King Faraduel and his army. The company rode away from Sarchara Island, Lord Faraduel led Carador and the others onto the Southern Bridge.

"Arados," informed Carador riding next to him. "Did you hear of the construction of the two bridges?" he asked gingerly still embarrassed at his lack of knowledge of their existence.

"How can we be certain Arush'n'aug flew to Caracross and not to Aussarok?" began Selldar. "I mean, if we ride to Caracross now, and Arush'n'aug is not there, wouldn't that mean we would have to ride to Aussarok?" he asked concerned.

"No actually, by our lack of knowledge, they must have been constructed quite recently, maybe the news has not been spread too widely yet, he replied maintaining his horse.

"Yes, I undoubtedly believe you're correct," Carador groaned.

"If Arush'n'aug is not at Caracross, then we will head back to Aromer Mountain, we dare not enter the realm of Saratrox at this time," announced Lord Faraduel.

"It cannot hide from Aromer Mountain for long, it will eventually have to return, I for one suggest we wait for its inevitable return," said Arados.

"I agree," began Carador. "Also, if we travel to Aussarok, Saratrox may have a trap for us."

"Then let's ride faster!" said Dalan. "We cannot waste more hours tracking this beast!"

The company departed from the southern bridge, arriving back on the vast grounds of the Camalon Fields. The sound of hundreds of hooves from the army of Faradown shook the Earth. The army rode further through the vast plains for roughly an hour, until the Ruins of Caracross came into their view.

It is here, at the great ruins of Caracross, that their final battle with the Great Black Dragon, Arush'n'aug was about to begin...

CHAPTER XI

* * * * * * * * *

ARUSH'N 'AUG'S LAST STAND

The Sons of Freedom, now along accompanied alongside with the army of Faradown, stood abruptly at the ancient ruins. They scouted the area for any sign of Arush'n'aug, unfortunately, chance was not on their side, and Arush'n'aug was nowhere to be seen. In return, only the dreary sight of grime was visible, spreading for miles in Camalon, to no apparent end.

Faraduel sighed. "Do you see anything?" he asked Arados and Farond, seeing as they both were elves. Arados and Farond, both scouted the area, with their exceptional sighting abilities, the chance for them to locate any presence of Arush'n'aug was great.

"We cannot tell from standing here, we must enter Caracross and get to the walls," notified Arados.

"Very well, we shall garrison in Caracross for now, be on your guard, my friends."

Arados and Farond nodded giving a quick tug at their horses' reigns commanding them forward. The bright sun was set high in the blue sky, no clouds present. The heat was effective on the soldiers, knowing full well that when the time of battle comes upon them, they will have to make best of the warmth.

The army moved forward, towards Caracross. The ground rumbled like an earthquake with every step the steeds took.

"Hanel, tell the men to dismount and take their horses inside the walls, keep them on the lower grounds, they will be safe there," Faraduel ordered.

"I will, my lord," said Hanel, turning around and giving the order to the closest horsemen, whom as well, told those close to them.

"Carador, you will be in charge strengthening

the walls and gate. This place may have been destroyed years ago, but it can still perform what it was designed for."

"Very well, I'll give the orders, but everyone will help in strengthening."

"Good, Carador," smiled Faraduel.

The army entered the ruins. Immediately, they dismounted their horses and kept them sheltered on the bottom level as they were ordered. The soldiers garrisoned the walls, towers, and homes, keeping a sharp eye out for Arush'n'aug, which they know is sure to come.

"You, soldiers!" began Carador. "Take what rubble you can find and fill that gap," he said pointing to large missing portion at the front wall. "Drop debris down from the wall, it will prevent any unwanted entry."

"Right away, sire!" they acknowledged. Loyal soldiers they were, as the thirty immediately performed what they were ordered to do.

"You three," Carador pointed to three knights who had just dismounted from their steeds. "Keep a straight lookout from up there!" he pointed to the top most ruined tower in Caracross. "It is your duty to report anything unusual, you will man the horn."

The three nodded and bowed. "Quick! Upwards!" they commanded each other, and swiftly took off.

Carador looked around himself, making sure everyone was doing their part. The soldiers upon the walls were either keeping a continuous lookout or maintaining damages in the walls. The knights garrisoned in the homes were forging weaponry and, assembling arrows. He looked at the ruins around himself, imagining once a great refuge that this place had once been, and how quickly Arush'n'aug destroyed it, leaving it to wither below the dark clouds. He was eager to avenge those who had fallen here in the past. Carador feels the greatest task he could ever perform is to be the slaying of Arush'n'aug. Every single step, and order that he had planned or taken, was all about this.

Carador approached and looked up upon a destroyed statue. It was a sculpture of Earicadal, the first King of Androuge, sitting upon a horse, with his sword raised above him, representing a Calvary charge. However, both the horse's head and the king's head were absent. Earicadal's head replaced with a jawless human skull, with an Androugen helmet still in possession. The sword now had the banner of Aussarok tied to it, the red flag with a black two-headed crow embalmed upon it. This was but a taste of the cruelty of Saratrox.

Carador knelt and gave a quick prayer, to the memoriam of his bloodline that was but withered, being the last of it. He stood up and climbed upon the statue to remove the skull and the tattered flag and replacing it with original head it had been sculpted with. Carador looked up to the reformed statue, it was now the symbol of hope and prosperity, hope that one day the land will be safe again for all those who inhabit.

"You there, Faradownian!" yelled Carador turning to a knight who looked unproductive. "If you seek a task, then go inform your king that the west wall needs more improvement!"

"I will, sire, right away, sire!" he said taking off to report to Lord Faraduel.

"Carador! Carador!" yelled Teradorn catching up to him.

Carador bewildered, wheeled around. "Yes,

Teradorn, catch your breath, what news do you bring?" Carador asked continuing to walk, glancing around, convinced that everyone was doing their part.

"Farond, Arados, Dalan, and I wish for you to help us barricade the front gate, we uh-, we already closed it, yet it now needs to be strongly secured. If Arush'n'aug brings Sarugs with it, we need to prevent them from breaching the gate," he said wiping his sweaty forehead. He had been working hard.

"Very well, Teradorn, let's go!" he said changing his direction.

"Where are the others?"

"Helldar and Selldar supplied the soldiers with arrows and spears. And the others I believe are with you, strengthening the gate?"

"Yes, that is correct," nodded Teradorn looking around himself, rather panicked.

"Is something wrong, Teradorn?" asked Carador.

"Huh? Oh no, I was pondering what I should do when Arush'n'aug arrives, you know, like how I should fight, or what orders to give out," he cracked a smile.

"You'll do fine, Teradorn, you are a magnificent fighter, I've seen what you can do," Carador smiled giving him a pat on the back.

Teradorn breathed. "You're right, everything will soon be right."

"Come on then," started Carador.

Teradorn quickly followed behind.

Both Carador and Teradorn headed back to the front of the fortress where the garrison was also complete. The progress was tightening, openings in the walls of the ruins were filled, and gates were sealed off, assuring no entrance from unwelcome foes.

Carador walked over to the newly fortified front gate, where Faraduel gave his soldiers orders.

"Faraduel! How much more?" he shouted.

"The fortifications are all but complete, now it is time to man the towers and the walls, scouts report Arush'n'aug is on its way here."

"Are there any Sarugs with Arush'n'aug? It's likely there could be, Arush'n'aug has called upon them for help in the past. And are you sure your scouts were not seen?" he feared.

"None reported, yet always expect the unexpected, Carador," he replied. "I only send my top spies for such espionage, I am certain they were unseen."

Carador nodded. "Right, and now I believe is the time."

Over the course of half an hour, the Faradownians and *the Sons of Freedom* fortified the walls of Caracross. Each level, tower, and wall, fully manned for the inevitable upcoming siege by Arush'n'aug.

Lord Faraduel and Carador resided upon the main wall, high enough where they had a clear view of the Camalon Fields and would be the first to know when the enemy was to arrive.

Arados, now in command of the archers of Faradown, situated upon the front wall of Caracross, the main sanctum for archers in the Stronghold, it was one level lower than the main wall.

Teradorn, Farond, and Dalan resided in the courtyard, securing the front gate, one of Arush'n'aug's major objectives.

Helldar and Selldar stood rank upon the

spearmen along the walls, ready to give any order when necessary, they stood side by side, prepared for anything.

* * * * *

Another hour had passed, the clouds were now overcast, standing boldly above the grounds of Caracross and the Camalon Fields, thunder cracking in the sky, angrily shaking the Earth below, no drizzle.

The company stood calm, awaiting whatever doom was to come before them, if their death was in defense of Earacill, it would all be worth it to them.

It was then that they realized that it wasn't the thunder in the sky which shook the Earth, yet rather the massive shadow south, on the horizon. This clearly was no cloud but the enemy they have been waiting for, Arush'n'aug, the Great Black Dragon.

Its size grew more and more colossal, the closer it approached. Deep down, the soldiers, even *the Sons of Freedom*, had a profound fear for this beast, knowing of it and its infamous damages and terror brought upon all

Earacill in the past. Fortunately, this fear was not going to affect their valiant efforts this midday. Their love for their friends, family, and hometowns was much greater than that of their fear of Arush'n'aug.

"No Sarugs," whispered Faraduel to Carador.

Carador looked at him. "Then we do not need the spearmen down in the courtyard," he whispered back. "They should disperse and join us upon the walls.

"Yes, Yes, of course," Faraduel said agreeing. "Gordoff, Hanel!" ordered Faraduel.

"Yes, my lord?" they both said quickly to his summon.

"Tell the men to break formation, it will not be needed, for Arush'n'aug comes alone."

"We shall!" they said quickly and nobly, leaving to follow their orders.

"What are our plans then?" asked Carador dumbfounded.

"As soon as Arush'n'aug is close enough, the captain archer, Arados, will command the archers to fire upon Arush'n'aug, which will in return anger

Arush'n'aug. In its retaliation, Arush'n'aug will most likely strike towards them, during this action, my spearmen will attack, which will then throw Arush'n'aug of course, and the archers will fire once more. Arush'n'aug will not know who to strike at first."

Carador nodded, understanding. "What of myself and your swordsmen?"

Faraduel looked at Carador. "It appears we will just have to wait and see, now won't we?" he smiled.

Carador took a deep breath and smirked. "Right," he drew his sword from its sheath, giving one last good look at it, feeling its blade, it remained as razor sharp as it did the first time he felt it back in Anlar.

Down below on the main tower, Arados told the archers of the plan, each of them knowing what order to give out and when, they might have a chance to rid themselves of Arush'n'aug permanently.

"-And after the spearmen strike upon Arush'n'aug, we fire again, this will throw Arush'n'aug of course, it won't know what to do,"

Arados confirmed this to the men.

"It is an honor to have the best archer from Anaron at our side, sir!" a Faradownian archer shouted. "Together we can overcome and destroy Arush'n'aug once and for all!" he grinned widely hoping to impress his captain.

"We will just have to wait and see, Faradownian, we will see..." replied Arados.

"Go! Go! Go!" a host of Faradownian spearmen shouted to one another. Arados turned his head to look at the men as they ran up the stairs and began to join the archers upon the walls.

The spearmen had dispersed from their positions down below and began to fuse with the archers, as Lord Faraduel ordered them to, for they now needed no defense down in the courtyard, strangely enough, Arush'n'aug comes alone, having been accompanied by Saratrox's soldiers in the past.

Helldar and Selldar made room for the spearmen to garrison the wall. They watched many men run past them, and three of them, familiar, stood next to them.

"Room for three more?" asked Teradorn to Helldar as he, Farond, and Dalan took position next to him.

"Likewise," Helldar smiled.

Arush'n'aug now came in sight of all the soldiers in Caracross. It stopped its flight, and hovered above them, its massive wings shook the ground with each flap, and the dirt upon the Camalon Fields flew awry, in every direction.

The soldiers stared up at the monster, nervously yet calm enough to stand their ground, Arush'n'aug stared back at them. This happened for a good ten seconds or so, and then it quickly ended with Arush'n'aug committing its infamous war cry screech, that unwillingly threw every soldier of course and begun to cover their ears in pain.

"Damn!" cried Carador quickly covering his ears, forgetting Arush'n'aug had such a deadly cry.

Arush'n'aug quickly seized its cry and darted down towards the stunned archers, now having a clean path of attack.

Arados quickly recovered from the attack and saw Arush'n'aug coming towards them.

"Archers now!" he yelled quickly, having to quickly remind them of their plan. "Aim for the chest and neck for the most effect!"

A good portion of the archers fired upon Arush'n'aug, yet not all had recovered from Arush'n'aug's battle cry, and only half as many arrows as expected were fired. The ones that managed to take flight, impacted the beast, and had only partly through Arush'n'aug off course. In return, it managed to blow a great flame at the main wall, burning a host of archers in the path. They screamed and cried as the hellfire burned threw them, painfully melting their flesh, they threw themselves off the walls to their death, a desperate act to rid themselves of the immense pain.

"Spearmen!" roared Lord Faraduel, to remind all soldiers of the battle plans.

The noble spearmen responded quickly and hurled their spears into the air to wound and throw Arush'n'aug of course. The spears, being as heavy as they were, did not soar as anticipated, nor did they puncture deeply if at all, and Arush'n'aug was able to shake them out.

"Archers! Again!" ordered Arados as he fired a poisoned arrow towards Arush'n'aug's chest, followed by a few hundred more.

They effectively impaled Arush'n'aug, having

more arrows successfully launch this time than before. Arush'n'aug staggered mid-flight at the number of arrows that had pierced it, however, this mere prick was nothing more than an irritation, and angered Arush'n'aug as a result.

Arush'n'aug soared downwards again and breathed another great flame towards Arados' tower. Arados quickly spotted the flame flowing towards him.

"Drop!" He shouted to his men, he quickly threw himself to the ground, and laid flat, a few other archers managed to copy his action in time, the rest unfortunately, did not suffer such a similar fate. Arados, covering his head with his arms, slowly poked his head up as he heard the screaming of his fellow soldiers around him, engulfed in flames, dropping like flies around him.

Arados and others recovered from the attack and quickly stood back up. He unfortunately witnessed one poor soul, screaming, while aroused in flames, stretching one arm outwards towards him for help, Arados watched as his outstretched arm disintegrated into ashes before him, and the archer dropped. This was merely a sample of the damage

Arush'n'aug is capable of.

"Recover!" Arados ordered to the freighted archers. Boldly, they did as they were told.

Over towards the main wall, Arush'n'aug battled the spearmen and archers there, not only blowing flames, but using its own tail and arms as weapons.

Arush'n'aug tail-whipped a group of spearmen upon the wall, the force of the whip was so great, that it sent the men flying off the walls to their deaths below.

Arrows and spears continued to hurtle in the sky, some successfully striking Arush'n'aug, and others not. Arush'n'aug whipped around grabbing a crowd of archers with its great claws and threw them upwards, hundreds of feet into the sky, only to fall to their deaths.

The arrows and spears strategy were not accomplishing much; a more hands-on strategy might be an enhanced tactic.

"Faraduel, my King," Carador started.

Faraduel looked to Carador. "Yes Carador?"

"This strategy is not going as we have hoped for. However, I have a plan, I am going to make my final attempt to stop Arush'n'aug, this might just work, however, I might be sacrificing myself in the process, a chance I'm willing to take for you all. Farewell, my friend," he said and took off running down the main wall, intentionally fast enough so that Faraduel could not stop him.

"Carador wait!" Faraduel shouted to him, yet it was no use, he was too far ahead.

Back on the front wall, Farond was able to shield Dalan, Teradorn, and himself from Arush'n'aug's flames using the Twin-Vipers.

"Is that the best you can do?" growled Farond towards Arush'n'aug as he repelled the flame with his knives.

Arush'n'aug seized fire and attempted to tail-whip Farond, it was a successful attack, however, an unfortunate spearman had taken the hit instead, sending him flying towards Farond. The spearmen crashed into Farond and Farond crashed into Helldar sending Helldar and the spearmen to fall off the wall, Farond was able to recover.

"Helldar!" cried Selldar, fearing for the death of his brother. "You will not harm him again!" he roared facing Arush'n'aug head on, his sword parallel to bridge of his nose, prepared to strike Arush'n'aug head on, knowing it was pure suicide.

"Selldar, no!" roared Carador approaching from behind. He was running towards both with the Emerald-Star in his right hand and the flask of water he recovered from Farrow Forest in his left.

Arush'n'aug opened its massive jaw to blow one last flame planning to engulf Selldar where he stood.

At the last second, Carador opened the flask of water and threw it into Arush'n'aug's mouth, while at the same time, throwing Selldar to his knees and using his shoulders as a step as he threw himself off the wall and landed upon Arush'n'aug's back.

The miracle water poured out of the flask and landed within Arush'n'aug's throat, not only did this action extinguish Arush'n'aug's flame, it also prevented either of them from getting burned alive. Black smoke flowed out of Arush'n'aug's throat and it began to shriek in pain, being no longer able to blow fire from within its throat towards any of the soldiers in Caracross.

Carador then proceeded to stab the Emerald-Star deep into Arush'n'aug's back and used the hilt of the sword as a grip so that he may hang while in flight with Arush'n'aug.

Arush'n'aug's flight pattern was shattered, and it began to fly into the walls and the towers of Caracross, knocking the standing soldiers down.

Carador now grabbed a hold of Arush'n'aug's horn and removed his sword from within its back. He began hacking away at Arush'n'aug's neck, desperately trying not to let go or suffer falling to his death below.

Arush'n'aug head on, flew into one of Caracross' towers, resulting Carador to lose his grip and flying off towards the back, he luckily, managed to grab a hold of Arush'n'aug's scaly tail now. The scales were the size of dinner plates, making them easy to grab a hold of.

Carador attempted to climb back towards the head, using the arrows impaled in it as leverage, however, they snapped if he tried to grab on to them, no luck. Carador grabbed tight on the scales, he promised his path was not going to end here.

Arush'n'aug felt Carador's grip on its own tail and thought of a method to release him. Arush'n'aug changed its direction and now headed towards one of the empty watchtowers. It sharply turned a sharp ninety degrees to steer clear of the tower, but allowed its own tail to smash into it, with Carador still holding on. The force of the impact caused the tower to crumble behind it, while at the same time caused Carador to fully lose his grip and he was launched forwards, towards Arush'n'aug's body, where he happened to grab a hold of Arush'n'aug's arm. He drew his sword and began hacking away at Arush'n'aug's chest. The two now flew over the watchtower where Arados resided, knowing this, Carador called for Arados to help.

"Arados! Arados!" he cried, knowing that they were close enough for Arados to hear his cry for help, while witnessing the entire event. "Aim for his eye!" He staggered while trying to avoid his claws from slashing him.

Arados heard the order and quickly strung an arrow and carefully aimed for Arush'n'aug's eye.

"Aim for the eyes!" Carador cried again, unaware that he had already heard the demand.

Carefully aiming, Arados fired a poisoned arrow towards the eye, but alas, it missed.

"Arados!" cried Carador, fearing that both their efforts were futile.

Arados carefully aimed again and fired, this time, the arrow successfully struck Arush'n'aug straight in the eye, Arush'n'aug screeched in pain. Now half-blinded, Arush'n'aug lost control of its sense of direction, and no longer could fly steadily to do the immense pain.

They both were heading straight for a tower directly to the right of the main wall, Carador saw it in front of him and he knew Arush'n'aug couldn't avoid it. If Carador did not release his grip now, then he knew he would end up being a bloody mess upon the tower.

With a few last seconds to think, Carador took a deep breath, closing his eyes, and released his grip, letting Arush'n'aug smash into the watchtower, Carador's sword remained lodged in Arush'n'aug's body. The tower shook enormously and was greatly crippled, yet it was strong enough not to collapse into ruin. Carador landed on top the same tower that Arush'n'aug had uncontrollably crashed into. Arush'n'aug, now with a deformed wingspan and mangled lower jaw, landed below in ruin. Its body crushed and covered from the falling debris.

Carador steadied himself on top the tower

now, one false move and the tower would collapse along with him still on top. However, even though he remained still, the weakened tower began to crumble straight down.

Carador had one chance to jump from the crumbling tower onto the front wall of Caracross. Teradorn, Farond, Dalan, all watched in disarray as the tower came crumbling down and watched nervously what was to become of the outcome for their friend, and leader.

With barely enough room below him, Carador took a last quick breath and jumped, successfully landing on the wall surrounded by his fellowman.

They cheered his name as they witnessed him survive every obstacle he encountered in the last and most long five minutes. Carador gave a quick grin as the ground behind him erupted in a cloud of smoke from the collapsed tower.

"You, my friend, must have been blessed by Aruanor to have successfully survived all of that," bellow Teradorn.

Carador let out a weak laugh.

Arush'n'aug might have been defeated, however, Carador had one last thing to do.

"Follow me," Carador ordered.

The army rushed down to the sight of Arush'n'aug's death. Carador, being down, first managed to recover the Emerald-Star from within the beast's chest. It was covered in debris and dust, which would take much time to return its former shine.

Arush'n'aug's corpse was now reduced to ash, all that remains, are its scales, hundreds of them, now scattered throughout the area.

"Everyone here today, you are heroes, you are all responsible for defeating Arush'n'aug, you made history this day. I command you all to keep one scale from Arush'n'aug for yourselves. A reward, for what you all have accomplished here today," announced Carador to all, as he took his own scale, and wiped the ash off.

Carador wiped his blade dry and returned it to its sheath. He walked back to Faraduel, receiving pats from fellow Faradownians along the way.

"Well, I'm glad all that is finally over," breathed Carador.

Faraduel laughed and gave him a hug, being both gracious that Arush'n'aug has been destroyed and that Carador and his companions have survived through it all, next to Faraduel, the six *Sons of Freedom* companions stood by his side, their hearts filled with glee and success as they witnessed Arush'n'aug's death and their own survival.

Carador looked to his seven friends, the six *Sons of Freedom*, and King Faraduel, and cracked a weak smile.

"Now let's go home," he said nearly passing out.

PART III

* * * * * *

HARD TIMES AHEAD

"With Arush'n'aug out of the way, Aussarok has lost its finest soldier. And the great city of Androuge was rewarded with a new king. This had reunited the Three Kingdoms and will bring them back into power. Now Earacill's future is in the hands of Carador and the Sons of Freedom..."

CHAPTER XII

✳ ✳ ✳ ✳ ✳ ✳ ✳ ✳ ✳ ✳

THE REUNITED KINGDOM

On the third of October 2935, Arush'n'aug, the Great Black Dragon, was slain. The first enemy to the citizens of Earacill had been vanquished by Carador and *the Sons of Freedom*. The fall of the Aussarokian Empire has begun, however, Arush'n'aug's defeat was the mere first step as Saratrox the Defiler is at full strength and will surely be seeking his revenge.

Caradorian returned to his homeland, Seragone, in Androuge, followed by King Faraduel and his six companions who aided him along his quest. In Androuge, the citizens of Seragone returned and began planning their reconstruction of the great city. The Elder Council in the Temple of Anastar agreed that Caradorian Caracross had the blood of Kings and was worthy enough to take throne of the kingdom. Seen in his ability and his successful quest of the slaying of Arush'n'aug, they find the Hero-knight an asset to lead the free nations of Earacill against Saratrox and most definitely find a way to overthrow him and restore peace to the war-torn land.

On this day, Caradorian Saladar Caracross accepts lordship over the kingdom of Androuge, having been against the title all his life, he now realizes it was his destiny to reign lordship over the land, and that he would undoubtedly lead the world to the long-anticipated peace and freedom they so strongly deserve. With Caradorian the King of Androuge, Androuge has become empowered once more by the Council of Earacill and is reunited with the great kingdoms of Anaron and Faradown. These events now will set in motion Saratrox and the fortress of Aussarok for a full-scale war against Androuge and its allies.

Lord Caradorian will seek the assistance once again of his friends and military to recover the lost shards of Saratrox's crown, the only true cause to his defeat. Carador will ultimately attempt to complete his destiny and destroy Saratrox before his plan of attack is carried out, with none other than the help of the brave *Sons of Freedom*.

As for now, Caradorian has an unfinished chess tournament with an old friend which needs closure...

END OF BOOK I

TO BE CONTINUED IN: *THE SHARDS OF THE CROWN*

APPENDIX I

* * * * * * * * * *

CHARACTERS, LOCATIONS & ITEMS

CHARACTERS

*CARADORIAN: \ "Kär"a"dor"ee"an *

CARADORIAN: The founder, and leader of *the Sons of Freedom*. Caradorian Saladar Caracross was the son of Caragorian Caracross. He was born in Seragone, the capital city in the kingdom of Androuge, in the year 2900, in the early years of the Third Century in Earacill.

He was the only descendent of Caragorian (2881-2915) and Morwen Caracross (2885-2920). Caragorian was well acquainted with the King of Faradown, Arog, and Carador had become best friends with his son, Faraduel, at the age of five. Faraduel was ten at the time. In the year 2915 Lord Caragorian was slain by Sarugs, and Carador kept it a secret for years that he was the King's son, he wanted to be a healer for the wounded when he was old enough, not have the responsibilities of lordship.

Carador's mother, Morwen, also kept it a secret for Carador. The King of Faradown, Arog resigns lordship, and Faraduel takes up the throne, becoming the new king.

Years went on (2920) and Carador became a Healer of the Temple of Anastar at the age of twenty, as he had planned. Unfortunately, his mother, Morwen, had died from leukemia the following year, Carador, in return, had tried to heal her, but nevertheless, failed.

He remained a Healer for seven years afterwards, however, doubt has always struck him at the task, having failed to save his mother; he began failing his healing courses.

Carador shortly later left his healing courses all together to become a knight, wanting to help people, for the good of the world. He trained for the next five years with a sword and shield and later was given to the opportunity to become a Knight of Androuge, he gladly accepted.

During his training and testing, Androugen Hero-knights knew he was born to become a fighter, and Carador quickly passed through the courses and tests at the top of his class. He was given the unlikely opportunity to become a Hero-knight of Androuge, a Hero-knight being the highest rank achievable for a soldier. Hero-knights are given authority to lead armies into battle and lead the campaigns.

For three years Carador had kept the rank of Hero-knight, boosting his ego throughout the kingdom. Through this time, Androuge still remained a kingless city. Carador was ordered by the Elder Council of Androuge to lead an army, commanded by himself, to the heart of dark fortress of Aussarok, home of Saratrox, as to test their strength. Carador knew it would be a dangerous task, nevertheless, he followed orders and the led an uneasy Androugen army to Aussarok and prepared to strike the fortress, Anaron and Faradown's forces had aided them. It truly was impossible for *the Three Kingdoms* to defeat Saratrox and Aussarok, however, they are still capable of causing some damage to its forces.

The battle raged on, long enough for the united allies to damage the forces of Aussarok, nevertheless, the army of Androuge would soon have to fall back, or face defeat.

A year later (2935) of the Third Century, Carador travels to Anlar in Faradown for the current weekend to celebrate his old friend, King Faraduel, for his fortieth Birthday.

While in Anlar, Carador finds in a shop, the great sword of the former King Tharagor, the Emerald-Star for sale and wishes to purchase the legendary blade, although the swords price was much too high for his budget. To purchase the legendary sword, Carador forced himself to compete in a dangerous tournament, held in Anlar, to win the required money, he had no trouble passing through the tournament and winning the prize to buy the sword.

Having been only one day away from his home: The Great Black Dragon, Arush'n'aug, strikes the Androugen city of Seragone, making this the third strike executed by Arush'n'aug in history (28,

1129, and 2935). Arush'n'aug has been a threat, and a personal enemy not only to Earacill, but to a loyal patriot such as Carador himself.

After returning home and witnessing this atrocity for himself, the enraged Carador returns to Faradown to protest the dire act, in hopes that the citizens are reminded of what a threat Arush'n'aug is, and that soldiers will join him to slay the beast.

Lord Faraduel orders Carador to travel to the town of Banlafar, and discuss this with the leader, Arien.

Arien accepts the terms and attempts to bring together a meeting, however, the plan is foiled when the summoned warriors are captured and imprisoned, by Sarug scouts.

While imprisoned, Carador befriends his cell mate, Arados, one of the soldiers rallied by Count Arien. Over the course of six hours, Carador and Arados devise a breakout plan and put it to use, successfully breaking out and freeing countless other wrongfully imprisoned heroes of Earacill, each one having been rallied by Arien to discuss the matter at hand. Carador had told them his story and seven of these freed prisoners, including Arados, agreed to travel along with Carador to the lair of Arush'n'aug, thus Carador establishes *the Sons of Freedom*.

The group of eight return to Banlafar and debrief the situation to Count Arien who then grants them permission to travel to Aromer Mountain and make a futile attempt to stop Arush'n'aug.

The Sons of Freedom then travel out of Banlafar on the following day, and make a nonstop trip to Aromer Mountain, the lair of Arush'n'aug. Carador and his companions encounter various obstacles and adversaries in the process. When all hope seemed lost, the army of Faradown, led by King Faraduel arrives at the slopes of

Aromer Mountain to accompany *the Sons of Freedom* and fight off Arush'n'aug for the time being.

The eight including the army of Faradown travel to the Ruins of Caracross the make their final stand against Arush'n'aug. After much thought and strategies, Carador and *the Sons of Freedom* successfully slay Arush'n'aug at the Ruins of Caracross, resulting in destroying Saratrox's greatest soldier, and giving the people of Earacill hope that they will soon be at peace. *The Sons of Freedom* make it their life goal to now rid Earacill of Saratrox.

Carador finally accepts lordship over Androuge after the event, knowing this will be best for the country, and reunites Androuge with the kingdoms of Faradown and Anaron, with *the Three Kingdoms* as one, they might have a fighting chance.

With Carador as king, *the Three Kingdoms* are back into power.

ARADOS: \ *"Âr"a"dos* \

ARADOS: The Sons of Freedom's Archer. Arados was born to Prince Ariel of Arcon Realm. Arados was born in the year 7357 in Arcon Realm, three millennia prior to Earacill.

As a child, Arados was raised to enjoy life the fullest extent, proving his love for the Earth, not before his seventh winter, Arados began questing different regions and territories in his homeland, sometimes even getting himself lost deep within forests, or trespassing on forbidden land even without having the slightest idea. Even with the wilderness at his side, Arados became depressed, wanting to seek more and occasionally leaves his home when he is rather in a state of depression, or stress, wondering elsewhere to sketch the different plants and animals he would encounter, studying their behaviors, and becoming more acquainted with the wildlife.

In his teenage years, Arados had already perfected his gifted skill of archery. Over the years, it had become his obsession. He would use his handcrafted Yew bow every chance he got, whether it be for sport, or for subsistence.

Many years pass for Arados, having each day repeat its cycle and Arados became filled with restlessness and what he considered to be hopelessness. He yearned for new adventures, or even the chance to return to his old childhood activities, of questing new land, and so Arados decided to follow in the footsteps of his idol, Tharagor, the first of his kind to make an extraordinary journey.

Over the next year, Arados had planned a trip of his own and followed in the path of Tharagor, sailing south to discover Earacill for himself. Earacill had been discovered for a little over one hundred years, yet Arados never had the motivation to travel to their Realm for himself, knowing of Arush'n'aug and the threat he poses upon the inhabitants who reside there. Arados decided to himself that he could be of support to the people of Earacill. His long and skillful years of archery and hunting would become of good use to the frightened villagers and would help the limited number of soldiers.

And so, Arados had set sail with a handful of other elves, out of Arcon Realm, and arrived upon Dynasty Realm in the year of 108 of the First Century. Arados traveled to where he would fit the most in, and he resided in Archara of the kingdom of Anaron. His first task was to prove his worth to the one elf he admired the most, and Arados was successful in proving worthy enough of his skill and he had become a high archer for King Tharagor, and a great addition to the soldiers of Anaron. Throughout the rest of the First Century, Arados fought alongside his fellow soldiers in all Anaron's battles, with his old Yew bow.

In the year 140, King Tharagor is slain during the great battle upon the plains of Camalon against Saratrox. Tharagor wielded a bow, a legendary bow known as Sky-Piercer. The bow was enchanted with miraculous powers. Arados had dreamed of owning that bow ever since he first witnessed King Tharagor use it in battle. After King Tharagor's death, Arados musters up the courage and makes a dangerous effort to the steal the priceless artifact, to keep for himself, a crime that would be punishable by death. Sky-Piercer bared a close resemblance to his own Yew bow and he had switched Sky-Piercer with it, no one had ever noticed the difference.

Over the next two millennia, Arados remand a loyal soldier to Anaron and to the kings that ruled over time, carrying out any service asked upon him, and fighting in any wars he was asked for service in. Arados' day of reckoning finally fell upon him in the year 2935, after Arush'n'aug's third strike upon the kingdom of Androuge.

Arados was given a high order from the current King, Earathell. He is summoned by the Count Arien to travel to the city of Banlafar to debate over the recent attack and that a fellow individual seeks the best warriors in the land. The enthused Arados gladly accepted the task, and makes a hasty travel to Banlafar, however, during his travels he was ambushed by Aussarokian scouts, and after putting up a valiant effort against the Sarugs, Arados is bounded and imprisoned deep within Farrow Forest where he personally meets an unconscious Carador. Carador awakes one hour later and quickly explains everything at hand to Arados.

Roughly one day later, Arados and Carador devise a strategy and manage to break out of the prison with many other wrongfully imprisoned soldiers. The escape was led by none other than Carador, the man they were sent to debate with. After the successful escape, Arados agrees to travel along with Carador and six other prisoners. Arados joins *the Sons of Freedom*.

The eight companions travel to Aromer Mountain on their quest to slay Arush'n'aug, which they successfully accomplish two days later at the Ruins of Caracross, with the support of the army of Faradown led by King Faraduel. This marked the fall of Saratrox's greatest soldier, and Arados, along with Carador and the five other members are considered the Heroes of Earacill. Arados and *the Sons of Freedom* will remain together as companions until Saratrox and Aussarok are forever destroyed, and Earacill is long last at peace.

TERADORN: \ *"Tehr"a"dorn* \

TERADORN: *The Sons of Freedom's* Hunter. Teradorn was the son of Tarador was born in 2695 in the kingdom of Faradown. He lived with his father throughout his childhood, one day Teradorn's father had robbed a market, he was being pursued by guards ordering him to stop, Tarador was cornered in a busy location, to avoid being caught, Tarador equipped a knife from behind, it was concealed from the guards. As the guards came closer to arrest him, Tarador quickly revealed the knife and attacked the four guards with it, killing them. Witnesses saw the crime Tarador committed and they reported it all throughout Faradown.

When Teradorn heard of the murders his father committed, at the age of fourteen, he ran away from his home and began living the remainder of his adolescent years living on his own, and hunting his own food, he never once: bought food from stores.

At the age of eighteen, Teradorn became one of Earacill's greatest hunters, his trademark was his ability to hunt only with his sword. Teradorn was capable of sneaking upon animals from behind and stealthily taking them down. He was given the name:

The Phantom Hunter. Teradorn never took his name seriously, although the citizens who knew his ability believed it.

Teradorn returned to Faradown and lives alone. He hopes he will never see his father again, nor does he know if he is still alive, he was never caught.

Many years later (2935) Teradorn receives an unexpected letter from the Lord Arien of Banlafar. He was instructed to head to Banlafar for a great debate. He agrees and heads out of Faradown the following day, and is ambushed and imprisoned, he then breaks out with several others. Teradorn accepts the duty to become one of *the Sons of Freedom* and joined with the leader: Carador.

Teradorn knew this would be his greatest quest, although it was also the deadliest. Teradorn and the other seven head out of Banlafar and begin their greatest journey to hunt Arush'n'aug.

FAROND: \ *"Fär"ond* \

FAROND: The elven warrior in *the Sons of Freedom*. Farond is the son of Farradol, a former soldier of a once great elven city in Arcon Realm. Like his close friend Arados, Farond was also born in Arcon Realm in the early years of 6842. He was once a worthy fighter in Arcon Realm. After his military training, Farond and Farradol joined an old friend, Tharagor, in his exploration to Earacill.

Farond never creates a boundary for himself, he fights usually alone apart from when he helped establish *the Sons of Freedom*. Farond was one of first elves to arrive in Earacill, in its foundation in the first year. He traveled along with the first elves to Dynasty Realm, after he grew tired of Arcon Realm, and wanted to become an explorer, and travel to new lands to observe what there is to see and learn about the different parts of the world.

His lifelong dreams were quickly shattered as he now is trapped in Earacill with the threat of Saratrox present, his life goal now is to destroy Saratrox.

Farond did his service in 2935 and helped Lord Caradorian slay Arush'n'aug and became a well-known hero in Earacill.

DALAN: \ *"Da"lon* \

DALAN: The dwarven warrior from *the Sons of Freedom*. Dalan was born in 2651 in the Manor Mines to Harten, a famous miner in the mines. Dalan was known to be the youngest dwarf ever to become a warrior. He would train for weeks, then months, learning everything about the art of war. His friends had nicknamed him: *The God of War*, as he was unstoppable to anyone. He was awarded a grand battle-axe for his skill by the dwarf's in the Manor Mines, which he still uses today.

Dalan was a brawny dwarf. His weapon of choice is a legendary battle-axe he received in placement over his old war hammer. Dalan commonly wears a helmet, which did not conceal his rather rugged face, and has a rather long dark brown, greasy beard. He resides with all the dwarfs in Earacill in the Manor Mines, which is the only land constructed by the first dwarfs in the year 300.

Dalan quickly became one of *the Sons of Freedom* to follow along Carador and the others on their quest. He believed that he would become of great support to Carador and the seven for the journey, and his support for them did them well.

HELLDAR: \ *"Hel"där* \

HELLDAR: The human Paladin in *the Sons of Freedom*. Helldar was one of the first to fight alongside with Carador on their quest in 2935. This Paladin lives and serves Faraduel in Faradown, and his Faraduel's highest fighting Paladin. Helldar lives with his brother Selldar in Faradown. He despises Arush'n'aug a lot and soon hopes to slay it himself. He was fortunate when he heard of a council being held to solve Arush'n'aug's threat. Helldar was pleased to hear he would be called upon to the council and help with the cause.

SELLDAR: \ *"Sel"där* \

SELLDAR: *The Sons of Freedom's* Assassin. Selldar was one of the companions to fight alongside with Carador on his quest to slay Arush'n'aug. Selldar is an assassin who goes out and legally assassinates anyone he is told, for this quest he has joined his brother Helldar to go out and assassinate Arush'n'aug with Carador and his fellow companions. Selldar was born the same year and day

2910 as his twin brother Helldar, Selldar lives with Helldar in Faradown, Selldar and Helldar rarely see each other for they have two different trades. Selldar was summoned for the council, for the senate thought as him as a great assassin and would do well along with Carador. He joined along, for his brother went along and for he was ordered to slay Arush'n'aug.

FARADUEL: \ *"Fära"dooul* \

FARADUEL: The current King of Faradown. Faraduel is the son Arog. Faraduel was born in the year: 2695, Faraduel is best friends with Carador, since early childhood. Faraduel agrees with Carador to form a council in Banlafar, he sends word to Arien to form a council on the first and the council is created. Faraduel heads out of Faradown with an army unnoticed by Carador, to join Carador and fight along with him, for Faraduel believes he can help with an army. Faraduel's army arrives while Carador and his companions are in fight with Arush'n'aug on the doorstep of Aromer Mountain. The Battle at the Ruins of Caracross begins when he arrives.

*ARIEN: \ "Ar"ien *

ARIEN: The current Count of Banlafar. Arien makes part of the senate in Earacill along with the King of Faradown: Faraduel, the King of Anaron: Earathell, and now the King of Androuge: Carador. Arien was close friends with Tharagor and joined him on his quest to find new land. Arien and his family arrived in Dynasty Realm from Arcon Realm with Tharagor and other elves. Tharagor gave him the power and made him ruler of Banlafar. Arien and Tharagor created the first laws in Earacill. Arien has ordered the debate for Carador concerning Arush'n'aug's threat.

*HARKEN: \ "Härk"en *

HARKEN: The last companion of the seven warriors to fight with Carador and end Arush'n'aug's threats. Harken is a berserker, whom was born in Barlafar in the year of 2651, he was a half-giant born from normal human's, although he grew to great heights. He was a great warrior his size gave him a lot of power. He has joined Carador on his quest, for enjoyment of killing, which he seemed to adore doing the most in his spare time. He was killed on *the Sons of Freedom* quest in 2935.

*ARUSH'N'AUG: \ "Âr"a"sh"näug *

ARUSH'N'AUG: Saratrox's greatest warrior, one of two of Earacill's threats. Arush'n'aug, was also known as The Great Black Dragon, for its dark and hideous color of steel scales. Arush'n'aug was formed together from the ashes of Aromer Mountain, after it burned to the ground, and then risen again, like the Phoenix bird. Arush'n'aug has been attacking cities and people for as long as it has been around. It has managed to attack every great city twice, destroyed the Stronghold of Androuge: Caracross, and attacked smaller towns as well. Its latest attack, the attack on Androuge has angered Carador into forming a council and sending a legion of the best warriors in Earacill to slay it. Carador and seven others set out of Banlafar on December first and accomplished their deed by slaying Arush'n'aug on the third of December.

KINGS, RULERS, & STEWARDS

*THARAGOR: \ "Thar"a"gowr *

THARAGOR: The first founder of Earacill. Tharagor was born in his hometown back in Arcon Realm. He was a town's citizen, who had a dream to leave his land and go in search for a new one. He discovered Earacill while sailing south. Tharagor spoke out about Arush'n'aug and insisted on making a stronghold or city to ward off any attacks. This started the construction of the greatest elven city, the city of Anaron, stronghold and city of the elves of Earacill. Nineteen years pass, and the great city is complete, and Tharagor is made first King of Anaron. Around eighty years later the elves of Earacill brought their magic from Arcon Realm with them. In which it led them into forging a magical sword for Tharagor in the Cave of Anlaw. It was a blade like none other. A year later Tharagor's son, Morather is born in Anaron. Starting a royal bloodline for the elves in Earacill.

Few years later the blacksmiths complete forging the Emerald-Star and is given to Tharagor as an heirloom. Years later, King Tharagor and his legion ride to Androuge. Saratrox and his forces ambush them. King Tharagor and his legion are slain. The Emerald-Star is passed onto his son.

EARICADAL: \ *"Ehr"eh"ca"del* \

EARICADAL: The first King of Androuge. Earicadal was the founder of Earacill for the race of mankind. He constructed the high city of Androuge. On March of the year 298, King Earicadal passes at the age of sixty-three. His son Beldar is made second King of Androuge.

EARATHELL: \ *"EÂr"a"thell* \

EARATHELL: The third and current King of Anaron. After King Morather's death Anaron was forced to keep the bloodline alive. In which they made Morather's nephew: Earathell the new and current king.

SARATROX: \ *Sar"A"trâ"ks* \

SARATROX: The Shadow Lord of Earacill. Saratrox the Defiler was no human, elf, or dwarf. Fate can only describe him as *"The Walking Phantom."* He was one lone race. Saratrox seduces life to obey and order his commands. His army is made up of men-turned-evil called Sarugs.

Saratrox himself was human at one point in time, born under the birth name of Agasell. He was continuously abused and neglected by his father since his early childhood. Agasell never learned the path to integrity, only darkness. At age sixteen Agasell murdered his abusive father. He was hunted down he was imprisoned for twenty years being yet again abused. Filled with malevolence, anger and sorrow Agasell enchanted strength and broke out of his prison chamber.

Saratrox committed a massacre in his homeland, he was then captured and executed. With all Agasell's dark memories, ideals and emotions, his spirit form never died. He was reborn as Saratrox, a spirit with the ability to talk, fight and even move. He has become a Phantom that would never stop his crimes. For five ages Saratrox corrupted living beings from every corner of the earth, building an army that would soon overtake the earth and rule it alone.

Many years pass and Saratrox and his army construct the dark fortress of: Aussarok in the south, their imperial nation is born. It became a much greater threat than Arush'n'aug could ever be.

Saratrox is given a crown. It is enchanted with power. It gave Saratrox the dark powers to corrupt any race, to his will. With that, Saratrox corrupted hundreds of thousands of humans, elves, even animals in his old world, he then brought himself and his servants to Earacill. Years later, after the seductions, the crown itself had betrayed Saratrox and attempted to seduce him, the crown nearly killed Saratrox. Its dark magic would work on any whoever bears it. Saratrox commands his servants to destroy the crown and hide the shards deep within the Cave of Anlaw. They successfully reach their destination and the shards were hidden it in the cave. Saratrox's weakness was the crown itself, if the shards were to be returned to him, and used against him. It would destroy him.

After hearing of its successful disappearance, Saratrox cursed the Cave of Anlaw for none ever to withdraw the shards from deep within the cave. The shards of Saratrox's crown would destroy him.

BELDAR: \ "Bel"dar \

BELDAR: The second King of Androuge. Beldar was the first and only son of Earicadal. King Beldar convinced King Tharagor to join in any wars, and he agreed. On the year 478 Beldar passes and his son Vermis is third King of Androuge.

VERMIS: \ "Vurm"is \

VERMIS: Former King of Androuge. After ruling Androuge for thirty-five years King Vermis insists on making the town of Barlafar, a twin town to Banlafar to be made next to Banlafar. King Vermis constructs Caracross, a stronghold and refuge for the people of Androuge. King Vermis, Lord of Androuge plans to attack Aussarok one more time, and if they fail, then never again. Two years pass, and King Vermis resigns from lordship of Androuge. His son: Carsor is made fourth King of Androuge.

*CARSOR: \ "Kâr"sowr *

CARSOR: The Grandfather of King Caradorian. Carsor's first task as king was to construct the Temple of Anastar in Androuge. Carsor's son: Caragor was born inside the Temple of Anastar. Few years later, Aussarok attacks Androuge, testing their skills and techniques. Androuge quickly repels Aussarok. Androuge's defense is high. King Carsor and prince Caragor quickly ride to Anaron and Faradown and warn them for a possible attack on their two cities. Anaron and Faradown built their defense and assemble their armies. In 2902 came the passing of King Carsor while visiting Faradown.

*CARAGOR: \ "Kâr"a"gor *

CARAGOR: The late King of Androuge. In his early years, Prince Caragor sent an army to Aromer Mountain to fight Arush'n'aug. Faradown's army joined them in for their revenge. The army attacked Arush'n'aug for the second time. Neither is victorious. Neither is defeated. Caragor's son:

Carador was born in Androuge on the year 2900. At the beginning years of the Third Century.

Caragor is made fifth King of Androuge. And Aussarok attacks Faradown, however, Faradown gets reinforced from soldiers from Androuge. Faradown and Androuge repel Aussarok. During Faradown's victory celebration Faraduel takes the lordship over Faradown and is made king at the age of eighteen. A new dynasty for Faradown is made.

Following the celebration, King Caragor and his personal bodyguards ride to Faradown and give his congratulatory hand to Faraduel and the citizens of Faradown. On his way, however, Ruthless Sarugs had ambushed King Caragor, he along with his soldiers: is slain. It was a day of celebration for the people of Earacill, it now had turned into grieves. The knowledge of Caragor having a son was all but forgotten by all, except for two.

*SILITHOR: \ "Sil"eh"thor *

SILITHOR: The first King of Faradown. On Silithor's seventeenth Birthday, he plans to construct a new city for mankind in the west. This city would be called: Faradown. Silithor's plan is debated and comes to into being. After three years, Faradown in constructed and is protection for the west.

Silithor is made the first King of Faradown on the following year. On the same year, however, Silithor and his wife have their first son: Darleer, starting a dynasty for Faradown. King Silithor is slain in battle.

DARLEER: \ "Dâr"leer

DARLEER: The second King of Faradown.

MORATHER: \ "Mowr"a"theer

MORATHER: The second King of Anaron. Morather became king after his father's death. Five years after his death, king Morather of Anaron seeks revenge on Aussarok. He assembles and army to strike at the fortress of Aussarok. In return Morather's army is defeated at the grounds of Aussarok, Morather with them. The Emerald-Star lies in the Camalon Fields, never found. For the dynasty of Anaron not to fall, they make Morather's nephew: Earathell, the next King of Anaron.

LOCATIONS

ANDROUGE: \ *"An"drowg* \

ANDROUGE: One of *the Three Kingdoms* in Earacill in the east, followed along with the kingdoms of Faradown and Anaron. Androuge was the first city in Earacill made by humans in the year of their arrival in 259 of the First Century. It is known as the: City of Silver Knights, for its white architecture. Earicadal was promoted to be the first King of Androuge after his decision of constructing the city. The elves declared war on Androuge and the race of mankind. Arush'n'aug's first assault on Androuge and Anaron let the elves and the human's friendship begin and have their peace for they apparently are at war with a much greater threat.

After King Earicadal's passing in 287, his son Beldar is made second king. In 475 Beldar's passing as come upon him, and his son Vermis is made the third King of Androuge. Carsor son of Vermis is made fourth king after King Vermis resigns in 2604. Caragor is made fifth king after King Carsor resigns. Androuge is left to Stewards after King Caragor is slain by Arush'n'aug and the dynasty is broken. Carador son of former King Caragor becomes sixth king after slaying Arush'n'aug in the current year of 2935. Androuge remained kingless for years, for no one had known that Caragor had a son. Until after Carador becomes the sixth King of Androuge. Androuge is ranked Earacill's highest city of the three.

*FARADOWN: \ "Fâr"a"dawn *

FARADOWN: The second of *the Three Kingdoms* in Earacill in the west. The first humans in the land constructed the city in 286 of the First Century. Faradown's main color of its buildings and architecture is sky-blue which can be seen reflected of in the sunlight around ten miles away. The base of the city lies upon the footstep of the mountain. The upper city starts on the mountainside and ends at the summit of the mountains. Anlar rests upon the summit. Behind Anlar is Mt. Stager piercing five hundred feet into the sky.

Silithor is made the first King of Faradown, after warning the men about the dragon: Arush'n'aug and its possible threat to them. King Silithor and his Steward son, Darleer are slain by Arush'n'aug in 365 at the end of the First Century starting the Second Century, breaking their dynasty, and allowing ordinary citizens overrule Faradown by becoming the cities Stewards. The Steward Arog is allowed the new king. After the passing of Arog, his son, Faraduel is made King of Faradown in 2908, thus starting a new dynasty for Faradown.

ANARON: \An"a"ron\

ANARON: The third of *the Three Kingdoms* in Earacill in the north. Tharagor and the first legion of elves from Arcon Realm constructed the great elven city of Archara in the kingdom of Anaron in the year 15 of the First Century. Archara's foundation was built at the foot of a mountain, while the great castle was built upon the mountain. Anaron could be mistaken for Faradown if glanced upon quickly or vice versa, although if glanced upon again, the difference can be recognized immediately.

Tharagor is made the first King of Anaron in the year 16, one year after the kingdom was constructed. The elves begin to forge the legendary sword: The Emerald-Star for Tharagor as an heirloom. In the year 18, Prince Morather son of King Tharagor is born. They lived the remainder of their lives in Anaron. For over one hundred years they lived until one day in the year 140 Tharagor is slain in the Camalon Fields. Prince Morather takes the throne of Anaron.

*AUSSAROK: \ "Oos"a"rok *

AUSSAROK: The dark fortress of Saratrox in the south, constructed in the year 100 at the end of the First Century, after Saratrox's appearance. With a rich Gothic theme to it. He constructed the fortress and it is Earacill's greatest threat. Aussarok's primary color was black.

*BANLAFAR: \ "Ban"la"fâr *

BANLAFAR: The first town crafted by the elves in the second year of the discovery of Earacill. And the first town constructed in Earacill. Banlafar is a small elven town. Banlafar has a twin town of Barlafar north of it, constructed by humans in 510 of the early Second Age. Banlafar's first and only Count is Arien and would remain the Count of Banlafar for years to come. Banlafar is special for its golden color and many surrounding waterfalls. The Great Council was held in the town of Banlafar, here also all ancient artifacts of Earacill remain in the town for the safest of keeping.

*AROMER MOUNTAIN: \ "Ar"o"mir "Mawntin *

AROMER MOUNTAIN: The dark mountain and the home of the Great Black Dragon, Arush'n'aug. The mountain had risen from ashes of Mt. Farshard after it collapsed and turned to ash in the third year. Aromer Mountain rose in the year 5 of the First Century.

*CARACROSS: \ "Kâr"a" "kros *

CARACROSS: Refuge for people of Androuge. Caracross was named after the bloodline of the Androugen kings. Caracross was first constructed in the year 125 of the First Century, before Androuge was fully constructed. Some years after its construction the first battle with Arush'n'aug took place in 127, during that battle, Androuge was defeated and Caracross was never bothered to be rebuilt. It is now formally known as the Ruins of Caracross.

FARROW FOREST: \ *"Farow "Forist* \

FARROW FOREST: Forest south of Faradown, one of the two only remaining forests in Earacill.

THE DEAD LAND: \ *"The "Ded "Land* \

THE DEAD LAND: Scorching hot ashes and rubble of land surrounding Aromer Mountain that had failed to rise with Aromer Mountain. The land remains heated while Arush'n'aug and Aromer Mountain have power. The Dead Land's horror gives out to whoever decides to cross into it harsh and piercing sounds and voices that people would only imagine hearing. The Dead Land's heat gives out steam, which lets it to be almost impossible to see anything ahead of them, once within it.

THE GREAT LAKE: \ *"The "Greyt "Leyk* \

THE GREAT LAKE: The River separating Aromer Mountain and the Dead Land from the rest of Earacill. The Great Lake was originally a lake. After a massive landslide a hundred years ago, the lake was pressed together and broke of a piece of Earacill, which that island is now named Sarchara. The island of Sarchara separates Aromer Mountain from the rest of Earacill.

BLOODLIПE

CARACROSS: \ *"Car "ah" kross* \

CARACROSS: The Caracross bloodline was always known for the tradition of bearing one single child, in which Carador was born with no siblings or cousins that he can relate to. The bloodline was first created by Earicadal Caracross, Androuge's first king. Following Earicadal's reign came, Beldar, Vermis, Carsor, Caragor, and now exists by only Caradorian Caracross.

SILDORIAN: \ *"Sill "door "ien* \

SILDORIAN: The Sildorian bloodline follows the ancestry of humans from the western kingdom of Faradown taking over lordship of Stewardship after the last living heir passed.

WEAPONS & ITEMS

*THE EMERALD-STAR: \ "The "Emuruld "Stâr *

THE EMERALD STAR: The Emerald-Star may be considered the most historical and the most famous of all legendary swords. It was forged by the greatest elven blacksmith of all time, in the mysterious Cave of Anlaw. It was forged for King Tharagor in the year 19 of the First Century. It then became an heirloom to Tharagor's dynasty.

   The Emerald-Star has seen its share of combat. Its high polished Triton double-bladed edge glows Emerald green when its user is enraged with anger, for the benefit of superhuman strength. Its Emerald handle regains your strength when weary of war or traveling. Its inscription reads: *"THE EMERALD-STAR: THE SWORD OF LEADERSHIP"*

SKY-PIERCER: \ *"SkI "Peersur* \

SKY-PIERCER: The legendary bow of the King Tharagor. Sky-Piercer was stolen by Arados after Tharagor's death in 2045. It is the strongest and fastest bow ever crafted in Earacill. The bow received its name from its height range to abrade the sky. Sky-Piercer has the power to set arrows in position of dismissal on fire or inject the arrow with Viper venom. Fire or poison flows from the inside of Sky-Piercer, then it flows through its string, and injects into the back of the arrow moving quickly to the arrowhead.

TWIN-VIPERS: \ *"Twin "Vi"purs* \

TWIN-VIPERS: The Twin-Vipers are the knives of Farond. Farond himself forged them, he had given them the magical power to absorb fire and heat from whatever it pierces into. They are the only weapons Farond would ever use. For they are his first weapons and will always be. Farond has never even held a bow or a sword. Without Farond's Twin-Vipers, he would have never a reason to fight again.

ORLIES: \ *"Owr"lees* \

ORLIES: Onion like vegetables found underneath trees. Orlies come out twice a year at nightfall and die within the next day. Orlies cannot be purchased in any stores due to their short shelf-life.

GORNBERRIES: \ *"Gorn "berees* \

GORNBERRIES: A soft red-orange fruit growing in almost any tree in Earacill. It has the mixture taste of Strawberries and peaches. Gornberries taste appetizing in almost any meal cooked.

SORFOIL: \ *"Sowr"foyl* \

SORFOIL: Herb used for texturing soup or can be eaten with any meat product. Sorfoil herb can also be used in assembling potions. Its taste is crucially acetic when eaten alone.

ANDROUGEN ALE: \ *"An"drowg"en "Eyl* \

ANDROUGEN ALE: Finest ale brewed in Androuge, Androugen ale was first located in the Sapphire

Mountains, north of Androuge.

BARION ALE: \ *"Bear"ehn "Eyl* \

BARION ALE: Ale brewed in the caves of Barlafar.

RELIGION

ARUANALOGISM: The religion of Earacill.

ARUANALOGIST: A believer and follower of Aruanor.

ARUANOR: Deity of Earacill.

ARUANALOGISM: The ancient religion was first founded days before the start of the First Century, precisely during the time of when Earacill was first discovered. Aruanalogism was created by the first elves after their long and treacherous journey to the unknown land. They believed it was their prophecy to create it the religion, their God, Aruanor, had led them to its discovery. The elves' first exploration to the new land was a deadly one, they believed that they would never reach any destination in their condition. They prayed deeply that they would soon overcome the storms before them and reach their destination. Their prayers were answered, the great storms died down, and days later they successfully arrived upon the shores of a new land: Earacill. The elves believed that there was a God whom had rescued them from certain death. From within their hearts, they had named it:

Aruanor, which in their language mean *Pathfinder*. The elves knew that Aruanor is not its real name. Aruanor was praised and worshiped by the elves in Earacill.

With the elves' knowledge of Aruanor, they passed it down to race of humans and dwarfs who all took it for granted. With the race of humans now believers and worshipers, Aruanor's good deeds fell upon them, and they too successfully thrive in Earacill.

Years later, after the coming of Saratrox and Aussarok, many of the races had lost all faith and accuse Aruanor for bringing this treachery to their new and peaceful land.

Numerous forgot the religion. Many Aruanalogists still thrive about, knowing that it is not Aruanor's fault. Aruanor itself did not bring this dark act upon his believers. Many citizens know this, and they still have faith in Aruanor.

Saratrox is a strong enemy to Aruanor, he at the same time despises him and fears him. Aruanor knows this and will never help Saratrox with his dark deeds. Aruanalogists desperately try to bring the faith of the religion back and preach to them that Arush'n'aug was not of Aruanor's creation, some go back into belief.

All hope now is that Saratrox and Arush'n'aug will be dealt with, and that Aruanalogism will fully return in Earacill.

MILITARY RANKS

LEVY: Forced into Military service, at knife-point if necessary. Unranked soldier.

MILITIA: Recruit without training. Eighth class knight.

SPEARMEN: Lower class professional soldier. Seventh class knight.

FRONTIERSMAN: Axe wielding men who will charge occasionally without command.

MERCENARY: Trained in warfare and willing to sell services for a nominal fee.

SQUIRE: Apprentice knight. Sixth class knight.

KNIGHT: Average recruit trained for war. Fifth class knight.

CONQUEROR: Advanced soldier on horseback. Fourth-class knight.

PALADIN: Highly trained soldier protector of a kingdom. Third class knight.

CHAMPION: Heavily trained soldiers and battle strategists. Second class knight.

HERO-KNIGHT: Superiorly trained soldiers used to command armies and fight on the front lines. First class knight.

ARMOR

PATCHWORK: Worn by Militia.

BRONZE: Worn by Squires.

IRON: Worn by Knights.

STEEL: Worn by Conquerors.

TITANIUM: Worn by Paladins.

TRITON: Worn by Hero-knights, Champions, and Paladins.

APPENDIX II

* * * * * * * * * *

A BRIEF HISTORY OF EARACILL

History of course, starts with the beginning. *The Three Kingdoms* era starts back before the first foundations of Earacill. History will bring us back to as early as the finding of this new land. It began with one elf's vision of freedom and solitude away from his home world of Arcon Realm. This elf, accompanied by a few others who wished to join him, journeyed the Earth, in exploration and blissfully stumbled upon a new peaceful world, inhabited by only its preserved wildlife, this world is none other than *"Earacill,"* or nicknamed *"Dynasty Realm."*

This is the start of the First Century: The Age of New Beginnings, of which the first millennium in Earacill is appropriately named. The First Century mainly revolves around the discovery and foundation of Earacill, and how it quickly becomes inhabited by three common races in the world: elves, dwarfs, and humans.

In the First Century, these three races, refused cohabitation and started wars with one another, they claimed that only one race was allowed lordship over these lands in these times. However, it is not long as they soon put aside their differences and become allies with one another after they are attacked by a threat they were unaware of: the great dragon, Arush'n'aug, who alone, was born out of ash and shadow.

As mentioned before, a few elves from Arcon Realm ventured out in search of a new land. This exploration had begun by a young determined elf named Tharagor, who now has gone down in history as one of the most iconic figures in the elven world. During Tharagor's and his crew's journey, strong winds and storms brought them into grave danger. They desperately prayed that they would soon be free of the storms and arrive to their destination. Their prayers were granted, the storms died down and the elves then set foot upon Earacill, claiming it for themselves. They believed there was a God that had blessed them and helped them through their struggles, and from within their hearts they called it: Aruanor, which in their language means "*Pathfinder*." Aruanor was praised and worshiped by the new, inhabited elves in Earacill.

The elves quickly discover food, trees, stones and other resources that they would need if they were to reside here for the rest of their lives. The elves worked day and night to construct the first town on their newly found land. It took them one year to complete. They called the town: "*Banlafar*," which to them means "*Land Afar*." Afterwards, Banlafar needed a ruler. It came down to Arien, one of the first explorers to become the Count, many disagreed with this decision and felt that Tharagor justified the position, yet Tharagor refused the seat.

During the first week of March in that year, Earacill had its first major earthquake in the southwestern province. That earthquake had in resultant, crumbled Mt. Farshard, the former home of the great Phoenix bird. The destruction of this mountain had now killed the last of the Phoenix birds that resided in Earacill, they were now all but extinct. Mt. Farshard had disintegrated into ash, as do the Phoenixes.

Two years later, a miraculous and unexplained event had occurred where the ashes of Mt. Farshard were present. It had risen once more out from within its ashes! The ever-present magical power of the Phoenix birds gave it a new life and caused it to rise once again.

Mt. Farshard, however, never looked the same. It had lost its previous beauty due to the extinction of the Phoenixes, and the elves refused to call new mountain, Mt. Farshard. They were forced to rename it to which they chose: Aromer Mountain.

Aromer Mountain in return, had attempted to resurrect the Phoenixes, although the original enchantment had backfired. The virtue and purity once present inside the mountain, had vanished. The ashes of the Mt. Farshard rose into a large, dark figure. This was no intended Phoenix, but rather a raging black dragon, with scales as dark as the night, and nearly half the size of the mountain. This was a creation of an ancient deity, who attempted the extinction of the Phoenix bird. Arush'n'aug, it was called, having the body of an ancient vessel, the skull of a prehistoric dinosaur, and resting upon its mutilated head sat a raging horn, as sharp as a sword. With claws made of keratin, and its black scales, being stronger than steel, could not be penetrated simply. Its bat-like wings had reached a commanding wingspan of nearly twenty-five feet. It was born with red, blazing, and fearful eyes. A trail of razor sharp black spikes decorating it, which rested upon the dragon's back. The elves had feared Arush'n'aug, and the certainty of the destruction it was to cause.

Twenty-five years later, and the first voice broke out, concerning Arush'n'aug. This mere potter insisted on making a stronghold or other fortification to ward off any possible assaults. This marks the construction of the greatest elven city, the city of Archara in the kingdom of Anaron, the stronghold and great city of the elves of Earacill.

Nineteen years pass, and the great city is complete, and Tharagor, Earacill's discoverer is crowned the King of Anaron, after having turned down the seat in Banlafar prior.

Around eighty years later, the elves of Dynasty Realm were able to revive their magic they have justly brought from Arcon Realm with them. Consequently, it led them into forging a magical sword for their king in the Cave of Anlaw. It would be a blade like none other, strongly polished from Triton stone. Its Emerald hilt would have the power to regain its owner's strength when weary in battle or travel. The Triton blade would turn into Emerald when one is filled with rage or fury, for more strength. The mighty sword was to be called: The Emerald-Star.

A year later Tharagor's son, Morather is born in Anaron. This began a royal bloodline for the elves in Earacill. Prince Morather would be the heir to the new dynasty, and Earacill is nicknamed "Dynasty Realm."

A few years later, the blacksmiths complete the forging of the Emerald-Star, and it is presented to Tharagor as an heirloom and a weapon. To their surprise, Arush'n'aug had not attacked the citizens of Earacill, not once and the beast was not considered much of a threat anymore and the citizens continued with their daily duties.

Years pass on, and more elves arrive from Arcon Realm after it has been announced to them of Dynasty Realm's discovery. They too, planned to spend their lives here. Although in 258 something unexpected happen, surprising and upsetting the citizens of Anaron. The first arrival of humans from Legion Realm, located in the north, arrive and discover Dynasty Realm for themselves.

The humans find the proper terrain where they construct the city of Seragone in the kingdom of Androuge, a larger and more powerful city than Archara, it was to become the capital city in Dynasty Realm. Earicadal Caracross, the founder of Earacill for mankind, is crowned the king over the kingdom of Androuge.

The elves promptly journey to Androuge and to Seragone, and protest as to dismiss the humans and ask them to return from whence they came, though the humans refused to, upsetting the established order. The elves then declare war on them, in attempt to keep Earacill for themselves as they had planned from the beginning.

Due to this war, Arush'n'aug devised a plot of its own wit. As the elves were now distracted by another foe, Arush'n'aug left its post at Aromer Mountain and attacks they city of Archara. Shortly after the destruction of the elves' city, Arush'n'aug attacks Seragone as well. It is then that elves and mankind realize that Arush'n'aug is a threat and a much larger threat than one another and are forced by fate to join forces to protect themselves and their families.

The elves' and human's alliance begin, and they join forces together to destroy Arush'n'aug and are willing to live together in peace.

One year later, the citizens of Earacill prevent any more arrival travelers into Dynasty Realm until Arush'n'aug is destroyed. However, the soldiers from Arcon and Legion Realm demand to enter Dynasty Realm to help the cause, they have no choice but to welcome them, and their army grows double in size. A year passes and Earicadal's first and only son: Beldar is born, starting a dynasty for Androuge and mankind.

Ten years later, Earicadal's cousin, Benemorn has his first son: Silithor. The same year, Benemorn purposes to the Elder Council of Androuge to construct a new city of mankind in the west. This city would be called: Anlar and would be the capital for the kingdom of Faradown. Benemorn's plan is twice debated before it finally passes.

Seventeen years later (59) Anlar's construction is completed and is now a barricade in the west. Silithor is crowned the first King of Faradown at only seventeen years of age. The following year, King Silithor and his wife, Ju'niis, have their first son and daughter: Darleer and Mania, starting a dynasty for Faradown.

Five years pass, and on March of the year 65, King Earicadal passes at the age of sixty-three. His son, Beldar is crowned the second King of Androuge.

Half a decade later, marks the dwarf's first arrive to Earacill from an unknown location to both elf and human. They come to Androuge and Faradown in peace, presenting foreign gifts to the kings and royalty in both Androuge and Faradown as a gift of friendship. They do not waste their time presenting gifts to the elves, knowing they would most likely toss them aside.

The elves were hoping this day would never come, when dwarfs would live in Earacill alongside the elves, for they are not fond with one another. However, both humans and elves warn the dwarfs of Arush'n'aug and its great threat. They join forces with the other two races and are prepared to fight alongside whenever necessary.

Seven years after their arrival, the dwarfs construct the Manor Mines in the Sapphire Mountains, north of Androuge. The Manor Mines is the heart of treasure and gems in Earacill. Half a century later, the dwarfs construct an actual town for themselves known as: Farist, which was a small village by the sea of Farbad.

Few years afterwards, the first legion of elves and humans march to the Dead Land surrounding Aromer Mountain in a feeble attempt to slay Arush'n'aug. They however, fail to do so. Being the ones slain in the process, the brave soldiers that day do not go forgotten. King Silithor is slain in battle. Prince Darleer takes up the throne.

A black colossal vessel approaches Earacill from the south, carrying on board an evil race of beings. This army came upon Earacill with only one goal in mind: conquer and destroy any living thing residing there, as it has already accomplished this deed in both Legion and Arcon Realm.

This is an alliance of corrupted-soldiers-turned-evil, led by the dark ruler, Saratrox. Saratrox has successfully destroyed both Arcon and Legion Realm with no warning, giving the warriors no time to fight back.

The survivors from these attacks were seduced by Saratrox and have become his Sarugs. Saratrox was no living being. Fate would describe him as *"The Walking Phantom."* He was one lone race. Saratrox seduces life to obey and order his commands. His army consists of thousands of prisoners he captured during the siege of Arcon and Legion Realm.

Saratrox himself was human at one point in time, under his birth name Agasell. He was continuously abused and neglected by his father since early childhood. Agasell never learned the path to integrity, only darkness. At age sixteen, Agasell murdered his abusive father. He was hunted down he was imprisoned for twenty years being yet again abused. Filled with vice, anger and sorrow, Agasell enchanted strength and broke out of his prison chamber.

He committed a massacre in his homeland, he then was captured and executed. With all Agasell's dark memories, ideals and emotions, his spirit form never died. He was reborn as Saratrox. He remains a spirit with the ability to talk, fight, and all else. He is a Phantom that would never stop his crimes.

For five ages Saratrox seduced all living races and beings, including animals, from every corner of the Earth, building an army of prisoners which he had captured in the assaults, which was now large enough to fully overtake the Earth and Saratrox would rule it forever, Earacill is all that remains for him.

Years pass and Saratrox and his army construct the dark fortress of: Aussarok in the south, their imperial nation is born. It became a much greater threat than Arush'n'aug could ever be. With the citizen's knowledge of their former homelands destroyed, the citizens of Earacill could not call for reinforcements who once resided there, and they cannot flee Earacill to return to their former lands.

After Agasell's rebirth as Saratrox, he was given a crown, which is enchanted with great power. It gave Saratrox the dark powers to corrupt any race, to his will. With that, Saratrox corrupted hundreds of thousands of humans and elves in his old world, he then brought himself and his servants to Earacill. Years later, after the seductions, the crown itself had betrayed Saratrox and attempted to seduce him, the crown nearly killed Saratrox. Its dark magic would work on any whoever bears it. Saratrox commands his servants to destroy the crown and hide the shards deep within the Cave of Anlaw. They successfully reach their destination and the shards were hidden it in the cave. Saratrox's weakness was the crown itself, if the shards were to be returned to him, and used against him. It would destroy him. After hearing of its successful disappearance, Saratrox cursed the Cave of Anlaw for none ever to withdraw the shards from deep within the cave. Saratrox's crown would destroy him.

Two years later, after Saratrox's construction of Aussarok, many of the races lost all faith and belief in Aruanor for bringing this treachery to their new and peaceful land, the religion was forgotten by many, although many Aruanalogists are still around. Aruanor itself did not bring this dark act upon its believers. The believers know this, and they still have faith in Aruanor.

The First Century ends.

The Second Century begins: The Age of Woe. In this age, *the Three Kingdoms*, and the free cities built upon the land, are mortally in danger with Saratrox and his corrupt army. The dark overlord and his finest warrior constantly attack Earacill to successfully bring *the Three Kingdoms* into ruin.

The cities are rebuilt, although they are never as powerful as they once were in their first construction. The cities are not powerful enough to launch an assault upon Aussarok to bring Saratrox along with Arush'n'aug down, and their armies are now too few. They will forever have to deal with the attacks until something can finally cease the great threat.

Seventy-five years pass and on March of 475, King Beldar passes. His son, Vermis Caracross is crowned the third King of Androuge. After ruling

Androuge for thirty-five years, King Vermis insists on making the town of Barlafar, a twin town to Banlafar to be constructed next to Banlafar, the plan was to make trading with Anaron and Androuge simpler.

Two years afterward, Arush'n'aug plans to attack Androuge for its second time. King Vermis plans the construction of Caracross, a stronghold and refuge for the people of Androuge. Arush'n'aug pursues the soldiers and villagers of Androuge into Caracross where they fought the Great Black Dragon. With no aid or reinforcements from Faradown or Anaron, the army of Androuge is defeated at Caracross, and Caracross fell into ruin, and was never bothered to be rebuilt again. The elves visit Androuge and bring aid to its citizens for their defeat at Caracross.

Years later, King Tharagor and his finest Champions ride to Androuge. On their way however, Saratrox's forces ambushed them. Saratrox single-handedly slays King Tharagor and his small legion. Tharagor's beheaded corpse and the Emerald-Star are recovered, and the proper funeral was set for the next day. The Emerald-Star was passed onto Morather.

Five years since his father's death, King Morather of Anaron seeks revenge on his father's death. He faultily assembles and army to strike at the fortress of Aussarok, out of pure rage rather than strategy. In return Morather and his army are defeated at the grounds of Aussarok. The Emerald-Star lies in the Camalon Fields, never found.

One hundred years later however, Morler, an elven shop owner from Anlar finds the Emerald-Star in the fields, little to his knowledge did he remember it was the sword of King Tharagor. Morler kept it in his armory for sale, largely overpriced.

For the dynasty of Anaron not to shatter, they crown Morather's nephew: Earathell to be the new King of Anaron.

Carsor Caracross, son of Vermis is born. King Vermis, Lord of Androuge plans to attack Aussarok one more time, with an entirely different strategy. Should they fail, then never again will they attempt. The army of Androuge is victorious and scars the enemies, however, in the long run, this was a mere scratch, and Aussarok still remains strong.

Two years pass, and King Vermis resigns from lordship of Androuge, his son: Carsor Caracross is crowned the fourth King of Androuge. Carsor's first task as king is to construct the Temple of Anastar.

The Temple of Anastar he plans would be a house for the wounded, and a haven for those in fear. It is also used as a meeting ground for assemblies, celebrations, and a chapel for Aruanalogists.

On the same year however, Arush'n'aug attacked Anlar for its second time, damaging the newly restored city. The casualties were lower than usual, although the damage was higher.

Twenty years pass, and within those years, the Temple of Anastar was completed. And Carsor's son: Caragorian Caracross was born inside the Temple of Anastar. Caragor is how he was referred to.

Yet another two decades pass, Prince Caragor sends an army to Aromer Mountain to fight Arush'n'aug. Faradown's army joins them for revenge against the former attack. The army attacks Arush'n'aug for the second time. Neither is victorious, and neither is defeated. They have adapted to the war lifestyle and have enough experience to survive attacks.

A year later, the dwarfs expand their mines, and their mines become the richest region in Earacill. Within the Manor Mines, Dalan son of Harten is born.

Some years later, Aussarok attacks Seragone, testing their defense and techniques. Seragone's soldiers quickly repel Aussarok. Their defense is high, and their soldiers professionally trained.

King Kiligon and Prince Korather quickly ride to Anaron and Faradown and warn them about a possible attack on their two capital cities. Anaron and Faradown built their defense and assemble their armies, although Saratrox's army never came.

Five hundred years later. Earacill celebrates half millennia with no warfare. Unfortunately, a few more days pass and both Arush'n'aug and Aussarok happen to attack Anaron and Androuge. These were the biggest attacks confirmed, destroying their great cities, leaving them to be rebuilt. Their cities would never be as strong as they once were. Dynasty Realm begins to fall parallel to Arcon and Legion Realm, all part of Saratrox's plan.

The dwarfs in the Manor Mines discover Triton. The dwarfs begin to construct Triton weapons and armor, for the perfect protection against their enemies, they share and sell Triton to the elves and humans. A few years later, the Manor Mines open a jewel shop.

Faraduel son of Arog is born in 2895 in Faradown.

After three years of the dwarf's discovery of Triton in their mines, enemy Sarugs invaded the Manor Mines and managed to steal the dwarf's treasure for themselves. This started the first army of dwarfs. The first ever dwarven army marches upon Aussarok and fight back. They successfully take back their stolen treasure.

Earacill's population begins to fall from non-stop deaths caused by Aussarok and Arush'n'aug. Their threat grows larger together than ever before.

The Second Century ends in the year 2706.

The Third Century begins: The Age of War.

The Third Century is the current age in Earacill. It mainly focuses on the great battles over Dynasty Realm. This is the era that would determine if the land was to be forever destroyed by Saratrox in the same way he had destroyed Arcon and Legion Realm, or if Dynasty Realm will have its redemption and destroy Aussarok and Saratrox and grow back into power as it once was, being now the last realm on Earth. The Third Century is the era that would determine the final fate of Earacill.

At the beginning years of the Third Century, Caragorian Caracross is crowned fifth King of Androuge. Along with that, this marked the birth of Caradorian Saladar Caracross, to the son of King Caragor in Seragone. Two years after the birth of Caradorian, former King Carsor passes while visiting Faradown.

Following the coronation of Caragorian, Aussarok attacks Anlar, however, Faradown gets reinforced from soldiers from Androuge. Faradown and Androuge's forces repel Aussarok, they assumed that Aussarok was now testing Faradown. During Faradown's victory celebration, Faraduel takes lordship over Faradown and is crowned the king at the young age of eighteen. A new dynasty for Faradown is made.

Following the celebration, King Caragor and his personal bodyguards ride to Faradown to give his congratulatory hand to the young king and the citizens of Faradown. On his way, however, King Caragor was ambushed and slaughtered by Sarugs. These Sarugs acted without any orders from Saratrox. King Caragor, along with his soldiers, is slain.

It was a day of celebration for the people of Earacill, yet it now had turned into a day of grief as well. The loss of the current King of Androuge, resulted in the fall of *the Three Kingdoms*. This unregistered attack had thrown off Saratrox's final siege plans. His final plan of attack was to attack Androuge, Anaron, and Faradown at the same time, with the entire population present to guarantee no survivors, and bring Earacill forever into ruin.

With *the three kingdom's* unison broken, the armies would become disbanded with no law to follow, and camps of rebels would form. A full-scale attack would then not succeed in the death of every man women and child. This would give Earacill an upper hand and delay Saratrox's final attack.

The knowledge of King Caragor having a son was forgotten, and Carador's mother never admitted in having a son. She secretly raised young

Caradorian alone, without the Elder Council's knowledge. She did want to risk Carador's existence in fear that the enemy might discover him and capture or possibly slay the last of the bloodline. Morwen would admit to Carador's lordship when the time would be right.

Few years later, Helldar and his twin brother Selldar are born in Anlar.

Carador's mother dies from sickness at Carador's age of twenty. The secret could only now be exposed by Carador himself.

After three years. Arush'n'aug attacks the Manor Mines and the dwarfs fight off the Great Black Dragon. The casualties were low, and only minor damage was caused from Arush'n'aug.

At the age of thirty, Carador is promoted to the rank of Hero-knight, the highest-ranking soldier.

Four years later, Hero-knight Carador and the army of Androuge, with the alliance from Faradown, try one more full measure attempt to destroy Aussarok and the dark armies.

One year later, Arush'n'aug heavily attacks Androuge for the fourth time in history, upsetting and enraging Carador. He then plans to form together a legion of the most skilled warriors in Earacill to slay Arush'n'aug once and for all. After his ride to Anlar to discuss the matter at hand, Carador is ambushed and imprisoned where he discovers and unites the newly imprisoned warriors there to breakout.

After they succeed, these escapees join alongside Carador and form *the Sons of Freedom*. A small platoon of recent history's greatest warriors that Earacill has ever seen. *The Sons of Freedom* are successful in their task to slay the mighty Arush'n'aug in the year 2935. After its defeat, the seven prepare themselves and their homelands for much more far down the road.

APPENDIX III

* * * * * * * * * *

THE TIMELINE OF EARACILL

The First Century: The Century of New Beginnings

1 - The discovery of Earacill (Dynasty Realm) by Tharagor along with the first elves from Arcon Realm.

2 - The elves establish the foundations of Banlafar.

3 - Mt. Farshard collapses after Earacill's earthquake, and it is reduced to ash.

3 - Aromer Mountain rises from the ashes of Mt. Farshard. Arush'n'aug is formed from the ashes of Aromer Mountain.

5 -   Tharagor travels to the north and lays out plans for the first kingdom of Anaron.

15 -   Tharagor constructs Archara in Anaron, and the legion of elves begin.

16 -   Tharagor is crowned first King of Anaron.

16 -   The greatest blacksmiths begin forging the Emerald-Star in the Cave of Anlaw.

18 -   Birth of Morather son of Tharagor, in Anaron.

19 -   The Emerald-Star is completed being forged and is given to Tharagor as an heirloom.

21 -   Arrival of Farond from Arcon Realm.

25 -   The first arrival of humans, led by Earicadal, from Legion Realm arrive.

25 -   Humans construct the Seragone in

Androuge in the east, and it becomes the
new capital city.

25 -   Earicadal is crowned first King of
Androuge.

26 -   The war between elves and human begin to
gain control over the new land.

28 -   Arush'n'aug attacks Anaron and
Androuge, Farond's father is slain.

28 -   The elves and mankind's friendship begin
and join as one to slay Arush'n'aug.

30 -   Elves and humans prevent arrival to
Earacill for they believe the land remains
too cursed.

31 -   Birth of Beldar, son of Earicadal, in
Androuge. The royal lineage in Androuge
begins.

32 -   Saratrox takes control of Arcon and Legion
Realm, corrupting the remaining

inhabitants to his will.

42 -   Silithor son of Benemorn is born.

42 -   Benemorn suggests the inception of a second kingdom in western Earacill. Humans establish Faradown in the west.

59 -   Benemorn's son, Silithor is crowned first King of Faradown at only seventeen years of age.

60 -   Darleer son of Silithor is born.

65 -   The passing of Earicadal and his son Beldar is crowned King of Androuge.

70 -   The first arrival of dwarfs.

72 -   The dwarfs construct the Manor Mines.

83 -   Humans construct the town of Farist in Faradown.

86 -   Birth of Vermis, son of Beldar in the east.

87 - The first legion of elves and mankind march to slay the dragon and are defeated.

90 - Silithor is slain by Arush'n'aug.

100 - Saratrox arrives to Dynasty Realm in an age long attempt to destroy it as he successfully has with both Arcon and Legion Realm. The dark fortress of Aussarok is built and is the prime evil of people in Earacill.

100 - Saratrox scrambles his armies in Aussarok.

101 - Saratrox's crown attempts to kill him, he gives the order for it to be destroyed and the shards hidden in the Cave of Anlaw. Saratrox clouds the Cave of Anlaw in a curse for the shards to never be recovered.

101 - Aruanalogism is forgotten by many, for they believe Aruanor is the cause of Arush'n'aug and Saratrox.

102 - King Beldar convinces King Tharagor to

join in any battles, and their alliance is born.

108 - Arrival of Arados from Arcon Realm.

110 - Birth of Prince Versor, son of Vermis, in Seragone.

113 - The passing of King Beldar, his son Vermis is crowned King.

122 - Barlafar is constructed by humans next to Banlafar.

125 - Caracross is constructed as a stronghold and a refuge for Androuge for future attacks from Arush'n'aug.

127 - The first war against the Arush'n'aug begins at Caracross.

128 - The war ends, the men are slain and Caracross stands in ruin.

129 - The elves come to Faradown and Androuge

for aid.

132 - King Vermis passes from disease in Spirit Village.

132 - King Vermis' son, Versor, is crowned king.

134 - Birth of Jeremiah, son of King Versor, in Seragone.

140 - The Battle of the Camalon Fields begins, and Tharagor is slain by Saratrox.

140 - The Emerald-Star is passed onto Morather.

143 - King Morather plans a full-scale attack on Aussarok, Aussarok is aided by Arush'n'aug.

144 - Morather's and his army are defeated.

155 - Birth of Corthair, the son of King Jeremiah in Faradown.

173 - King Morather is slain in the Camalon

Fields and the Emerald-Star lies there.

180 - Birth of Celcir, son of Corthair.

180 - Morather's nephew: Earathell is crowned King of Anaron.

274 - Birth of Fornair son of Celcir.

275 - Morler finds the Emerald-Star.

283 - King Celcir sends a legion to end Aussarok's threat forever. Arush'n'aug aids Aussarok.

285 - King Celcir's army is lost at Aussarok, the threat remains.

302 - Fornair becomes King of Androuge after Celcir resigns.

303 - Second attack on Faradown begins by Arush'n'aug.

304 - Fornair plans and constructs the Temple of

Anastar.

323 - Kelthor, son of Fornair is born in the Androuge.

332 - Fornair leads all legions of Androuge to Aromer Mountain. Faradown's legion joins Androuge's.

336 - Second attack upon Arush'n'aug begins.

341 - Kelthor weds.

347 - Former King Celcir passes.

352 - The dwarfs expand the mines, and it is the richest region in all Earacill.

363 - Faradown is warned from a potential attack from Aussarok.

364 - Faradown remains unharmed.

384 - Androuge drives back Sarugs.

394 - Birth of Kiligon, birthplace unknown.

403 - Triton is discovered by the dwarfs in the Manor Mines.

408 - Saratrox's final attack plans begin.

410 - Dynasty Realm calls upon any remaining survivors from both Arcon and Legion Realm for aid.

410 - Few respond to Dynasty Realm's call and leave the desolate wastes of their old world.

419 - Birth of Korather, son of Kiligon.

510 - Birth of Farah, daughter of Earathell.

524 - The Manor Mines open a Jewel shop.

The Second Century: The Century of Woe

1129 - Arush'n'aug attacks Anaron, while

Aussarok attacks Androuge.

1200 - Both Arush'n'aug and Aussarok are fought back.

1545 - Life in Earacill begins to decline. Armies turn into rebels. Cities are destroyed and never rebuilt as powerful as they once were.

1632 - The first surnames are represented in Earacill.

The Third Century: The Century of War

2845 - Birth of Dalan son of Harten, in the Manor Mines.

2858 - Birth of Carsorian Caracross, son of Serador Caracross.

2881 - Birth of Caragorian Caracross, son of Carsor Caracross.

2895 -   Birth of Faraduel son of Arog, in
          Faradown.

2895 -   Sarugs invade the Manor of Mines and
          steal the dwarf's treasure.

2895 -   Birth of Teradorn son of Tarador, in
          Faradown.

2897 -   The largest assembly of dwarfs ever attack
          Aussarok head on, and they recover their
          fortune.

2900 -   Birth of Caradorian Saladar Caracross, son
          of Caragorian Caracross, in Androuge.

2902 -   The passing of King Carsor while visiting
          Faradown.

2905 -   Carador and Faraduel's friendship begins.

2906 -   Caragor leaves Androuge, and heads to
          Faradown for advice.

2907 - Caragor is crowned the fifth King of Androuge.

2910 - Birth of twins Helldar and Selldar, in Faradown.

2913 - The Siege of Anaron begins by Sarugs.

2913 - Anaron calls for aid from Faradown and Androuge.

2913 - Anaron and Androuge soldiers fight of the Aussarok army.

2913 - Faraduel claims throne of Faradown after King Arog resigns.

2915 - Caragor is slain by Sarugs without Saratrox's commands, Androuge's dynasty falls resulting in the breaking of *the Three Kingdoms*. Saratrox's final attack plans are thwarted.

2920 - Morwen Caracross dies from sickness, the knowledge of Carador's royalty is lost.

2923 - The dwarfs are attacked by Arush'n'aug and repel its efforts.

2933 - Carador and the army of Androuge and few allies from Faradown lead on assault on Aussarok to weaken it.

2934 - The army slays many and damage Aussarok, however, the imperial nation still stands strong.

The Current Year

2935

September

Day

28 - Carador visits Faradown for a day.

29 - Carador returns to Seragone and finds it destroyed.

29 - Carador leaves Androuge and heads back to Faradown.

29 - Carador leaves Faradown and heads to Banlafar.

29 - Faraduel and a legion of soldiers depart Faradown to aid *the Sons of Freedom.*

30 - Carador is captured and imprisoned.

30 - Carador and his fellow inmates escape.

October

1 - Carador establishes *the Sons of Freedom.*

1 - *The Sons of Freedom* depart Banlafar and travel to Aromer Mountain.

2 - *The Sons of Freedom* reach Aromer Mountain and are attacked by Arush'n'aug.

3 - King Faraduel reaches Aromer Mountain. The Second Battle at the Ruins of Caracross begins.

3 - Arush'n'aug is slain by the Carador and the Sons of freedom at the Ruins of Caracross, and Aromer Mountain crumbles into ruin. The threat of Arush'n'aug ends.

3 - Caradorian Caracross is crowned the new King of Androuge. The bloodline of Androuge prospers.

3 - Saratrox's final siege plans fall back into effect.

APPENDIX IV

* * * * * * * * * *

THE ANDROUGEN
LANGUAGE

HISTORY:

The language of Androugen was first invented in Androuge during the First Century by the first king, Earicadal, after Saratrox's rise to power. It is currently the third language in the world.

The first King of Androuge invented this language as a language of peace and wisdom. The language is spoken through Earacill, all races utter it, Saratrox and his Sarugs are the only ones who cannot speak the language, which the people of Earacill use to their advantage. Strategists and commanders are given authority to plan attacks or assignments without the fear of being spied upon by their enemies.

Androugen is one of Saratrox's biggest concerns, knowing his inability to speak the language will lead him to lose valuable information on his enemies. If Saratrox was to ever learn the language, all hope of undercover assignments will be lost.

ANDROUGEN FONT:

ABCDEFGHIJKLMNOPQRSTUVWXYZ
ABCDEFGHIJKLMNOPQRSTUVWXYZ

BASICS:

I: Sa

You: Ye

He:	Fu
She:	Serie
It:	Un
Is:	En
In:	An
On:	On
A:	Ah
This:	Mas
That:	Mus
We:	Shen
When:	Shew
They:	Asen
Good Morning:	Farradeeto

Good Afternoon:	Farraunso
Goodnight:	Farranee
Please:	Sego
Thank You:	Sunki
You're Welcome:	Bengo
Yes:	Shae
No:	Na
The:	Sah
What:	Spauk
How:	Beh
Sir / Mr.:	Mensa
Madam / Mrs.:	Fensa
Miss:	Feensa

BASIC PHRASES:

I Want:	Sa Ent
I Don't Want:	Sa Na Ent
Where?:	Velent?
Where Is?:	Velent En?
How Much?:	Beh Maut?
How Much Does It Cost?	Beh Maut Ess Un Mensu
Time:	Deen
What Time?:	Spauk Deen?
At What Time?:	Ma Spauk Deen?
You Have?	Shew Caus?
Do You Have? / Have You?	Da Shew Caus?

I Understand:	Sa Revoro
I Don't Understand:	Sa Na Revoro
You Understand?:	Shew Revoro?
It Is? / That Is?:	Un En? / Mus En?
Is It? / Is That?:	En Un? / En Mus?

IMPORTANT WORDS:

Water:	Vessa
Drinking Water:	Misten Vessa
The Food:	Sah Massa
The One:	Mus Vun
That One Over There:	Mus Vun Seben Dah
The Counter:	Sah Munker

The Key:	Sah Seen
The Town:	Sah Fense
The City:	Saj Feia
A Map:	Ah Nua
Open:	Dase
Closed:	Sedose
Go:	Rus
Stop:	Siet
Move:	Daku
Life:	Anastar
Death:	Anlaw

DIRECTIONS:

North:	Sana
South:	Pona
East:	Mooth
West:	Saath
Northwest:	Sanasaath
Northeast:	Sanamoth
Southwest:	Ponasaath
Southeast:	Ponamooth
Straight Ahead:	Leen Umbar
The Corner:	Sah Beiner
Around The Corner:	Daru Sah Beiner
The Side:	Sah Isen
The Other Side:	Sah Ethier Isen

TIME, GENERAL:

A Moment:	Ah Revest
A Day:	Ah Dah
A Week:	Ah Maik
A Month:	Ah Norn
A Year:	Ah Yaht
Today:	Latag
Tomorrow:	Matag
Yesterday:	Shatag
Now:	Negg
Not Now:	Nah Negg
Not Yet:	Nah Leug
This Year:	Mas Yaht

The Next Year:	Sah Nu Yaht
The Last Year:	Sah Pein Yaht
In Two Days:	An Kai Dahs
Two Times:	Kai Intas
Three Times:	Sai Intas
One More Time / Again:	Fuun Nagu Inta
On Time:	On Inta

NUMBERS:

1	Fuun
2	Kai
3	Sai
4	Neir

5	Com
6	Nex
7	Feur
8	Lus
9	Neen
10	Comph
11	Fuunfun
12	Kainai
13	Sainai
14	Neirseir
15	Comsun
16	Nexdex
17	Feurfur

18	Lusleen
19	Neeinnun
20	Comphfuun
21	Kaifuun
22	Kaikai
30	Comphsai
31	Saifuun
32	Saikai
33	Saisai
40	Comphneir
50	Comphcom
60	Comphnex
70	Comphfeur
80	Comphlus

90	Comphneen
100	Sunda
101	Sundafuun
102	Sundakai
115	Sundacomsun
200	Kaisunda
220	Kaisundacomphfuun
300	Saisunda
400	Neirsunda
500	Comsunda
600	Nexsunda
700	Feursunda
800	Lussunda

900	Neensunda
1,000	Miesen
1,100	Miesensundafuun
1,200	Misenkaisunda
1,500	Miesenconsunda
1,700	Miesenfeursunda
10,000	Comphmeisen
100,000	Sundameisen
1,000,000	Milla
1,000,000,000	Billa

A PREVIEW INTO BOOK II: *"THE SHARDS OF THE CROWN"*

It had not taken much. The slaughter of fifty Sarugs at the gate had given him some credibility, but it required some charisma as well.

Deltun was happy with his assignment. Of course, the chance at three-hundred-fifty thousand Bansers had sealed the deal indefinitely. The path to the home of the new king, Caradorian, would be a long one, but he, driven by his sheer will to accomplish the task before him.

Three-hundred-fifty-thousand Bansers for the simple assassination of the new King of Androuge was worth it to him. Deltun was unaware that this "Carador" was the one hero who had broken him out of prison in Farrow Forest two weeks before.

Deltun suffered from Hyril Syndrome, a rare

disease of the lungs, which caused one to have a deadly case of coughing. With the three-hundred-fifty-thousand Bansers he was promised for Carador's assassination, he could but cure this disease finally, and as a Mercenary, he was willing to oblige.

The land seemed bleak, devoid of hope. Deltun gave no care to this, as he had dealt death his entire life. At his feet, a wolf trotted along, his coat light gray, with darker patches, almost black in some areas. Deltun stopped at a small creek, falling to his knees to drink. He dropped his sword by the creek, along with his pack.

"Siyas," Deltun grunted. "Settle down."

The wolf hung his head low, lying down near the travel pack. The breeze was cold and unforgiving, as it whipped against the man. He drank deeply from the creek, only until he was content. Siyas rose with break neck speed, his teeth bared, as he let out a low growl. It took nothing more than a quick motion for the wolf to settle. Next to Deltun, stood a group of men, four of them to be specific. They wore dark red robes, while being diversely armed. Deltun rose, as the tallest of the men held the sword in his hand.

"Beautifully crafted, this will fetch a great price at the market." The men chuckled, as Deltun let out a soft laugh of his own. The man took a step closer, and Deltun slowly drew back. "You seem confident, for a man bearing the clothes of nobody above a beggar," the chorus of laughs came just in time.

In an instant, the man had drawn back, as blood now flowed freely from his nose, while at the same time, losing the sword out of his grasp.

One of the men swung at Deltun, only to let out a cry of pain, as the jaws of Siyas drew deep into his leg. This gave Deltun time to swing around, hitting a bewildered man in the abdomen. He fell to the ground, gasping for air. Deltun smirked with satisfaction, as he whistled sharply. Siyas let go of the unfortunate man's leg, his fangs now dripping freely with blood. He extended his sword in the direction of the final man, who had managed to draw his bow, and prepared to fire an arrow.

"Walk away, Siyas does not take kindly to

bullies," Deltun spat with a grin, noticing the man's fear induced- unstable posture.

The wolf drew closer, and so did Deltun. The man abandoned all will to fight, as he dropped the bow, sprinting over the creek, out of sight. Deltun fell to the ground again, Siyas laying his head on his knee. He briskly stroked the wolf's head, much to his satisfaction. "Good boy."

The journey had hardly begun as Deltun noticed his low supplies. Siyas seemed content, sniffing about happily, chasing the occasional squirrel. Deltun felt annoyed at their slow progress. He was eager for the rest of his money. He was a mercenary, the most hated profession of all those in the land. Since he was young, his father had left, in an attack on Aussarok. Deltun never knew of how his father died. With cruel fate, his mother died of illness not but a season later, leaving him alone, at the age of nine. He was constantly picked on by the children of his village, fueling anger deep within his being, which had yet to extinguish.

Over the years, he made a living as a delivery boy, taking goods from one side of town to the other, earning enough money to keep himself fed. At seventeen, he had applied for the legions, as his father had. To his great dismay, he was declined the opportunity, claiming he was of no physical condition.

Years on the street had brought him a severe illness. He was always short of breath, making deliveries near impossible in his later life. He began to save money to move north, in search of a cure. His ambitions halted as he encountered a cloaked man, in a local pub. The man had told Deltun his tale, of his neighbor who had stolen his wife, children, and home. All the cloaked figure had left was his fortune of three thousand Bansers, an amount of money Deltun had never seen in his life. Therefore, as history tells us, Deltun accepted the mission. He murdered the adulterer, and soon after, reaped his bounty.

It was a habit Deltun would never rid himself of.

KEVIN R. ESSER

www.facebook.com/kevinesser90
www.linkedin.com/in/kevinesser90

Manufactured by Amazon.ca
Bolton, ON